Also by A.J. Pine

THE MURPHYS OF MEADOW VALLEY
Holding Out for a Cowboy
Finally Found My Cowboy

HEART OF SUMMERTOWN
The Second Chance Garden

THE COWBOY
of my
DREAMS

A.J. PINE

sourcebooks
casablanca

Published by Sourcebooks Casablanca, an imprint of Sourcebooks
P.O. Box 4410, Naperville, Illinois 60567-4410
(630) 961-3900
sourcebooks.com

Printed and bound in the United States of America.
BVG 10 9 8 7 6 5 4 3 2 1

For Mindy

Chapter 1

WILLOW MORGAN WAS USED TO SLEEPING IN strange beds. Hell, sometimes that *bed* was a mattress tossed in the back of a tour van, especially when the cost of a motel far outweighed the cost benefit of sleeping in the van. Now that her paying gigs were paying actual money, she still slept in her vehicle. But these days it was a slightly more upscale tour bus with a slightly more upscale bed. She at least had an accordion door she could close and pretend like she was in an actual room...that wasn't moving.

So watching her older brother, Colt, sprawl out like a starfish across the king-sized mattress in the very much not-moving master bedroom made her feel like this was way too...extra.

"See?" Colt said, patting the spot next to him. "You could fit three of you in here."

Willow shook her head and laughed, then plopped down next to the giant man of a brother who still acted like a goofy teenager around her.

"I would have been fine on the bus," she insisted as they both stared at the ceiling fan slowly spinning above them.

"For two months?" Colt scoffed. "You're going to finish recording an album and prep for a concert on a bus?"

Willow elbowed him in the ribs. "Come inside next time we're on the fairgrounds. It's pretty damned luxurious for a moving motel." Though in truth, hiding the nondescript bus in the freight lot thirty miles away gave her a safe enough distance from the public Willow Morgan for at least the next couple of months.

Actual motels and hotels weren't her style. As her career had grown, Willow tried to maintain as much privacy as she could muster. One tabloid scandal when barely anyone had known who she was had taught her early enough to do whatever was needed to keep her life *to* herself. And yes… she could have finished the album on the bus. But it would have been lonely. Here, at least, she could host her brother and sister-in-law and their family for dinner. She could hop on one of the Murphy horses and ride until her life felt like hers again. Maybe then she could finally finish the last song she'd promised her label, the one that still refused to come.

Colt sighed and crossed one dusty cowboy boot over the other. "Oops," he remarked with an apologetic laugh, then decided to dangle his feet off the side of the bed instead.

Willow elbowed him again.

"Ow!" he replied with a laugh. "That one hurt."

"Serves ya right for treating my new place like your mudroom." She tilted her head toward his.

"Does that mean you'll stay?" he asked.

She sighed. "Eli and Beth really don't mind giving up their guesthouse for two whole months?"

Her brother rolled his eyes. "It's a *guest*house. And he and Beth are in Vegas letting Beth's parents fawn all over their new grandbaby, so you've got the whole property to yourself for the next week—horses, chickens, and all."

Willow nodded. "Horses, chickens, the whole place is mine for an entire week. Got it."

Colt propped himself up on one elbow, so Willow did the same.

"I'm really glad you're here, Wills," he told her with a smile that still broke her heart sometimes, reminding her of the years they'd spent apart after their mom died and Willow had been adopted while Colt bounced around foster care until he was eighteen.

"I'm sorry it's been so long since we had some time together," she replied, her voice thick.

He responded by rumpling her hair. "Still waiting on you to write a song about reuniting with your long-lost big brother. But all I hear are these angry breakup songs. Catchy…but angry."

She sat up and whacked him in the head with a throw pillow.

"*Ow…again.*" They both stood, and her brother furrowed his brows while scratching the back of his neck. "Speaking of…um…angry breakup songs… Is there a list of asses that need whooping to avenge whoever hurt my baby sister?"

She picked up another pillow and raised her brows. "I can still get you," she warned. "Even across the bed. I have excellent aim."

He held up his hands in defeat. "All right. All right. I'm just trying to make it clear that if you need someone to look out for you, you should take advantage of having me close by for the next few weeks before your big concert."

She dropped the pillow and put her hands on her hips. "And what if I'm perfectly capable of taking care of myself?" she asked, chin up and shoulders back.

Colt strode around the bed and over to where she stood, gripping her gently by the shoulders and giving her a soft squeeze. "I know you are, Wills. I guess I like to fool myself into thinking that even at twenty-nine years old, you still need your big brother."

Her expression softened as she grabbed his hands and lowered them, reciprocating his reassuring squeeze. "'Course I need you," she promised him. "Just not to fight my battles for me." He opened his mouth to respond, but she cut him off. "And *no*, I don't have any battles that need fighting at the moment. It's a figure of speech. I'm just saying I've got this thing—this *life* or whatever—under control. Okay?"

He nodded. "Okay."

———

Willow hadn't written anything that day, though she chalked it up to travel, getting settled, and plain old exhaustion. Except now that it was past midnight and she was finally snuggled into the bed that truly could fit three of her, sleep refused to come.

She grabbed her phone off the nightstand, ready to dive into a four-hour TikTok rabbit hole that would at the very least keep her occupied until daylight. But before she'd even unlocked her screen, a crash sounded outside her room—something shattering against the hard kitchen floor—followed by a muffled voice.

What had she told her brother? That she had this whole life thing under control? Yeah, that was before she'd considered someone breaking and entering into a secluded, *locked* guesthouse on very private property.

She so did not have *this* under control.

"Shit," she hissed under her breath before crawling out of bed wearing nothing but a ribbed tank top and her most comfortable underwear...men's boxer briefs.

"Weapon, weapon, weapon..." she mouthed silently to herself as her eyes scanned the dark for any sort of protection. She found it in the way of a ceramic vase on the dresser that Colt's wife, Jenna, had filled with beautiful wildflowers that Willow now scattered—along with the water that was keeping them alive—on the rug at the foot of her bed so the intruder wouldn't hear her pouring anything onto a hard surface.

She inched toward her closed bedroom door and heard the unmistakable sound of the knob turning, the latch unlatching.

The mix of fear and adrenaline coursing through her blood was so potent that Willow thought she might levitate off the floor or lose consciousness completely. She really, really hoped the universe would grant her the former rather than making her a sitting duck for whatever lay on the other side of the door.

She held her breath as the door creaked open and her would-be assailant stumbled inside.

It all happened so fast, like something out of a vaudevillian silent comedy. Willow raised the vase above her head as a man lumbered toward the bed. She sucked in a breath just before striking, allowing barely enough time for him to turn. Their eyes met, and as she swung the vase, she heard him groggily say, "Willow?" Then the vase shattered against his temple, and he fell backward against the mattress.

In the moonlight she could see blood trickle down his cheek and onto the duvet.

She flipped on the light and gasped.

"Ashton Murphy, what the *hell* are you doing in my room?" she asked.

His eyes fluttered open and locked on hers. "I missed you too, darlin'," he replied, pushing himself up to sitting. But then his eyes rolled backward. "No hospitals," he mumbled, then collapsed again.

Willow swore and rushed toward him, dipping her head to make sure the man was still breathing, only to be greeted with an exhale so clearly full of bourbon she was stunned it didn't get her drunk on contact.

"I swear to god, Ashton Murphy," she began through gritted teeth as she battled the deadweight of his legs to swing them onto the bed. "If you die on my watch and they give me a lie-detector test, it won't matter that this was very clearly self-defense. They're gonna lock me up for life." Just because she'd never *planned* on killing the man, she'd maybe—at one of her lower points—*fantasized* about it.

She propped a couple of pillows under his head and then retrieved a first aid kit and a damp towel from the bathroom and got to cleaning him up the best she could.

"Ash…" she said softly at first. "You're gonna have to wake up and hold a conversation with me if you don't want me to call 911. Whether you're just drunk or drunk and concussed, I need some proof of life, or you're shit out of luck."

No response, but luckily the cut on his temple seemed happy enough with a butterfly bandage and had all but stopped bleeding.

"*Ash*," she tried again, this time a little louder, and received something akin to a snore in reply.

"Ashton Murphy, you lying, cheating asshole of a human parading as a man, wake the hell up, or I'm calling an ambulance and every TMZ reporter I know!"

Ash's eyes flew open, and he bolted upright, knocking Willow right in the forehead with his own.

Willow swore.

"I'm awake!" Ash exclaimed.

Great. So, no manslaughter charges for tonight, but now Willow was pretty sure *she* was concussed too.

"Next time," she grumbled, "I'm staying on the damned bus."

Chapter 2

ASH WOKE TO THE CACOPHONY OF CABINETS opening and closing, metal clanging, and water running. He tried to open his eyes, but the light felt like a knife stabbing his irises, so that option was out. Instead, he decided to roll over, bury his head in whatever pillows he could find, and pretend that whatever was happening beyond his closed lids was not, in fact, happening. Except when he rolled, he dropped to a hard floor with a painful thud.

"What the…?" He seemed to be tangled in some sort of yarn-based creation with holes of varying sizes that had cuffed one of his hands and possibly a few of his toes. So now, instead of ignoring the outside world and sleeping off his hangover, he was battling with a blanket after falling off of a bed that seemed way too small.

He finally freed himself, rolling the sorry excuse for a blanket into a ball and tossing it back on the… couch?

Where the hell was he?

Ash tried to blink the light away, but it was relentless. So he pressed the heels of his hands to his eyes and somehow climbed to his feet so he could get his bearings. The first thing he saw was a window and, beyond that, a field that led to a chicken coop. He spun slowly, recognizing the building that led to the fenced-in field: his oldest brother Eli's veterinary clinic. As he continued his slow rotation, he stopped short at what he knew now was the guesthouse kitchen that should have been empty. Instead he found a woman standing on the other side of the breakfast bar, facing him. She wore a flour-coated apron, hair in a wild bun atop her head, and…was that a goose egg on her forehead?

"Could you put on some pants and cover that thing?" she asked, blowing a loose brunette lock out of her eyes.

Ash glanced down to his boxer briefs where he was sporting some significant morning wood. He was in the middle of formulating a witty yet sexy comeback when the voice and the hair and every one of his five senses flooded with recognition despite the years since he'd last seen her.

"*Willow Morgan.*" Her name was a declaration rather than a question. He grabbed a throw pillow from the couch and used it as a shield to hide his erection. "Did we…? I mean… What are you…?"

She cracked an egg with one hand, let the contents fall into a bowl in front of her on the counter, and then dropped the shell into what he hoped was a garbage can beside her. Then she groaned.

"Don't flatter yourself, Murphy. The only thing

that *we* did last night was concuss each other. Only difference between my injury and yours, though, is that *you* deserved it."

Ash's vision cleared even as the pounding in his head raged on. He found his jeans crumpled in a ball on one end of the couch and took his time climbing back into them, though not bothering with the zipper or button.

He brushed the tips of his fingers over his right temple and winced as he felt the bandage and the tender lump beneath it.

"What the hell did you hit me with?" he asked. "And *why*? Also, what are you doing in my brother's guesthouse?"

Willow's jaw tensed. Despite the bump, Ash was pretty sure he saw a vein pulse beneath the skin on her forehead.

"A vase," she began, holding up a thumb. "Because you broke into *my* bedroom." She added her index finger. "For the next couple of months or so, depending on what's next after the festival, I *live* here." She nodded her head back toward the front door. "Thanks to your little destructive entry last night, you now owe your brother and Beth *two* vases."

"Shit," Ash mumbled through gritted teeth. Then his fingers wandered toward his head wound again. "Did you knock me out and then patch me up?"

Willow crossed her arms—her bare, lean arms

that bore the muscles of a musician who always had a guitar strapped to her back. "Had to make sure I didn't kill you once I saw who my *intruder* was."

The corner of Ash's mouth twitched. "You disappointed that vase wasn't heavier?"

She narrowed her dark-brown eyes, then picked up a red spatula and pointed it at him. "Do you really want me to answer that?"

He strode toward the breakfast bar and the woman who, for all intents and purposes, had tried to kill him the night before. She couldn't have been more than five foot three, but what she lacked in stature, she made up for in attitude and the voice he knew came from deep in her soul. He'd known it the first second he ever heard her sing all those years ago.

"Are you really gonna hate me forever?" he asked.

She went back to whatever her concoction was, furiously stirring with her spatula.

"I don't know," she remarked without sparing him another glance. "I'll let you know at forever o'clock." She cleared her throat. "Obviously, you can't stay here, but I can call my brother. I'm sure they can get you a room at the guest ranch."

Ash scoffed. "I came here to lay low. I can't stay in a big, public tourist trap like that."

She rolled her eyes but still hadn't bothered to meet his gaze again. "Someone's gotten a little big for his britches, hasn't he?" But after a few more vigorous stirs of what looked like some sort of thick batter in the bowl, she finally looked up and sighed. "I guess your presence would be a pain in the ass over there."

He slapped his hands against the counter, then winced as his head responded with an extra throb. "I guess it's settled then."

"What's settled?" Willow asked.

Ash shrugged. "*You're* going to stay at the ranch instead while I hole up in *my* family's guesthouse."

She stopped midstir and finally looked at him again, which—from this close—made something jolt deep in his gut, even if her look was more of a glare.

God, he wished he could remember the details of the night before. He wished he could remember a lot of nights that he didn't, but he was also grateful for others that would remain a mystery.

She opened her mouth, most likely to breathe fire and scorch him right where he stood, but he was offered a limited reprieve thanks to a frenzied knock on the door followed by another voice he knew all too well.

"Ashton Murphy, open this door and show me proof of life, or so help me, god, I am going to murder you where you stand."

He offered Willow a shrug. "Sorry, Morgan. Looks like you'll have to get in line."

He strolled to the door, still shirtless with his

unzipped jeans resting on his hips, and threw it open to find Sloane Edwards, his manager and publicist, in a fitted checkered pantsuit, crisp white blouse, stilettos that probably made it near impossible to walk from her rental to the door, and her blond, chin-length bob styled perfectly. Not a hair out of place, including the blunt bangs that hung just below her brows. Yet somehow Ash knew—as he always did—that she was at her wits' end.

"Sloane!" He threw his arms open as if the two of them always greeted each other with a bear hug. (They did not.) "You found me!" *Already.*

She stormed past him and into the guesthouse, pivoting to face him only after he'd slammed the door closed.

"You're not answering your phone," she offered instead of any traditional greeting. But then again, Sloane never wasted time on unnecessary words. He liked that about her.

"I'm using a loaner," he replied. "Not even sure what the number is." Ash also liked that for the past however many hours, Sloane—or anyone else, for that matter—had not been able to contact him directly.

"Arrested?" she added to her non-greeting. "Again?"

He held up his hands to show her that he was, in fact, handcuff free, and flashed her a grin. "They let me off with a warning."

She crossed her arms. "After your team paid for the damage to the hotel room. And by *team*, I mean *me*."

"And by *you*, you mean *me*, right? Whatever card you gave them draws from my account, doesn't it?" He waved her off. "Besides, you say *damage*. I say *incidentals*. Whatever is in the hotel room is fair game as long as it's paid for, and as you just informed me, I *paid*."

"Incidentals, huh?" Sloane raised her brows. "Did you throw the hotel phone at the wall? No. Out the window? No again. At the seventy-five-inch 4K television that used to be mounted on the wall but is now a pile of broken glass? Ding! Ding! Ding! We have a winner."

Ash shrugged. "Tried the cell phone first, but all that did was bust up my phone." Hence the loaner.

Sloane tried to level him with her gaze or maybe…melt him with invisible death rays? He wasn't sure.

"I guess you're lucky that *some* people are actually feeling sympathy for you right now."

Ash clenched his teeth and let a breath out through his nose, suddenly devoid of any snappy comebacks.

Sloane sighed. "Divorce sucks, Murphy. I get that. Even more so when it's in the public eye, but you chose this life and all that comes with it. And you chose me to make sure you manage that public eye better than anyone else out there."

Suddenly remembering where he was, Ash darted a glance over his shoulder to find that Willow was gone.

"Who's that?" Sloane asked, nodding toward the floor-to-ceiling windows that looked out on the open field.

Ash followed her gaze as Sloane strode straight up to the glass, using her hands as a visor against the morning sun as she peered out toward the chicken coop. Her mouth hung open as she pivoted back to face him.

"Tell me that is *not* Willow Morgan out there." But Sloane's lips were already curling into a grin, and Ash could see the diabolical wheels turning in her head.

"It's not what it looks like, Sloane," he told her, an echo of the very same words he'd spoken when she barged into his tour bus bedroom four years earlier.

"Oh yea?" Sloane asked, her blue eyes brewing up a publicity storm. "Because to me it looks like a comeback." She sauntered over to the couch, stretched her arms across the backrest, and crossed her legs. "Put on a shirt, Murphy. Because we are about to spin."

———

"No," Willow told them, pacing back and forth in front of the breakfast bar. "Absolutely not. I'm here to work, not to be the next notch on a player's belt."

Sloane swiveled back and forth on a breakfast barstool, drumming her perfectly manicured nails on the counter as if Willow's protestations meant nothing.

Ash stood by the couch with his arms crossed over his chest, guessing he wasn't as good an actor as Sloane was. He hated his publicist's plan as much as Willow did, but he also knew that if he dared to open his phone up to any entertainment website or social media outlet that he'd likely find his name—and another record of less-than-stellar public behavior—trending.

"I'm not asking you to actually sleep with him," Sloane replied with a laugh. "We'll leave that to speculation. All I'm asking is for periodic photos to be 'leaked' by outlets of my choosing and for the two of you to debut a song together at the cute little festival where you're performing a couple of months from now."

"Come on, Sloane. Acoustic Acres is projected to get at least 20,000 a day with Willow headlining," Ash interjected.

Willow's brows shot up, and for a second she glanced at him with something other than ire or disdain.

Sloane grinned. "Imagine what those numbers would be if we hinted at Willow inviting a special guest onstage for a yet-unreleased song." She pressed her palm to her chest. "I'm not only asking this for

Mad Man Murphy over there…" She nodded her head in Ash's direction.

He winced. *Mad Man Murphy?* Did she make that up, or was that one of the little gems he'd find online once he found his phone?

"But think about what this might do for *you*." Sloane sighed. "There's been some speculation about writer's block, and I'm not saying I'm buying into it. But your label did push the release date, did they not? Think about what your fans would say if they caught wind of you 'collaborating'"—she put finger quotes around the word—"with country music's resident bad boy?"

Ash ran a hand through his hair and stepped between the two women. "No." He was the one shaking his head now. "We're not putting Willow in the middle of this. *I* got arrested last night. *I* messed up the whole end-of-the-marriage thing. *I* should be the one to figure out how to clean it up." He held his arms out and spun slowly. "That's why I'm here. I need to lay low in a place where cameras and social media and all of that bullshit can't find me. The last thing I want to do is drag Meadow Valley or anyone in town into the circus."

He stared at the woman who'd helped build his career and image over the past decade and silently pleaded with her to leave the whole ordeal alone. He'd—*they'd*—figure something out. Just not this.

"I'll do it," he heard from over his shoulder, and

Ash pivoted to find a resigned Willow still in her flour-covered apron, shoulders squared and chin held high.

"What?" he asked. "Wait…*what*?" he repeated. "*Why?*"

Willow cleared her throat and smoothed out her apron. Though all she really did was smear the flour farther across the fabric. "Sloane's right." Willow shrugged. "My album was pushed because it's not done. The label wants a *Billboard* country hit for the first single, and they're not convinced that hit is any of the other *eleven* songs I've already recorded." She let out a bitter laugh. "I can't believe I am this much of a cliché. Debut album is enough of a hit that they sign me for number two, and I go and fall into the sophomore slump."

She strode toward Ash and gently poked her index finger against his still-bare chest. Jesus, he could smell the sweet mix of sugar and butter, the coconut of her shampoo. It hit him in one intoxicating wave, making him lose the ability to speak, which he guessed was okay because Willow looked like she had a lot more to say.

She stared at him for several seconds, her chest rising and falling, the heat from her fingertip threatening to brand his skin.

"You sleep on the couch," she began. "And we *work*. Day and night, however long it takes."

Ash nodded.

"No drinking, no drugs, and—and no women or any other distractions in the house."

He wanted to tell her that there had only been two times in his life when he'd gotten blackout drunk and that somehow, thanks to the menacing asshole that was the universe, Willow Morgan had been there for both, even if the former was only via email. But what did it matter anymore? She saw him like every other person who read the tweets, posts, and comments. And on some level, he deserved it. So he simply said, "That's a lot of *no*, but okay."

She whirled on Sloane. "I choose where and when we snap a selfie. *I* post on my own social media. Both of you agree not to disclose our location to *anyone*, and nothing gets mentioned about any song until it's actually written and I have my label's permission to debut it at the festival. Are we in agreement?"

Willow glanced back and forth between Ash and Sloane. He was still too stunned to articulate any of the thoughts swirling around in his head, but Sloane was smiling like a hyena cornering her prey.

"We are very much in agreement," Sloane told her, extending her hand. But Willow didn't reciprocate.

"I want it in writing," Willow replied instead. "Signed by all parties involved."

Sloane slowly lowered her hand but laughed. "I like her, Murphy." She turned to face him. "Dare I say it might actually be a *good* thing that A.B. posted her engagement news last night before we had a chance to announce the divorce? Your…*reaction*…might actually earn you the sympathy vote. Poor, jilted Ash Murphy. We get your fans to eat this up and then BAM! You rebound with Willow Morgan and a duet!"

"It's *not* a rebound," Willow and Ash said at the same time.

Well, good to know she was adamantly opposed to that sort of connection between them. He wouldn't want to mistake her agreement for any sort of forgiveness or reconciliation. This was work for Willow, and that was all it would be for him. She'd get a song, and he'd get an image makeover. Again.

Sloane shrugged and then flicked a piece of non-existent lint from the shoulder of her suit jacket and grabbed her phone from the counter. "I'll have a draft of the contract sent over this afternoon." She pointed at Ash. "You stay out of trouble, especially the kind that involves handcuffs and fingerprints." Then she turned her attention back to Willow. "And *you*… Well, you just keep being America's next country sweetheart, and we'll all get what we want out of this spectacular new arrangement. I'll see myself out."

And with that, Sloane sauntered toward the door and back out into the morning sun.

"What the hell just happened?" Ash asked after several beats of silence.

"I think..." Willow began, staring blankly toward the door through which Sloane had disappeared. "That I just sold my soul to the devil for a song."

Chapter 3

WILLOW GOT THE LAST OF THE TOFFEE SHORT-bread cookies—her and her brother's favorite—onto the cooling rack and untied her apron.

Moments after Sloane left, Ash found his shirt and shoes and disappeared somewhere outside himself.

"I need to find my phone," he'd mumbled before striding straight past her and out the door, which had given Willow way too much time to think. And because she hated thinking about things she didn't want to think about, she baked. Hence the whole early-morning shortbread-batter creation in the first place because sleeping in that big, beautiful, ridiculously comfortable king-sized bed had *not* been an option if all she could do was lie there and think about the fact that Ash Murphy was passed out on the couch on the other side of her door.

Except now the cookies were done, her quiet two months had turned into a fun house version of her life, and she still didn't want to be alone with her thoughts…or with the newly divorced Ashton Murphy, for that matter. Yeah, that little nugget of information had not escaped her notice.

A.B., or Annabeth Calder-Payne, was a Scottish tennis prodigy with an affinity for country music… or at least for a certain country music singer-songwriter who grew up on a horse ranch and charmed every woman in his orbit.

As the story went, the two supposedly struck up a secret relationship around five years ago after she won a tournament that happened to be in the same town where he'd had a gig, only going public a year later when news of their engagement hit all the online entertainment outlets on an early, rainy, we-should-stay-in-bed-all-day Sunday morning.

Bile rose in Willow's throat, and she yanked the apron over her head and tossed it on the couch.

This was why she shouldn't be left alone with her thoughts.

This was why she'd chosen to spend the next two months far from the world of country music… other than penning her final song.

And *this* was why she needed to get the hell out of this house and onto the back of a horse where she could outrun the events of last night, the mistake of a deal she'd struck this morning, and the memory of a rainy Sunday morning when for a tiny fraction of a moment, she was a naïve twentyfive-year-old up-and-comer who thought she was in love.

Though Willow had only met Eli once, years ago, and had yet to meet Beth in person, the three had been in contact for the past couple weeks leading to her stay in Meadow Valley.

"All three horses are healthy and fit for riders," Eli had told her. "Cirrus, the male, is a bit rambunctious. He likes to play. But once you get him going in the arena, he's all business. Midnight is a mama's girl. If it's not Beth, she seems to prefer female riders, but once she trusts anyone—man or woman—she warms up pretty quickly. And then there's Holiday, the newest member of the family. She was only meant to be a rehab after a ligament, but then again, so were the other two. Now I own three horses."

Willow had laughed, falling a little bit in love with each horse as he described them. "And you and Beth are okay with me riding while you're gone?"

"Of course," Eli replied. "Your brother claims you're a better rider than he is, and that's reassurance enough for me."

As she entered the barn now, she shook her head and laughed. Colt was always her biggest cheerleader. Not a day went by that she didn't thank the universe for reuniting the two after years apart... and for finally giving her brother the happiness he deserved with Jenna and their ever-evolving foster family. Willow wrote songs about the elusiveness of love and the inevitability of heartbreak because that was all she knew. But her brother was proof that for at least some, love was more than a few chords on a guitar, several verses of lament, and a powerful—often angry—bridge she usually sang so hard it burned her throat.

Willow strode down the walkway lined with stalls, ready to see which horse she connected with best, when she stopped short, her breath caught in her throat.

Out of three stalls bearing three nameplates to identify each inhabitant, the door labeled MIDNIGHT hung wide open with no mare in sight.

She bolted out into the arena and found it empty save for fresh hoofprints in the dirt, which she followed to the far end where they abruptly stopped. She absently brushed her finger over a fresh-looking nick in the wood on the top of the fence.

"Shit!" she hissed, a splinter sliding beneath the skin of her index finger. Willow quickly pulled it out with her teeth and then stormed back to the barn where she found herself pacing for the second time today, this time between Cirrus and Holiday's doors.

"Is this technically *his* family's ranch?" she asked the gelding and the mare. "Of course it is. But did he let his family know he was coming home to play house and upend my short reprieve between gigs?" She threw her arms in the air and glanced at Holiday's dark eyes as she whinnied and nudged her tawny-brown nose in Willow's direction. "No," she told the mare. "No, he did not. And now he's either off galivanting who knows where on Beth's favorite horse or…" The *or* made her stomach drop as if she'd just leaped off a cliff.

Or he chose the horse who doesn't take kindly to male riders, and the mare decided to teach him a lesson about his poor judgment.

Willow glanced down at the tiny spot of blood on her finger where the splinter had been and swore again. She couldn't believe what she was about to do, especially after striking a deal with Satan less than two hours before. She was going to go *save* Ash Murphy.

Holiday seemed to trust her off the bat, so as soon as Willow had her tacked and ready to go, she led the mare into the arena and walked her toward the place where Midnight's hoofprints stopped.

Holiday marched in place and snorted, shaking her head back and forth.

"You want to go find them, girl?" Willow asked, patting Holiday's withers and then stroking her nose. She was about to ask her horse if she thought she could make the jump when she noticed that only two sections of the fence to the left there was a latch, which meant a gate, which also meant that Midnight had not been led out of the arena. She'd taken off on her own.

The only thing that lay beyond the Murphy

property in the direction they were facing was the woods.

How much trouble could one man get himself into in less than twenty-four hours? She guessed she was about to find out.

She led the trusting horse through the gate and closed it behind her, already sure that riding one of Beth and Eli's horses off of the property was not what they'd had in mind when they entrusted their barn—and its inhabitants—to her. But Willow didn't have a choice now, did she? She'd already made one inadvertent attempt on Ash Murphy's life. If he ended up dead in the forest off the property where *she* temporarily lived and where a broken vase with her fingerprints all over it lay in the guesthouse trash, who would be person-of-interest number one?

So she hooked her boot in Holiday's stirrup and hoisted herself into the saddle. She gave the mare a gentle nudge with her heels and a reluctant "Ya!" Then the two were off toward the forest where—so help her, god—Willow better not have to drag Ash's corpse back to civilization.

———

"No!" Willow growled as she and Holiday came to a halt in a clearing. She dismounted from the horse and tied her off to a small tree, then pivoted back to where Ashton Murphy reclined against the trunk of a massive maple tree, boots crossed at the ankles, straw hat lowered over his eyes, and a black Friesian she assumed was Midnight grazing beside him, not tied to anything.

"NO!" she repeated, louder this time, but Ash barely stirred.

"You sure do like that word, don't you?" he mumbled from where he lay. Then he tipped his hat up and dared to flash her the cocksure grin that stared out at his adoring fans from his carefully curated social media posts. *Not* that she'd ever looked on purpose, but Willow couldn't help what showed up in her feed.

She opened her mouth to respond but caught herself just as she was about to utter the exact word he expected to hear. *No.*

"I thought you were hurt. Or worse," she admitted.

He straightened so he no longer looked half-asleep and crossed his arms. "And let me guess... You're disappointed to find me alive and well."

Willow fisted her hands at her sides and stifled an exasperated scream. Instead, she counted to five, exhaled a steadying breath, and decided that he could push her buttons all he wanted, but she would not push back. She couldn't live like that for two days, let alone two months.

"Eli told me that Midnight doesn't take to male riders as easily as female, and when I saw her hoofprints and a nick in the fence that indicated she'd jumped when you very well could have used the gate like any other civilized human..." *Nope,* she reminded herself. *Not gonna push.* "I did not want to find anyone *un*alive or *un*well...even if it was you." It might have sounded like button pushing, but it was the truth.

Midnight gave Willow a cursory glance and then, as if she were a cat rather than a giant equine, she spun once and then laid herself down beside him, resting her head on his lap.

"You've got to be kidding me," Willow said, letting out an incredulous laugh. "Actually, no. I should have known you'd have that horse wrapped around your finger the second she laid eyes on you. After all, she's a female, right?"

Willow's throat burned, and she spun back toward Holiday, who was happily chomping on some grass.

Maybe she was desperate for a song, but at what cost? Her pride? Her dignity?

"Willow, wait..." Ash called from over her shoulder, but he sounded closer than where he'd been lying beneath the tree.

She stopped a foot from her horse, and Holiday lifted her head to ask for a quick pat on the nose, to which Willow immediately obliged.

"I didn't know you were going to be here," Ash continued, close enough now that he could speak softly. "It caught me off guard, and I needed to get away for a bit to clear my head. I should have said something before leaving. I should have known that you were still you…that you'd worry."

She rounded on him, her gaze narrowed on his. "It was a few months four years ago, Murphy. You don't get to pretend like that means you knew me then, and you certainly don't know me now."

He nodded. "Plus a few more months of touring before we…" he reminded her. "But fair enough."

"Or that *you* seeing *me* creates any sort of need for you to clear your head," she added. Because what the hell did that mean, and why did she even care? She didn't. Not then and not now.

He nodded again. Ugh. Why was he being so agreeable? It made it a lot harder for her to hold on to her anger.

"I can go to your brother's ranch," he told her. "Or see if Boone and Casey can put me up…after he reams me for missing his and Casey's wedding."

"And Eli and Beth's," Willow mumbled. "Plus the births of their children."

He flinched as if she'd threatened to strike him with another vase, and for an odd moment, her chest ached at the possibility that Ash's absence from his family's life might not have been entirely by design.

But then she remembered he was an adult with free will and swallowed the lump of guilt rising in her throat.

Willow sighed. "We already established that you'd turn the guest ranch into a zoo. And last I heard, Boone, Casey, and Kara live in a two-bedroom apartment above her salon. Where are they going to put you?"

He shrugged. "I'm either a couch surfer in the guesthouse or a couch surfer over there. Hell, if Eli and Beth are gone long enough, I can probably crash over there."

She shook her head. "They're only in Vegas for a week. Don't you... I mean, haven't you talked to your brothers? Didn't they know you were coming home?"

Ash pulled his hat down further over his eyes so that all she could see of his face were the tip of his nose and the tight line of his jaw.

"*I* didn't know I was coming home until I did." He shrugged. "And I wasn't exactly sure they'd be happy to see me after—you know—missing all those things."

The words *I'm sorry* dangled from the tip of her tongue. But they were also words she'd waited *months* to hear from the man standing directly in front of her. Yet it was somehow four years after the fact, and she'd never heard a damned thing.

"It hasn't even been twenty-four hours, and I already have no idea how this is going to work," she admitted. "But I need a song. I need *the* song."

"And I, apparently, need yet another image refresh," he added.

Willow glanced over his shoulder to where Midnight now rolled back and forth in a small patch of dry dirt. She laughed. "I can't believe you had her eating out of the palm of your hand in a matter of minutes." She flicked the brim of his hat up, and Ash's eyes widened before he met her grin with his own.

"Come on, Morgan," he drawled. "You know it was seconds, not minutes."

She groaned. "Of course it was." She suddenly eyed him up and down, realizing that when he'd left the guesthouse earlier that morning, he was wearing a different-colored T-shirt, and there'd been no cowboy hat in sight. "Where's all your stuff?" she asked. "And where did you change?"

He glanced down at his fresh white tee and the same dusty jeans he'd thrown back on that morning. "Turns out," he began, his eyes meeting hers again. "That I got taken into custody before I had a chance to pack last night, but the hotel boxed up my belongings and dropped them on the front porch this morning. Grabbed a clean shirt and my hat on my way out the door and then tossed the box into the bushes. Didn't feel like the right time to unpack."

She'd already seen him nearly naked today, but for some reason the thought of him stripping off his old shirt for a new one—all on the way to hopping onto the back of a horse—knocked her a little off-kilter.

"What?" he asked, and Willow noticed she was staring at him.

She shook her head and let out a nervous laugh. "I feel like there's a lyric in there somewhere. *Didn't feel like the right time to unpack…*"

"*With the whole damned world cracking a whip at my back?*" he asked but didn't wait for her to answer. "*So I hopped on a horse and rode until dark…*"

"*Knowing with each step I'd never recapture the spark!*" Willow bounced on her heels, a grin spreading across her face. "Holy shit, Murphy. This might actually work!"

She pulled her phone out of her pocket and sang the words with a random melody into her voice recorder before she forgot them.

The song might work, she meant, of course. Living together for two months without killing each other? The jury was still out on that one.

Chapter 4

ASH RAISED HIS HAND TO KNOCK ON THE BED-room door, but it flew open before he made contact so that he was face-to-face with his new roommate who was wearing nothing but a white cotton robe, a towel dangling from one hand, and her dark-brown hair now wet and soaking the fabric on her shoulders.

"Oh!" Willow said, taking a step back. "I mean, hi. Did you need something?"

They'd ridden back to the barn together after deciding a couple lines of a song were good enough for day one. Once inside the house, Willow had disappeared into her room while Ash decided to make the front hall closet his, stashing his boxed belongings in the small space. He had an entire house worth of possessions in Nashville, but he couldn't remember the last time he'd spent more than a week there, let alone called the place home. So he traveled with the barest of essentials and bought what he needed along the way.

Right now, he needed a shower.

"So, here's the thing," he told her. "The bathroom out here has a toilet and sink, which is great. Love me a good toilet and sink." Inside, he cringed at himself. "But if I'm going to live here, I'm going to need to shower here too."

She stared blankly at him for several seconds before exclaiming, "Oh!" Again.

"Oh," he repeated, then raised his brows. "I can wait for you to get dressed if you want. Or…"

"Right," Willow replied. "No… I mean…"

"There you go with that favorite word again, Morgan. Are you saying I should find somewhere else to shower for eight whole weeks?"

She rolled her eyes. "Have you always been this impossible?"

"Since the day I left the womb." He winked. "So you're *not* saying that I *can't* shower? Because last time I checked, that there is a double negative, which translates to a positive, which means you better have left me some hot water."

She lifted the towel she was still holding, squeezed the ends of her dripping hair into it, and then tossed it on the bed.

He could smell her shampoo again, that familiar, intoxicating scent, and he hoped to hell he could find another brand of shampoo in the bathroom because how the hell was he supposed to walk around day to day smelling like her? Or more to the point…smelling *her* on *himself*.

She gently poked her finger against his chest for the second time today, urging him out of the doorway so she could slip past.

"The 'no' was for not needing to get dressed before letting you borrow the shower. I was going to grab a snack and have a seat on the back porch, let what's left of the sun air-dry my hair."

Ash swallowed as she sauntered past him, bare feet padding toward the kitchen.

"It's *our* shower now, Morgan," he called after her. "Which means I'm not borrowing anything other than some time in your room."

She waved him off, not bothering to turn around, and he shook his head and laughed.

Then he made his way into the room, kicking the door shut behind him and glancing at the still-unpacked suitcase sitting open atop the giant bed, at her jeans, T-shirt, and undergarments lying in a heap on the floor. In the bathroom, another towel hung on the doorknob. Bottles of lotion and face wash along with a tube of toothpaste and her toothbrush were scattered across the counter.

He laughed again. He might still be an asshole, but four years later, Willow Morgan still lived like a frat boy.

He hung the wet towel on a hook on the back of the bathroom door and then lined up her few toiletries against the backsplash below the mirror. Then he turned on the shower and peeled off his clothes, stepping into the hot spray in the hope of washing himself clean of the night before—not only the hotel, his arrest, and the surprise publicity of his divorce, but also of reuniting with Willow the way he did, drunk off his ass and scaring her like that.

Not that this was any sort of true reunion. It was a tolerance at best. Ashton Murphy knew resentment when he saw it, and he knew he deserved it.

So he rested his head against the cool ceramic tile of the shower wall, hot water and steam allowing him to start fresh, at least in the physical sense.

When he spun toward the mounted shelf of bath and shower products, he exhaled with relief to find a tall, dark bottle of a drugstore-brand shampoo simply labeled as shampoo, no frills or bells or whistles. That didn't stop him from grabbing the white bottle next to it, the one with words like *daily hydration* and *nourishing coconut milk*. He flipped open the cap and squeezed, releasing the scent of its contents into the steam so that the whole shower seemed to fill with Willow.

"You're a damned jackass," he said out loud, while silently answering himself with, *I know*.

———

Ash raised his hand to knock on the apartment door and realized that for the second time in less than twenty-four hours, he was an interloper in someone else's space, in someone else's life. He could turn around right now, pretend he was never here, and leave everyone in peace...maintain the status quo. Wouldn't everyone be happier that way?

He continued with the mental gymnastics, vaulting from one convincing excuse to another so that he wouldn't have to do the thing he didn't want to do, which was why when someone tapped him on the shoulder from behind, he nearly leaped out of his own skin, a string of expletives firing off from his lips as he spun to face his...attacker? Nosy neighbor?

"Language!" Boone Murphy exclaimed with a laugh, brows raised in admonishment. Next to him—and several feet closer to the floor—stood a blond, pigtailed, blue-eyed toddler who was now *repeating* that string of expletives like she was reciting her ABCs. "Oh shit," Boone added.

"Oh shit!" the girl mimicked.

And all the anxiety that had caused Ash's mental gymnastics in the first place dissolved into a fit of laughter as he watched his niece send her father into an all-out panic.

"Casey is going to kill me," Boone told him through clenched teeth. Then he reached past Ash and opened the apartment door, the small girl running ahead of him and down a hallway he assumed led to her room.

Boone followed the girl, jogging after her, and then returning fifteen seconds later.

"She's coloring," he informed Ash, breathing a

sigh of relief. "And no longer dropping f-bombs. Though she'll probably surprise us with a doozie at dinner." He crossed his arms and looked Ash up and down.

"What?" Ash asked.

"Are you a vampire or something?" Boone countered.

Ash's brows furrowed. "*What?*" he repeated, apparently having lost all other words that used to be in his vocabulary.

Boone shrugged. "Just figured the only reason a Murphy would have to *not* enter another Murphy's property would be because the undead can't enter without an invitation." He leaned forward and stage-whispered. "If anyone asks, Casey makes me watch *The Vampire Diaries* with her, but the truth is, on my days home with Kara, it's my goddamn favorite thing to binge while she naps."

"Goddamn favorite thing!" Kara exclaimed from her bedroom.

Boone threw his hands in the air. "I'm already a dead man, so if you're going to drain me of my life force, or whatever, you might as well put me out of my misery now." He stepped aside and motioned for Ash to enter.

Ash stepped over the threshold into one of his two older brothers' homes, a place he'd never visited before today. "I'm...uh...not going to drain you of your life force, by the way," he told Boone.

The older Murphy brother shrugged. "In that case..."

And then, for the second time in a matter of minutes, Ash was thrown for yet another loop as Boone pulled him in for a bear hug.

He just stood there, stiff, as his brother clapped him on the back and then grabbed him by the shoulders, pushing him an arm's length away so he could get a good look at the prodigal son now returned.

"What's the matter?" Boone asked with a wry grin. "Has superstardom beaten the ability to hug outta you?"

Ash cleared his throat. "No... I just... It was unexpected." But the truth was, Ash Murphy couldn't remember the last time he'd hugged someone...or that someone had actually hugged him without the gesture turning into some sort of transaction.

He finally had a chance to get a good look at Boone. His dark hair was longer than Ash had remembered, and there were lines at the corners of his brother's eyes that hadn't been there before. But Ash could tell those lines were evidence of happiness, of too much smiling when the Boone he'd known in his later teen years had been anything but.

The two men who stared at each other were strangers now, and Ash wasn't prepared for the virtual sock to the gut he felt as he realized this.

"You look good, Boone," he admitted, trying to hide the guilt from his tone.

Boone huffed out a laugh. "And you look like you just got hit by a truck." He nodded toward the butterfly bandage on Ash's temple, the one he'd had to reapply after his shower yesterday when he realized he probably should have gotten a stitch or two.

"Not a truck," he told his brother, absently brushing his fingers over the bandage. "A vase. My welcome-home gift."

Boone slipped past Ash and into the kitchen opposite the living area. Though all of it looked like one big room, with *big* being a generous term. It gave a whole new meaning to *open concept*, the term Sloane had used to describe the house he bought sight unseen simply to have a place of his own. Yet this little apartment felt more like a home than Ash's open-concept five-bedroom ranch ever would.

"You look like you could use a drink," Boone called from over his shoulder.

Ash spun to face him just in time to catch a cold aluminum can in his left hand. He was about to tell his brother that it was too early to start drinking, even for him, when he caught sight of the words *Raspberry Lime Sparkling Water* written in pink and green on the whimsically decorated aluminum.

"Oh," he said instead. "Seltzer. The un-spiked kind."

Boone cracked a can open for himself and then

strode back into the living room, dropping onto an oversized chair kitty-corner from the couch.

"I tend not to drink when I'm with Kara. Also, I think it's only decent to wait until there's a p.m. after the time." He nodded toward the couch to his right. "Why don't you take a load off. Unless, of course, you're just passing through."

Of course he was just passing through. Ash Murphy didn't belong in Meadow Valley anymore. He wasn't sure he ever did, not like Boone and Eli at least.

"I am," Ash admitted, making his way to the couch and sitting anyway. "I mean, I'm only in town until things in the press die down, and then…" His voice trailed off. And then *what*? Make another record, he guessed, after rebuilding an image he still couldn't figure out how to maintain even after ten years.

He sat but flinched when something hard poked him in the thigh. Peeking out from the cushion was the corner of a book. He pulled it free and produced a board book of Maurice Sendak's *Where the Wild Things Are*, and handed it to Boone. "I think this might belong to your swearin' sailor in the other room."

Boone laughed and dropped the book onto the arm of the chair, a sure sign it would end up in a similar spot in the not-too-distant future. "I've been wondering where that book ended up. That was Colt and Jenna's gift for Kara's first birthday.

Oh!" His eyes widened. "Colt's sister…Willow Morgan! Isn't she the one who…?" But Boone had the decency not to finish that sentence.

Just the mention of her made the wound on Ash's temple throb and the blood in his veins turn molten. He groaned at the simple sound of her name, at the irreconcilable way his body reacted to just the thought of her, and at the constant realization that if she *had* killed him with that vase, he probably would have deserved it.

"Can we talk about something else other than my tour?" he asked.

Boone shrugged. "Are you working on a new album?"

Ash pinched the bridge of his nose. "No," he answered with a sigh.

"On vacation? Hiding out from the paparazzi after your divorce? Not that I *knew* you were getting a divorce, by the way. But I guess that's par for the course since none of us knew you were getting married until Mom and Dad sent a reel that *they'd* been sent by your publicist."

Ash took a sip of his seltzer, swallowed, and then let out a bitter laugh. "There it is," he said.

Boone set his can down on the table between the chair and the couch and threw his arms in the air. "What the hell do you want from me, Ash?"

"What da hell do you want fwum me, Ash?" a tiny, powerful voice called from Kara's room.

Boone's jaw tightened as he exhaled through clenched teeth.

Ash leaned forward, resting his arms on his knees. "I want you to be pissed at me if you're pissed at me! I want you to yell at me or hit me or—I don't know—crack a vase over my head instead of acting like you're happy to see me when I've been such a shitty brother!"

"Shitty brother!" Kara called.

Boone growled and pressed the heels of his hands to his eyes.

Ash stood. "I shouldn't have come here."

The door flew open, and a woman with a stylishly messy blond bun burst into the apartment. "Mama's home!" she called. "Where's my Supergirl?" She strode toward Ash, beaming, then stopped short of throwing her arms around his neck. "*You're* not my husband," she said, matter-of-factly. Then she threw her hands over her mouth. "Ashton? Oh my god. Is that really you?"

And then she *did* throw her arms around his neck and squeezed him tight just as Kara came running out of her room yelling, "Mama! Mama!" and "Shitty brother!"

"Murrrrphyyy!" Casey cried, letting her brother-in-law go.

But Boone was already up and out of the chair.

"Sorry, Babe. I really am. But Ash and I were just about to...do a thing. Be back in an hour or so, okay?" He scooped his daughter into his arms, spun her once, and then blew a raspberry on her cheek as the young girl erupted into peals of laughter.

"You better run," Casey warned, holding her arms out for the daughter exchange. But then she jutted out her chin, placing her cheek in front of Boone's mouth.

Boone obliged, kissing his wife and then his daughter before grabbing Ash by the elbow and dragging him toward the door.

"You boys better behave," Casey told them as her husband opened the door. "And Ashton Murphy, you better come back here for a proper visit before you leave town again."

"He will!" Boone called over his shoulder as he ushered Ash through the door, pulling it closed behind him.

"Where the hell are we going?" Ash whisper-shouted, knowing full well now that Kara's super-hero ears were listening from the other side of the door.

Boone raised a brow. "You said you wanted me to hit you," he replied matter-of-factly. "So I'm taking you someplace where I can give you exactly what you asked for."

Chapter 5

"YOU'RE KIDDING, RIGHT?" ASH ASKED, THOUGH the fact that his brother was already wearing his headgear, mouth guard, and boxing gloves showed that Boone Murphy was not joking.

"Come on!" Boone replied as best he could with the guard covering his teeth. "It'll be good for both of us." He clapped his padded fists together and bounced side to side on his bare feet. Since Ash had been wearing boots, the older Murphy brother agreed they'd both fight shoeless to make it fair... and so Ash wouldn't ruin the floor of the boxing ring.

Oh and also...when Boone dragged him to the Meadow Valley Fire Station and the weight room and boxing ring out back, Ash only took off his boots and let Boone plop the headgear onto his head because he *thought his brother was kidding.*

Now he stood there with his own mouth guard in his left hand, a boxing glove in his right, and the second glove tucked under his right arm.

"Come on," Boone goaded again, this time tapping Ash lightly on the shoulder with his glove. "When was the last time you worked out all your poor-little-rich-boy frustrations?"

Ouch. Ash felt that one right in the gut.

"Piss off," Ash muttered in reply. "I'm not doing this."

Boone shrugged, undeterred. "Hey... I'm not the one who said you were a shitty brother. You figured that one out all on your own."

This time Ash chose a better four-letter word and modified his directive.

Boone nodded. "There we go." Then he tapped his brother's jaw with his glove. "What else you got?" The next shoulder tap felt a lot less *tap* and a little more *push*. "Shitty brother..."

The only way for Ash to push back was to free one of his hands, which was the only reason he shoved the mouth guard over his teeth. But all his one-handed shove did was knock himself off-balance and give Boone a reason to counter with a way less playful hook to the jaw.

Ash stumbled back a few steps, more shocked than pained, but still... Boone had hit him. Like... actually *hit* him.

"You *hit* me," Ash said, stating the obvious. "Like...actually *hit* me."

Boone barked out a laugh. "Look where we are, Bro! I didn't bring you here to play. I brought you here to work shit out, so let's *work* shit out!" He clapped his gloves together once more and then stormed toward Ash like a man on a mission, and that mission seemed to be to lay his brother out flat.

Ash scrambled to get the first glove on and then the second, barely giving himself the time he needed to block the next blow. But when he threw his hands up to protect his face, Boone's glove glanced off Ash's elbow and nailed him straight in the gut.

Ash dropped to his knees, not sure whether he was going to throw up or pass out from the air being knocked clear from his lungs. But when neither happened, and Boone went from the man on a mission to an Oh-shit-did-I-just-hurt-my-brother look in his eyes, Ash climbed to his feet and nailed his opponent with a left cross.

Gone was the concern from Boone's stare. They'd hit the point of no return. And it. Was. On.

⸻

Ten minutes later, both men collapsed on a bench outside the ring, Ash with a split lip and a bruise already blooming on the skin over his ribs, and Boone with a bloody nose he insisted was not broken.

After several moments of silence, save for the two men catching their breath and nursing their wounds, Ash finally asked, "So…did we work shit out?"

Boone shrugged. "I feel better. Don't you?"

Ash rolled his eyes as his brother plugged his

bleeding nostril with a wad of tissue. "You look like what your wife is going to do to *me* once she sees what I did to *you*. And in case you were wondering, it ain't pretty."

Boone nodded at him with a laugh. "I'll just tell her she should see the other guy. The question is, little bro, do *you* feel better?"

Ash sighed. He didn't know how to answer because he'd been knocked over the head *and* punched in the face, the gut, and the ribs all within the past twenty-four hours. It also was because he couldn't remember the last time someone had asked him how he felt, and his brain seemed to have lost the ability to compute what for many was such a normal question to answer.

"I don't know," he admitted. "I mean, it was kind of fun to pummel you now that you're not a head taller than me anymore." Ash laughed but then winced as he felt the cut on his bottom lip tug and likely start bleeding again.

Boone leaned back on the bench and tilted his head toward the sky. "I know what I see online is some curated mix of bullshit and truth. And I also know you're busy as hell and that it's hard for you to get back here, or maybe you don't want to." He straightened to face his younger brother again. "But you've got people here who care about you, man." He clapped Ash on the shoulder. "Enough to give a shit about the *real* story."

Ash nodded, but then he stood. "The thing is, Boone…" He licked his busted lip. "I send you and Eli tickets to every damned show. How long has it been since I've seen one of my brothers in the crowd?" He shook his head. "Maybe it's time to hit pause on how shitty *I've* been and take a good look in the mirror." He shrugged. "How's that for how I'm feeling?"

And then, prick that he already knew himself to be, Ash spun on his heel and left his brother staring wide-eyed as he strode away.

"Ash! Come on!" Boone called after him. "You wanna hit me again? I'll give you one freebie, no retaliation!"

Ash replied by holding up his hand and offering his brother a one-fingered salute.

"Are you staying at the guesthouse? I thought Eli said…" And then it all must have clicked because that was where Boone's words vanished.

Four years ago, Ash Murphy's career was on the rise.

And four years ago, he let the curated mix of bullshit and truth set fire to the best thing that had ever happened to him because he was too stupid to recognize the best thing *wasn't* his career.

"I fucked up," he'd told his brothers when they ambushed him with a joint video call after the announcement of his marriage.

"You didn't even invite Mom and Dad," Eli

had replied. "You didn't even *tell* them before it happened."

"Or us," Boone added.

"We eloped," Ash explained. "It all happened so fast."

But Boone and Eli had both called bullshit. They were the only people who knew that the woman in Ash's bed the morning of the big announcement wasn't his blushing bride. They were the only ones who knew that the Ashton Murphy they'd grown up with would never exclude his family from a family affair.

Except by then, he wasn't that Ashton Murphy anymore. And rather than admit what they already knew, he played along with the curated picture of his life that had been created for him—and in doing so had pushed the people who mattered most so far that they'd stopped trying to find a way back in.

He took his time heading back to the Murphy property, soaking in the solace on the stretch of country road that connected Meadow Valley's town square to the ranch where he'd spent more than half his life. No one gave a shit who he was in Meadow Valley, and for the first time since he'd had the audacity to think that there was something bigger for him outside the confines of his hometown, he enjoyed it.

"Change of plans!" Ash declared as he strode into the guesthouse, not even sure Willow was there, considering he'd slipped out after she'd gone for another ride on Holiday. But when an idea struck, he needed to say it out loud before he forgot it. The same went for writing songs.

Speaking of which… Willow *was* home, sitting on the far arm of the couch in a black tank top and jeans, her bare feet resting on the cushion as she fingered the frets on her guitar and strummed one chord and then another, her brows furrowed as she stared at her instrument.

"You writing without me?" he asked, a smile tugging at the corners of his mouth. Though this time he exercised caution so he didn't reopen the cut again.

"Change of what plans?" Willow countered, glancing up to meet his gaze. "Jesus, Ash!" In one swift move, she tossed the guitar onto the couch and strode across the room, stopping short when she likely found herself standing closer to her new roommate than she wanted. She fidgeted with the bottom of her tank before crossing her arms and glaring at him. "What was it this time? A midday bar brawl? A throwdown with a photographer who dared to get too close to the great Ashton Murphy?"

He flinched but then did his best to school his expression. "Why don't you tell me what you really think of me, Wills." He cleared his throat. "I mean *Willow*."

Her jaw tightened. "Only Colt gets to call me that."

Ash nodded once. "I know. It was a mistake. It won't happen again."

Though in his head he remembered the first time the nickname had rolled off his tongue.

"Okay... That's so weird. That's what my brother, Colt, calls me," she'd told him.

"Oh," Ash had replied. *"Then I won't—"*

"No," Willow interrupted. *"It reminds me of home... the name. And I think maybe I like you reminding me of home too."*

He was pretty sure home was the last thing he reminded her of now.

"So?" she asked, bringing him back to the present. "Are you going to tell me who you got into a fight with or not?"

Ash shrugged. "Does the *who* really matter?"

"I guess it doesn't." Willow sighed. "Are you going to tell me about this change of plans?"

He rounded the corner and stepped into the kitchen, grabbing a much-needed glass of water and downing the whole thing before answering her.

"Your terms with Sloane..." he began. "You choose the photos, you post them, no disclosed location, and no mention of a duet, right?"

She nodded slowly, her eyes narrowed, mistrusting.

"And nowhere in those terms does it specifically

say that my *face* has to be shown in any of those photos?"

This time she shook her head. "I signed it virtually this morning and sent it off to my agent for her signature as well. Your name is only mentioned as the song collaborator."

Ash raised his brows. "Then we don't identify me at all in the photos. You can tease the collaboration and leave the reveal for the concert. This is your gig. It should be about *you*."

She was fidgeting with the hem of her shirt again, still nervous. Still not ready to trust him. Not that he could blame her.

"But Sloane only wants to do this to clean up your image after...you know..."

He huffed out a laugh. "After I got publicly dumped, replaced, and arrested in the same night?" He set his glass in the sink and gripped the edge of the countertop, the veins in his wrists and forearms growing taut. "Maybe I need to sit in my mess for a bit until I can clean it up myself. Anyway, I'm pretty sure sharing the stage with *the* Willow Morgan is all the cleaning up my image will need." He relaxed his arms and ran a hand through his hair. "It's the best thing for the town too. Don't you think? The fewer people who know I'm here, the better."

Willow stared at him long and hard. He could see the wheels turning but couldn't read her expression.

"So you want to do what's best for me and the town?"

Ash nodded. "Yeah. I guess I do."

She backed away, slowly at first, but then scrambled back onto the couch, tossing her guitar strap over her shoulder as she started to strum again. Then she sang, her voice breathy and delicate yet at the same time a powerhouse of emotion that knocked Ash harder than any blow Boone was able to land.

Didn't feel like the right time to unpack
With the whole damned world
    cracking a whip at my back,
So I hopped on a horse and rode until dark,
Knowing with each step I'd never
    recapture the spark.

Everyone wants me to fix what I broke,
But it took me this long to get in on the joke.
Maybe I'll sit in my life, give it time to soak in
'Stead of letting 'em clean every mess I get in.

Willow shrugged when she was done. "Or something like that, I guess?"

"You don't need me for this," he told her. "You're too good on your own." It was the truth. He hadn't written or sung a note with that much of himself in the sound of it for years.

But she shocked him by shaking her head. "Look… I don't believe in muses or stuff like that…"

"And I am definitely no muse," he added.

She laughed. "Maybe not. But… I don't know. You being around is unlocking something up here." She tapped her temple. "Right when I was convinced I'd lost the key."

His pulse quickened as more of the song started to play in his head, parts they hadn't written yet. "Okay…" he told her. "Okay…" He made his way out of the kitchen to where she was. "I have a slight tweak for the melody if you want to hear it."

She started to lift the strap from over her shoulder but abruptly stopped. "You're a lefty," she said. "I forgot."

Except she didn't forget. Willow remembered he was a southpaw and wanted him to stay. She *wanted* to do this together.

"I'll get my guitar," he told her.

She smiled. At *him*. And even if this truce would only be short lived, he would gather every scrap she tossed his way, savoring each one.

Chapter 6

THE AFTERNOON PASSED IN A FEVER DREAM OF writing, strumming, rewriting, scrapping the whole thing, and starting again. Somehow Willow was both depleted and elated. Even though the song was still a mess—a jumble of lyrics that so far worked best as scattered verses rather than a cohesive song—she couldn't remember the last time writing had felt like this. She couldn't remember the last time it had been...fun.

Not that Ash Murphy was fun. He was...he was Mayhem from the Allstate commercials, leaving scandals and broken hearts in his wake, and Willow would not be foolish enough to get sucked into that kind of orbit again, not when she knew better.

She stood in the kitchen, nibbling on one of her shortbread cookies, when she heard singing coming from the bedroom. Correction...the bathroom. But Ash hadn't bothered to close the bedroom door.

After the pair decided to call it a day, Ash had disappeared into their shared showering space to clean up. He still hadn't told her what happened earlier that day, and Willow hadn't asked again. Whatever trouble he'd been up to was his business, not hers. She didn't care who split his lip or where he went when he wasn't in the guesthouse. Hell, she didn't care about anything pertaining to Ashton Murphy unless it concerned the song they were writing.

Which they weren't right now. So why, if Willow couldn't care less about her roommate's whereabouts or actions, did she find herself moving toward her bedroom? Why was she suddenly slipping through the door he'd left ajar, tiptoeing so she could hear better. So she could identify the song.

Her breath caught in her throat when the bathroom acoustics carried a familiar lyric out to where she stood.

"'This time I'll pick myself up when I fall...'" Ash crooned, his deep rasp of a voice adding a new layer of aching regret to the line. *Her* line. "'This time I'll block your number before you call. This time I'll hold the needle and thread. Jagged stitches 'cross my heart...cold sheets on your side of the bed.'"

Before her brain registered what she was doing, Willow stormed into the steam-filled bathroom and threw open the shower door.

She was greeted by a really great ass and sculpted back, but she would not let that get in the way of her fury.

It took a second for Ash to react to the gust of

cold air that must have rushed in to greet him, which meant a second more of him staining her song...*her* song...with his uninvited—albeit gorgeous—voice.

He finally flinched at the change in air temperature and spun to face her, but when he saw Willow standing there, he actually had the audacity to grin.

"You afraid I'm using all the hot water?" he teased. "Or do you want to join me that badly?"

He was lathered in body wash, but that did nothing to hide what he had going on between his legs. If any of the online tabloids wanted to know if Ash Murphy was a shower or a grower, Willow could probably make a pretty penny with her intel. But there was no way in hell she was going to boost his ego by publicizing that he somehow— and impressively—both.

"What gives you the right?" she cried over the sound of the shower's spray.

He blinked as water hit him in the side of the face and trickled down over his eyes.

"What?" he asked. "What did I do now? Wait. This is ridiculous." He slammed his palm against the shower knob, effectively turning the water off despite the fact that he was still full of suds. He crossed his arms over his bare chest.

Willow's mouth fell open. "What are you doing?"

"Freezing my ass off," he told her. "So I don't have to shout over the water to defend myself for..." He shrugged. "Whatever I fucked up between leaving the living room and now."

Her palms clenched into fists at her sides. "You were singing," she said coolly, though there was nothing cool about her heart hammering against her ribs.

Ash laughed. "Yeah. I know. I sing in the shower. So what?"

"So what? So *what*? So...so you were singing *my* song."

He laughed again. "Yeah. I know," he replied, parroting his own words. "It's a good song," he added matter-of-factly.

Willow's eyes widened, and she glanced left and right, then back at Ash as if suddenly realizing where she was and wondering how she got there. The argument in her head seemed so logical when it first took root, but now she knew her accusation was so way off base that it wasn't even on the field anymore.

"That's why we make music, isn't it?" he asked, his voice gentler this time. "So other people will sing it?"

She opened and closed her mouth to respond her fight-or-flight retreating because it knew she couldn't just up and admit why the incident had her stomach tied in knots.

Willow blew out a breath, her shoulders relaxing. "It caught me off guard," she told him, which technically was the truth. It just wasn't the whole truth. "It was never released as a single, so it kind of freaked me out that you knew it well enough to just...sing it."

"Hello?" a male voice called from *outside* the bedroom. "Anyone home?"

"Are you a ventriloquist?" Willow whisper-shouted to Ash. "Or do I need to grab another vase?"

"Just getting out of the shower!" Ash called, then returned his attention to Willow. "It's just Boone. My brother. Keep him company until I rinse off? I'll be two minutes."

Willow grumbled something under her breath though was secretly grateful for whatever divine intervention was getting her out of the whole yelling-at-a-very-naked-Ash-in-the-shower situation.

"Fine," she told him as if it were a burden to leave, then spun on her heel and headed straight back from where she'd come.

"Boone!" Willow said with probably too much enthusiasm for a man she'd met once a few years back. "It's nice to see you a—"

But when the other Murphy brother turned around to face her, she gasped at the slight bruising under his left eye.

"It was *you*," she added as realization hit her like a boulder. "*You're* the fight Ash got into earlier today."

Boone laughed, his bright-blue eyes crinkling at the corners. He was a slightly older version of

Ash, all dark hair, blue eyes, and the same rugged, rancher-ness. But there was something softer in Boone's presence compared to Ash's sharp edges. That was the only way Willow could explain it. Even when Ash was all smiles and teasing, she knew that if she wasn't careful around him, she might get cut.

"Fight?" Boone replied. "Is that what he called it? I like to think of it more as a brotherly bonding sort of thing. Was hoping after having a few hours to marinate on the situation, Ash would see it that way too."

"*Bonding?*" Ash asked accusingly, and Willow whirled to see Murphy brother number two rinsed and in a clean pair of jeans pulling a gray T-shirt over his head. Without the suds covering his skin, she caught a glimpse of what looked like his own slight bruising over his left ribs.

"Seriously…" Willow began, her gaze volleying back and forth between the two of them. "Why are men? Just…why?" She grabbed them each by the wrist and dragged them to the breakfast bar. She pointed toward the stools. "*Sit.* Both of you."

They sat.

She left them there and strode around the corner and into the galley kitchen where she grabbed the tin of her homemade cookies and plopped it down on the counter in front of them. Then she poured them each a glass of ice-cold milk. "You two are going to sit here like good little boys, eating your cookies and milk, and talking your shit out. NO. HITTING."

They both had the decency to look chagrined as they nodded.

"I'm going to give you boys some space and go groom the horses. If you do what you're supposed to do and feel up for it, you boys should go for a ride after. Pretty sure activities like that are more of a brotherly bonding sort of thing than whatever you two were up to this morning."

The brothers nodded again.

"She's scary," Boone said to Ash.

"Tell me about it," Ash replied. "The vase to the temple? My welcome-home gift?" He nodded toward Willow.

"No shit," Boone replied, then reached for a cookie, but Willow smacked his hand.

"*Not* until you ask your brother *why* he took a vase to the temple," she told Boone.

Boone sighed, then turned to Ash. "Why did you take a vase to the temple?"

Ash blew out a breath. "Destruction of property... Drunk and disorderly..." He waved a hand in the air. "It's my healthy way of dealing with public humiliation."

Boone swore under his breath, and Willow saw all manner of teasing leave his expression. "Why didn't you call?"

Ash shrugged. "Thought I'd sleep it off in the

guesthouse before letting you know I was home, but the mediator over there thought I was breaking and entering." He nodded toward Willow, then let out a mirthless laugh. "Pretty sure, though, that even if I rang the bell, things would have gone down in about the same way."

His eyes met hers in a flash of acknowledgment before Ash turned his attention back to his brother. Willow's throat tightened. What was he acknowledging? Her hurt? His regret? Singing "This Time" in the shower?

"Can I have a cookie now?" Boone asked, breaking the silence. "I can smell them, and my mouth is watering, and it kind of feels like *not* eating one will—I don't know—give my taste buds blue balls or something."

Ash barked out a laugh, and Boone shrugged.

Willow rolled her eyes. "I'm heading to the barn," she said, then waggled her index finger back and forth at them. "No…?"

"Hitting," both men mumbled.

"Good," she replied. "And no recess until you boys have served your full detention, which means working your shit out with *words*."

She gave them one final look that she hoped solidified her expectations before booting up and heading outside.

Willow had made it a couple of laps with Holiday in the arena when she heard hoofbeats behind her. She slowed her mare and waited to see which of the brothers approached first. But because she had zero patience, and something about the anticipation of Ash Murphy's presence made her more anxious than him sleeping on the couch outside her room, she made it approximately three seconds before glancing over her shoulder to see Boone atop his white gelding...and only Boone.

"Did I scare your brother off?" she asked with a nervous laugh when the older Murphy and his horse trotted up beside her.

Boone shook his head. "He'll be out in a bit. I guess inspiration struck, and he's out on the back porch writing before he 'loses the magic.'" He said the last part with finger quotes.

"Writing?" Willow asked, and she fought the knee-jerk reaction to jump straight to anger, still stinging from her misinterpretation of Ash's new injury when he returned home earlier that day. "On *our* song?" she added, trying to sound more curious than accusatory.

He shook his head again. "Nah. Said he's always working on his next album and has to write when the words come. He told me about the duet, though." Boone smiled at her, but even beneath the brim of his hat, she could see the hint of concern in his gaze. "I know we don't know each other well," he continued, motioning between them. "But I feel like I know enough to ask… Are you sure you want to go down that road with my brother?"

Willow's stomach protested before she could find the words, tying itself in copious knots, reminding her of just how unsure she truly was.

"No," she replied, because what would be the point in lying to Boone when he did know enough to ask the question. "But I need a song, and your brother needs another image refresh." She shrugged. "I know that tons of writers will tell you that there is no such thing as writer's block, but I've been blocked for…well…a while." How about two *years*? But this conversation didn't call for that much honesty. "And for some reason—probably stemming from a hideous crime I must have committed in a past life—the universe has decided to open the floodgates of creativity only when I'm verbally sparring with your brother."

Boone laughed. "I'm guessing that crime was hideous as hell." He tipped his hat and nodded toward the expanse of track in the straightaway ahead of them. "You up for a bit of nonverbal sparring? Maybe clear your head?"

Willow nodded back toward the guesthouse. "Did you boys work your shit out like I asked you to?"

Boone gave her a wink, and despite the vast differences she could already see between the brothers, they both had the same mischievous glint in their eyes. "It was a good start," he told her. "Admittedly better than me dragging him to the firehouse boxing ring and goading him into taking a swing at me."

Willow winced. Not only had she accused Ash of starting some sort of daytime brawl, but now Boone had to tell her the guy didn't even want to fight in the first place?

"Yeah," she finally said. "Nonverbal sparring it is." Then she gave Holiday a nudge with her heels as she called, "Yah!" And the mare took off, hopefully leaving Boone Murphy in the dust.

Chapter 7

ASH STOOD WITH MIDNIGHT'S REINS IN HIS HAND at the entrance to the arena. The mare whinnied and snorted as Boone and Willow raced by.

"I know, girl," he soothed, stroking her shoulder. "I want to get out there too, but can we just watch for another minute or two?"

Something in his tone must have calmed the mare because she let loose what sounded like a sigh and then all but stilled as Ash marveled at Willow not only holding her own against his raised-on-the-back-of-a-horse brother, but also smoking his ass, keeping at least a nose ahead of him at every turn.

She caught a glimpse of him as she approached the barn and pulled up on the reins, but she over-shot him due to Holiday's speed.

Boone, looking grateful for getting to call it quits, brought Cirrus to a halt right in front of his younger brother and his mare. He lifted his hat with one hand and swiped his arm across his forehead with the other.

"A heads-up that she was an ace in the saddle would have been nice!" Boone called down to him.

Ash laughed. "What's the matter, old man? You outta shape?"

His brother plopped his hat back down on his head and glared at him. "You want to take it back to the ring?" he challenged.

Willow and Holiday trotted back toward the two brothers. "What did I say about working your shit out?"

Ash stuck his foot in Midnight's stirrup and climbed onto her saddle. "No hitting. Isn't that right…old man?" he goaded his brother again.

Boone growled, but his shoulders relaxed. "Good. I don't have it in me for another round." Then he shook his head and laughed.

Ash laughed too. It would take a lot for his relationship with either of his brothers to feel even ten percent like it did when they were growing up. But laughing and harassing his brother—good-naturedly, of course—felt at least like a small step in the right direction.

"Should we all hit the trail to the clearing?" Willow asked as if she was just getting started with their riding adventure.

Boone raised his hands in defeat. "Count me out. Kara will be up from her nap soon. I promised her and Casey we'd play beauty salon before dinner, which basically means Kara gets to paint my face with her mama's makeup."

"Did you lose a bet or something?" Willow asked.

Boone narrowed his eyes at his brother and then

turned his attention back to Willow. "Not exactly. But every time my daughter learns a new...um... *colorful* word on my watch, *I* have to play client while Kara pretends to be her mama."

Willow's wide-eyed gaze volleyed between the two men until Ash finally spoke up.

"She might have gotten 'shit' from me, but 'goddamn' was all you. I think it had something to do with *The Vampire Diaries*?"

Boone mouthed a choice directive at his brother and then flipped him the bird in case he hadn't gotten the message.

"You still want to hit the clearing if it's just me?" Ash asked, ready and expecting to be turned down. But Willow surprised him with a shrug.

"I guess I wouldn't mind the company." She turned her attention to Boone. "Enjoy your makeover. I hope I get to meet Casey and your swearin' baby girl while I'm in town."

The departing Murphy grinned. "Casey would love that. My swearin' baby girl would too. How about when Eli and Beth are back in town? We can fire up Eli's grill, introduce you to the chickens... Colt and Jenna should come too, of course. It'll be one big family reunion."

"It's a date!" Willow exclaimed.

Ash cleared his throat. "Yeah. Great idea, big bro," he lied. Because finding his way back to some semblance of normalcy with his own brothers was one thing. But how much did Colt Morgan know about Willow's time on Ash's tour…or why she left? He guessed that in several days, he was about to find out. And he doubted there'd be boxing gloves or headgear to cushion any potential blows.

And with that, Boone and Cirrus disappeared back into the barn, leaving Ash and Willow to chase the soon-to-be setting sun on a ride to and from the clearing.

"Are we racing too?" he asked.

She shook her head. "Let's take our time."

Ash tilted his head toward the sky that was now swathed in streaks of blue, orange, and pink. Then his eyes fell back on her, a girl on her horse, backlit by the golden hour.

"What?" Willow asked, and he realized he was staring.

He huffed out a laugh. "Nothing."

She bristled. "Fine. Don't tell me what you were thinking when you obviously have something on your mind."

Ash grabbed the straw hat that had been resting on Midnight's withers and placed it on his head. "You don't really want to know what I'm thinking, Wills… Sorry. *Willow*." He tapped his heels and urged the mare forward. "Come on. Let's enjoy the ride."

And they did. At least, Ash did. They took it slow, just like she'd wanted, and made their way to the clearing in what for him felt like an almost comfortable silence. There was still tension between them, but he could feel something in her demeanor softening.

They had a bit of sunlight left when they reached their destination, so they both dismounted, tied off the horses, and then made their way to the giant maple. Willow lay down just outside the shade, tossing her hat to the side and crossing her hands behind her head.

"Do you ever watch the clouds at the end of the day like this? How they change color and shape and then sometimes disappear?" She tilted her head toward where Ash still stood. "Or am I the only weirdo who does that?"

Was that an invitation to join her? She wasn't telling him to piss off or hitting him over the head with pottery, so he decided that it was and lay down beside her. He set his hat on the grass between them, ensuring he was a safe couple of feet away.

"You're not a weirdo," he finally replied. "At least not for meditating with the clouds."

She grabbed his hat and tossed it at his head.

Ash laughed, and then they both sank into the quiet as wispy white cirrus clouds slowly sailed through a sea of pink until they seemed to vanish into mist.

"What if I did want to know what you were thinking?" Willow asked after neither of them had spoken for several minutes.

Ash answered her but kept his eyes trained on the sky above. "Then I'd probably have fed you some corny line that belonged in a song about how you looked beautiful backlit by the setting sun. But I know I have no right to look at you like that, so I kept my damned mouth shut."

He hoped she knew the bite in his tone was aimed at no one other than himself.

The air went still again for a handful of seconds before she said anything in response.

"Do you regret what happened four years ago?" Just like that, after two days of dancing around the elephant that was far too big to even fit in the room, Willow was done pulling punches.

"Every day," he admitted. Though she had to know that much. He didn't blame her for walking away from him and never looking back, but he'd made it clear on more than one occasion that he hated himself for how it all went down.

In his peripheral vision, he saw her roll onto her side to face him, but he wasn't ready to do the same. So he focused on the clouds while she apparently focused on him.

"Hating you is exhausting," she told him.

He sighed. "If that's true, then there must be a shit ton of exhausted people in my life."

She collapsed back onto her back. "Your brother doesn't hate you," she continued.

Ash crossed one ankle over the other and

laughed. "Is that why his first instinct was to kick the shit out of me after not seeing me for years?"

He didn't know why he was perpetuating this conversation. Ash hadn't talked to anyone like this since... Well, he didn't talk to anyone like this. He played the game, put on his public persona, gave the fans what they wanted, and gave his management team an ulcer. But it felt different when it was only him and her, just like it had four years ago. Even if the real him was a mess, he seemed to be dropping the act around Willow.

"It's getting dark," she finally said. "We should probably head back."

He nodded, grabbed his hat, and climbed to his feet. Then he held out a hand for Willow, and she surprised him by taking it. Once on her feet, she pulled her hand free.

"I'm not the naïve groupie you thought I was four years ago."

His eyes widened. "Willow, I never thought—"

"Let me finish," she interrupted.

Ash nodded and closed his mouth.

"For reasons beyond my wildest imagination, we work—as co-writers. But if we're going to survive as cohabitants too, I need to stop putting so much energy and effort into the Ash Murphy anti-fan club."

His brows furrowed. "Is that a thing?"

She nodded, expression earnest. "Oh yeah.

I'm the founder, president, and social committee chair. We have online meetups every Wednesday night and do a pub crawl the first Saturday of every month."

Ash stared at her, unblinking, and she left him hanging for several seconds until she finally burst out laughing.

"I know I deserved that," he admitted. "But you just made me realize that such a club probably does exist, and it's going to be really hard not to fall into a Google rabbit hole later trying to confirm it."

She shrugged. "If you sign up with my referral code, it's half off the joining fee." Then she strode toward Holiday, leaving him there to wonder...

"You're kidding, right?" he called after her, following her back to his own horse. "I mean, at least about being president and founder?"

She hopped into her saddle and took a page from the Ash Murphy book, answering him with nothing more than a mischievous wink. Then she nudged Holiday with her heels and took off for the ranch before he even had a chance to untie Midnight from her tree.

When he finally made it back to the ranch, Holiday was already in her stall, no sign of Willow in the barn. He guessed she hadn't wanted to take her time riding back with him...probably because it was Wednesday, and she had an anti-fan club meetup to attend.

He half expected to find her sitting at the breakfast bar, video chat open to greet the other members. But the house was empty, save for a page ripped from what he guessed was her songwriting notebook stuck to the fridge with a magnet.

Need some space. Heading out to see my brother and Jenna. Rain check on writing for tonight?

He nodded as if they were having an actual conversation. But that seemed to be the last thing Willow wanted. Space was good. Two days with Willow, and he was venturing into dangerous territory…in his head, the kind that made him wonder if her abandoning her hate might be the beginning of something like forgiveness.

Ash's stomach grumbled, and he pulled out his phone to check the time. Then he opened his texting app and fired off a quick message to Boone before he talked himself out of it.

Ash: How about I pick up dinner for you, me, Casey, and Kara and bring it over?

Why did seeing the flashing ellipses make him more nervous than if his brother didn't respond at all?

Boone: Will you let Kara paint your nails? Full

disclosure...she's 2. She does not stay in the
lines.

Ash let out a relieved laugh.

Ash: Was going to get my nails done later
this week, so she's actually saving me a trip.
And staying in the lines is so boring.
Boone: See you soon. Pick up whatever you
want, but I wouldn't kick a pizza out of bed.
Or an order of garlic knots.

Ash found himself unexpectedly grinning. Did
this mean his brother had forgiven him? Did it
mean he'd forgiven his brother? Or maybe after
their time in the ring and their forced chat—thanks
to Willow—they could simply move forward.

One thing Ash knew for sure was that he wouldn't
be eating alone tonight or with anyone who stood
to either make or lose money on whatever he said,
did, or sang next. He'd be with family, and tonight
that sounded better than any crowd cheering him
on from below the stage.

Chapter 8

WILLOW HAD MANAGED TO RAIN CHECK WRITING and sharing any sort of formal meal with Ash for three whole days. But her big mouth—signing herself up for a family reunion at Eli and Beth's place—made it impossible to get out of the barbecue with her newly returned neighbors, her brother and sister-in-law, plus Casey, Boone, *and* Ash tonight.

"Don't Eli and Beth want to settle in before hosting everyone? They just got back last night. With a *baby*," she'd reasoned to Colt when he'd called her with the "good" news that morning.

"They're settling in today, getting Maddie back on her nap schedule and seeing a few patients at the clinic," her brother had explained. "But it sounds like Eli is itching to have both of his brothers in one place for the first time in years, and he said Beth can't wait to meet you."

So…yeah. A big ole family reunion with all the Murphys and Morgans under one roof or sky or whatever. No big deal. Willow wasn't anxious at all.

Hence the multiple batches of toffee shortbread she'd baked while Ash spent the afternoon with Midnight in the arena.

"I was gonna ride today," she mumbled to herself while sliding the last cookie off her spatula and onto the cooling rack. But for some reason, after the other afternoon, in addition to writing and eating, she'd avoided riding with him.

President and founder of the Ash Murphy anti-fan club? What had she been thinking, teasing him like that? Even now, as she thought about the exchange, she had to suppress a grin.

The front door flew open, and she startled, flinging the spatula in Ash's direction.

"Whoa," he replied, holding his hands up. "Do I need to start making formal announcements of my arrival so I don't risk another concussion?"

Willow rolled her eyes. "I didn't throw the spatula *at* you. Just in your general direction."

He rubbed the spot on his temple where the ceramic-induced gash was finally scabbing over. "Is that where you aimed the vase? In my general direction?"

She wiped her hands on her apron, and then—with as much dignity as she could muster—strode to where the spatula lay on the floor at Ash's dusty-booted feet. She picked it up and offered him a nervous smile. "Sorry," she told him. "You just caught me off guard."

He crossed his arms and raised his brows, and Willow tried not to notice the sleeve of his T-shirt stretched over his biceps. Tried…and failed.

Because despite not being as naïve as she was four years ago, she was a human woman with eyes. And Ashton Murphy was an undisputed sight to behold, onstage or off.

He raised a brow. "For the spatula or the vase?"

She hugged the spatula to her chest and sighed. "Both," she admitted. "You scared the shit out of me that first night, but I know you didn't mean to. I should have apologized for hurting you, and I didn't. So...to clarify... I'm sorry for chucking the spatula in your general direction." She sighed. "And I'm sorry for knocking you out with the vase."

His blue eyes bored into hers, and it took everything in her not to look away.

"And scarring my otherwise flawless face?" he teased, brushing his fingers over his temple again.

Willow winced. "Ugh. Yes. That too. Though most people think scars add character, right?" She really had clobbered him, hadn't she? Clobbered him. Hated him. Avoided him. Was it enough, finally? Because Willow was so tired. How did she convince her heart to finally let go and leave the past in the past?

Ash took a small step forward and gave her a conspiratorial grin. "Are *you* most people, Willow Morgan?" he asked.

Willow's throat grew dry, and she had to swallow before she could reply.

"No," she told him. "I'm not most people."

He surprised her with a grin. "No," he agreed. "You're not." He brushed his hands off on his jeans. "I'm going to shower and then head over to Eli and Beth's a little early. Figure my official reunion with brother number two shouldn't be with an audience just in case Eli wants to offer a similar greeting to Boone's."

Willow winced. "You really have taken your share of beatings since you got home, huh?"

He leaned back and shrugged. "Probably deserved most of it, right?"

And despite the smile still on his scruffy, unshaven face, Willow felt a small tug in her chest. *She'd* been punishing Ash Murphy in her head and heart for years, but this was the first time she considered that maybe all this time he'd been doing the same thing to himself.

"No," she told him, though she wasn't sure where she was going with her disagreement yet. "I don't think anyone ever deserves to get hurt, Murphy. It just happens. That's life. You're either the hurt*er* or the hurt*ee*."

This time he was the one to protest with a shake of the head. "Some people are neither," he told her.

Willow sighed. "Aren't they the lucky ones?"

"They really are," he agreed.

Silence hung in the air for several seconds before Ash was the one to break it.

"So… I'm going to shower and get out of your hair."

Willow nodded. "Yeah. Of course. I'll leave you to it." She nodded back toward the kitchen. "I've gotta see a man about some cookies. Wait…that sounded like innuendo, and it was not innuendo. I really do have a lot of cookies to deal with back there, so…yeah. I'll leave you to your naked. I mean *shower*. Oh my god." She clamped a hand over her mouth and backed away. Slowly.

Ash watched her go until she bumped into the wall and waved him off with her spatula.

He laughed and disappeared through the bedroom door, making sure to close it behind him.

———

Willow fidgeted with the spaghetti strap of her pale-pink maxi dress. She'd worn the same dress onstage on more than one occasion and felt nothing but confidence in what had become her performance look—a simple dress and her calf-high boots. Tonight, though, she couldn't help wondering if it was too much or maybe not enough. Did it look like she was *trying* to look good? The follow-up question being, did she look like she was trying to look good for *Ash*? And why did she care one way or another?

"You are allowed to put in the effort simply for yourself," she told the woman in the bedroom mirror. But what kind of fool would she be if that wasn't the case?

Rather than overthink to the point of tossing on jeans and an oversized sweatshirt, she squared her shoulders and strode to the kitchen where she found the tin she had lined with wax paper and three layers of her late mother's famous toffee shortbread cookies. She dropped her phone in her pocket and with her other hand grabbed the bottle of red she picked up at the local market the day before, anticipating a quiet Saturday night in the guesthouse. She guessed now she'd have to share.

"The clinic will be closed, so just head around back," Colt had told her. "Everyone will be outside."

So, Willow exited the safety and cocoon of the guesthouse and ventured the handful of yards over to the rear of the Murphy Veterinary Clinic where she found a stamped concrete patio looking out on a fenced-in field where Holiday, Cirrus, and Midnight grazed. And gathered around a built-in grill stood four men, three of whom looked like the spitting images of one another from different stages in life, save for the unexpected addition of Eli Murphy's beard. The odd man out was, of course, her brother, Colt.

"Am I interrupting the bro portion of the evening?" she asked, stepping onto the patio and making her presence at this strange reunion official.

"Wills!" Colt called, striding toward her with his

arms outstretched, a bottle of beer dangling from one hand.

Willow held up her own hands, both occupied, and her big brother immediately set his beer down on a long wooden table set for eight and grabbed both the cookies and the wine, placing them next to his beer. Then Colt scooped his sister into a giant hug, lifting her off her feet as she yelped with laughter.

"Okay! Okay," she told him, her grin growing wider every second she was with the person she loved most in this world.

He set her back down on her feet.

"Don't you think I'm getting a little too old for that?" she asked him with raised brows.

Colt shrugged. "Not until I'm too old to do it without breaking a hip or something like that."

She laughed again, and from behind her brother she saw Eli approach. Boone waved from the grill, and Ash seemed to be preoccupied with something in the field beyond. Or maybe he was simply avoiding her like she had been avoiding him since the clearing.

"Willow!"

"Eli. Hi!" she replied, extending a hand. But Eli Murphy—who she'd only met once and didn't remember being the openly affectionate type—followed Colt's lead and drew her into a warm hug. "Oh," she said as the eldest Murphy gave her a quick yet warm embrace before taking a step back and offering her a welcoming smile.

"How's the guesthouse?" he asked. "Everything working okay? Do you have enough space to... um...to work?"

Ah. So that was where the warm greeting was probably coming from.

Is it okay that my brother crashed your stay, and if not, do you want me to toss him out on his ass? Because I'll do it. Just say the word.

At least, that was what Willow imagined as the subtext Eli was trying to convey.

"The house is lovely," she told him. "And there might have been some space issues at first, but I think I've got everything worked out," she assured him.

Eli let out a relieved breath. "Good," he replied. "Good. Wouldn't want the first review of our vacation rental to tank just because of a not-quite breaking and entering." He laughed.

Willow's eyes widened. "Vacation rental?" she asked. "I thought it was a family residence."

Eli nodded. "It is. I mean, it was going to be. But Beth grew up in the hospitality business, and you know your brother here knows a thing or two about running guest ranches."

Colt grinned. "Not that the Meadow Valley guest ranch is looking for competition, but the Murphy property is a great opportunity for more of an intimate ranch experience. And if the first review comes from someone who others might consider a celebrity…"

Willow's cheeks flushed. She was still getting used to the fact that people she'd never met knew her name and actually paid money to see her perform. She loved what she did, but she also appreciated places where she could separate herself from that person people only knew as a presence onstage… Places like Meadow Valley where she might get a knowing glance or two, but other than that—thanks to her brother being pretty damned beloved by the town he now called home—Willow could simply *be*.

"I would be honored to give the Murphy Ranch a glowing first review," she told Eli. "As long as there are no other surprise late-night guests."

Eli nodded toward where Ash and Boone still stood at the grill, Ash's back conveniently to the rest of them. "Thank goodness there's only one of him, right?" he teased.

Willow crossed her arms and nodded. "But I'm guessing you and Boone are pretty happy to have him back for a bit, huh?"

The eldest Murphy scratched the back of his neck and nodded slowly. "Yeah," he admitted, no hint of teasing left in his tone. "It's about time we all stood on the same piece of land. Four years is too long."

"Four years?" she asked, but Eli didn't have a chance to respond as one by one, three women emerged from the sliding door leading into the home attached to the back of the Murphy Veterinary Clinic.

Casey carried what looked like a charcuterie board to end all charcuterie boards. Jenna held a pitcher of sweet tea. And the third woman—the one who had to be Beth—carried a six-month-old girl with fine dark curls, bright-blue eyes, and a four-toothed grin.

Casey blew Willow a kiss as she strode by. Jenna kissed her on the cheek before dropping the pitcher of tea off at the table. And Beth—a woman she'd never met before—handed her the baby.

"It's the only way I can properly hug you," Beth told her with a sheepish grin. "Plus my two other baby handlers had their hands full, and my back is killing me."

And then Willow received her third hug in a matter of minutes...and a baby who seemed fascinated with Willow's face, exploring it with her adorable, chubby, and mildly sticky fingers.

"She's very tactile," Beth explained. "I hope that's okay."

"Back still bothering you?" Eli asked, sliding his hand across the small of his wife's back.

She wore a green camisole, dark skinny jeans, and black ballet flats that reminded Willow that she wasn't the only performer in the group, Beth having danced with the Radio City Rockettes, even while pregnant with Maddie.

Beth nodded, and Eli kissed the top of her head. Then he held his arms out toward his daughter, and the young girl clapped when she saw her daddy, reaching for and grabbing hold of his beard. "Ow!" he said with a laugh as he situated Maddie in his arms. "I'll take her to see the chickens and then get her ready for bed if you want to open the wine and take a load off."

Beth beamed at what Willow could tell were the loves of her life. "Her bedtime bottle is all ready for you on the counter, and I am going to take you up on the wine and the sitting and everything else you just said." She grabbed her daughter's foot and kissed her toes. Then she raised herself on her own tippy toes and kissed her husband too.

"Finish up the burgers and dogs!" Eli called to his brothers as he strode off toward the chicken coop at the far end of the field. "I've got a date with one of my girls!"

"What about Boone and Casey's little girl?" Willow asked.

"With my parents," Casey announced, approaching the group with two glasses of wine and handing one to Willow.

"And we are in between fosters right now," Jenna added, handing the third of four glasses of wine to

Beth, her shoulders slightly sagging. "Christopher just left for college, but he'll be home for the holidays, and we'll hopefully have a houseful by then."

Colt stepped behind Jenna, wrapping his arms around her waist and pulling her to his chest. "Just means we'll have to find something *else* to keep us busy at home until the bedrooms are full again." He dipped his head and kissed her neck, and Jenna's cheeks flushed pink.

This was... Wow. Willow was surrounded by so much love. It felt like a fun house version of her current life where she was always surrounded by others—her band, tour manager, and the few roadies who dealt with the minimal equipment with which they traveled. And while on tour, everyone was her best friend. They were a family of sorts. But when there was no gig, they all went their separate ways, back to their lives outside of the show. It was like summer camp, but for grown-ups.

But everyone here was family in the truest sense of the word.

"You okay, Wills?" Colt asked, and Willow realized she'd gotten lost in her head with everyone else watching.

"Yeah," she replied, holding up her glass. "It's just really nice to be here."

And as everyone seemed to settle into their roles of grillers, wine pourers—because of course there was more than the one bottle she brought—appetizer passers, and storytellers, Willow forgot that she'd second-guessed her outfit or whether or not she'd been softening toward Ash. She just enjoyed existing among brothers and sisters-in-law and people who—at least for now— didn't care who she was outside of this backyard.

"Thank you," she leaned over and whispered to her brother once dinner got underway.

"For what?" Colt asked.

"For not going all Neanderthal when you found out Ash was going to be here."

"I'm not going to ruin the night." A muscle pulsed in his jaw. "Do you forgive him, Wills?"

Do you regret what happened four years ago?

And Ash hadn't even hesitated to answer.

Every day.

Maybe it was more than being too exhausted to hate. Maybe there was more to his side of the story. Either way, they were sharing a house and writing a song, and Willow was ready to let go.

But did she forgive him?

She might have been talking to her brother, but when she glanced across the table to where Ash sat at the far end, she found him looking directly back at her, offering her a tentative smile.

"Yeah," she told her brother. "I think I do."

Chapter 9

THROUGH THE FLICKER OF ORANGE AND BLUE flame, Ash continued to steal glances at Willow from the opposite side of the stone firepit. The whole lot of them had grown quiet as wineglasses were topped off and Beth connected a Bluetooth speaker to her music-streaming app.

"I call it my perfect night playlist," she'd told them. It even contained a song here and there by Ash himself and a few of his favorite Willow Morgan tunes.

Except every Willow Morgan tune was his favorite, even the ones that hurt to hear.

Ash was the only one not hitting the after-dinner wine. He wanted a clear head tonight, wanted to avoid any missteps with this unplanned reunion with his brothers...and with her.

He noticed Willow shiver despite the heat of the licking flames. Without realizing what he was doing before he did it, Ash was circling the group, sliding out of the unbuttoned plaid shirt he'd been wearing over his tee, and draping it over the back of her Adirondack chair and thereby her shoulders.

"Fire's getting a little too warm for me," he told

her as she stared at him with wide, dark eyes. Then he continued up the path to the main portion of the patio where he poured himself another glass of Jenna's sweet tea even though he wasn't thirsty.

By the time he turned around to deal with whatever looks were thrown his way following his unplanned gesture, Colt was out of his chair and halfway to him.

"Was wondering when this part of the reunion would take place," Ash mumbled under his breath.

"Did you say something?" Colt asked when they were in speaking distance. He poured himself a cup of sweet tea as well, clearly wanting the rest of the group to think this was simply two thirsty men around the watering hole.

Except Ash knew none of them were thinking that.

"Nope," Ash replied. "Just thinking out loud. But I'm guessing you have something you want to say to me." It wasn't a challenge. Just a statement of fact. Whatever Willow's brother wanted to say to him—or possibly *do* to him—Ash told himself he had it coming.

"This is your brother's house," Colt began. "And for better or worse, my sister is working with you for the next several weeks, so I have to make peace with that. But I have to ask what the hell it is you think you're doing."

Ash took a sip of his tea. "Do you mean right this second? Drinking some delicious sweet tea."

He might have had it coming, but Ash Murphy wouldn't be Ash Murphy if he didn't push a button or two. His best defense was always offense.

"Don't," Colt told him, unamused. "Okay? Just don't."

Ash sighed. "She looked cold. I gave her a shirt. That's it. Transaction complete." He nodded at Colt's own long-sleeved button-down with a T-shirt peeking out from behind his collar. "You could have done the same, but you didn't." He shrugged. "So I did."

Even in the dim moonlight, Ash could see the other man's jaw clench. "She might forgive you, Murphy. But that doesn't mean I have to. And that doesn't give you license to mess with her again. I don't like you working with her, and I sure as hell don't like you living with her, but I guess the *transaction* works in her favor. But you need to swear to me that all you are after is the song and whatever it'll do for you professionally."

Ash wanted to give Colt the answer he wanted, but all he really heard in the guy's meant-to-be threatening big brother speech was one single word.

"Wait…" He felt like he could hear his heart beating in his ears. "Did you say Willow *forgives* me?"

"Are you two gossiping about me?" Willow's voice sang out from over her brother's shoulder.

Never in his life did he wish Willow Morgan would disappear from view, but right now, he wanted—no, *needed*—Colt to confirm what Ash thought he'd heard.

Except Willow stumbled, catching herself with a hand on her brother's shoulder.

"Whoops!" she said with a laugh. "I probably should have said no to that last glass of wine."

Ash had to fight every instinct, every twitch of his muscles, to not go to her, even if she was now wearing his shirt.

"You okay, Wills?" Colt asked, gently grabbing her elbow to help her steady herself on her feet.

Wills. It killed Ash that Colt got to call her that, that it was a privilege he'd once had but lost.

"Yeah." She nodded. "Just got a little lightheaded there for a second." She pulled her phone out of some hidden pocket in her dress and glanced at it with furrowed brows. "I didn't realize it was after eleven already. I'm thinking maybe it's time to head back to the guesthouse and sleep this off."

Jenna jogged up the path behind the Morgan siblings, and everyone else soon followed as Eli began the process of closing down the firepit.

Colt chuckled. "Looks like everyone just realized how late it is."

"I've got to be out the door early tomorrow for the farmers market," Jenna explained.

"And kids who get up at the crack of dawn," Boone chimed in as everyone made their way up toward the house.

"Y'all should come to the market!" Jenna exclaimed. "I mean, if you're going to be up and at it early anyway, why not enjoy some local produce? Some eggs from your favorite egg farmer?"

"Count me in," Willow replied, giving her sister-in-law a hug. "As long as I drink enough water tonight so I'm not cursing my past self in the morning," she added.

They all said their goodbyes by helping carry glasses and dishes inside. And maybe Ash was stalling or maybe he just wanted to help, but by the time he and Willow were making their way back outside and toward the guesthouse, they were the last two guests left.

"It's really good to have you back," Eli told him, pulling him in for a quick bro hug, and it continued to surprise Ash that even after all this time, his family was truly happy to see him.

"It's good to be back," he replied, and it was the truth.

———

Willow was steady enough as they crossed from the clinic property to the guesthouse, but once inside, as she tried balance on one foot to pull off her boot, she pitched backward, pinning Ash against the just-closed door.

"You all right there, Morgan?" he asked, his voice

a low whisper. He wondered if she could feel his heart slamming against his chest at the unexpected nearness of her. God, muscle memory really was an asshole.

"Yeah. Totally," she replied, but she hadn't moved.

Against Ash's better judgment, he grabbed her by the hips, setting her back on her two feet. His fingers twitched against the fabric of his shirt that she now wore, beneath which was the thin cotton of her dress and, beneath that, her skin.

He cleared his throat. "Come on," he said softly, then slid one hand to the small of her back and nudged her toward her room.

He led her to the bed, then grabbed her gently by the shoulders and spun her to face him. Maybe he'd steered clear of the wine that night, but the sweet scent of her shampoo mixed with what smelled like warm vanilla—her perfume—made him feel drunk just the same.

"Sit," he told her softly.

She sat.

Ash knelt in front of her, pulling off one boot and then the other, setting them next to her bedside table.

"Thank you," she told him with a tentative smile.

He swallowed, then nodded. "Why don't you do whatever it is you need to do to get ready for bed, and I'll get you some water and a couple of aspirin."

"Okay," she replied, though he could hear a hint of hesitation in her voice.

"It's just water and aspirin, Willow. I promise I'm not... I mean, I wasn't..."

"I know," she told him. "I know you don't think about me like that anymore. It's just...strange. Us being here like this. But I know you're just being nice, and I appreciate it."

He rose and exited the room without another word, heading first back to the front door to kick off his own boots and then to the kitchen for the water, aspirin, and hopefully the last shreds of his resolve.

For Ash Murphy, it was more than simply strange being under the same roof as Willow Morgan, let alone leading her to her bed to take off her boots. Words like *karmic justice* came to mind instead. Also, *complete and utter torture*.

He pulled a pitcher of water from the fridge and filled the insulated cup with a straw Willow was always sipping on throughout the day. Then he rummaged through the cabinets until he thankfully found one that housed a small first aid kit and bottles of various types of pain relievers. He laughed softly, thankful for his Boy Scout of a brother always being overly prepared.

He blew out a steadying breath before making his way back to Willow's room where the door was no longer wide open but not completely closed.

He rapped his knuckles softly against the wood. "Is it safe to come back in?"

"Yeah," Willow replied. "All washed up and ready for bed."

He nudged the door open with his shoulder and found her sitting cross-legged on the mattress tapping away on her phone. She wore a gray cotton tank top and matching shorts, and her hair was piled on top of her head in a messy knot.

"Just setting my alarm so I don't miss Jenna at the farmers market," she told him with a soft laugh. Then she plugged her phone into its charging cable and set it on the nightstand.

Her hair was wet around the frame of her face, and her makeup-free skin still damp. The sight of her like this—beautiful and so comfortable in her own skin—made it hard for him to breathe.

"Your water and aspirin," he told her, handing her the tumbler and opening his palm to reveal the two white pills.

"Thank you," she replied, her voice a breathy whisper this time, and for half a second Ash let himself wonder if he had even a fraction of the ability to disarm her like she did him.

She grabbed both pills, popped them into her mouth at the same time, and downed them with three large gulps from her straw. Then she froze.

"What?" he asked. "Was there a bug in the cup or something? I swear it was empty when I filled it."

Willow squeezed her eyes shut and shook her head. "No bug," she told him. "But unless the floor and ceiling just switched places, I think I'm a little tipsier than I thought."

Ash swore under his breath.

"Open your eyes, Willow," he gently commanded. "Please."

She did as he asked.

"Give me your hands, and focus on me." He held out his hands.

She instinctively swung her legs over the side of the bed as she placed her hands in his.

"Now put your feet on the floor, but keep your eyes on me. Always on me, okay?"

Willow nodded and slid to the edge of the bed, her gaze never straying from his. When her feet hit the floor, she blew out a shaky breath.

"Better?" he asked with a slight grin.

She nodded. "How did you know to do that?"

He huffed out a laugh. "When you party a little too hard a little too often, people like to give you advice on how not to choke on your own vomit while you sleep."

She wrinkled her nose.

"I know," Ash added. "Gross."

This earned him a laugh. "But you're not drunk now," she informed him. "I barely saw you take a sip tonight."

He shrugged. "Well, I've turned over a new leaf."

Willow nodded again.

"If you're okay…" he continued, "then I should let you get to sleep. Just make sure you finish the water before lights out."

He loosened his grip on her hands, but she responded by tightening hers.

"Stay," she blurted out. "I mean…just to make sure I don't spin out again."

Ash clenched his teeth and told himself this meant nothing. It was the wine and only the wine.

"Sure," he finally replied, taking a step back and nodding for her to crawl back into the king-sized bed.

"Okay, but you can't just stand there like a creepy vampire watching the underage high-school girl he wants to devour." She crawled back into the bed.

He laughed. "You want me to grab one of the breakfast barstools? How will that be any less creepy?"

She groaned and slapped the side of the mattress on her left. "Just sit for a minute, creeper. I'm sure I'll be out quicker than you can blink, but just in case…"

"Fine," he relented, then moved stiffly to the other side of the bed as she took several more sips from her tumbler. But when Ash positioned himself precariously close to the opposite edge of the bed, Willow pivoted to face him, her head nestling into her two fluffy pillows.

She yawned, and her eyelids drooped.

"I loved you once," she murmured dreamily, and Ash almost fell off the bed.

"What?" he asked, gripping the edge of the nightstand on his side to keep from toppling to the floor.

Willow sighed, her eyes fluttering closed. "Your song…" she amended, her voice light as air. "'I Loved You Once.' Was it about…? Was it about *me*?"

"It's just a song, Willow," he whispered, and she hummed a soft sigh.

"That's what I thought." The only thing to come from her lips after that was a soft snore.

"They're all just songs," he added, voice barely audible even to himself. "And they're *all* about you."

Chapter 10

Willow sat bolt upright in bed. She was going to be sick. Or maybe...

She fumbled in the dark in the direction of her bedside table.

"Yes! Thank you!" she whispered when she clasped the handle on the side of her tumbler and felt liquid move inside. She brought the straw to her lips and drank, and drank, and drank. She had a vague recollection of someone suggesting she finish the water before she fell asleep, but her thoughts felt like how trying to talk underwater sounded.

Good god. How much wine did she have at Eli and Beth's? Considering she couldn't remember her glass ever being empty, the answer added up to...a lot. It was still pitch-dark in her room, and when she tapped her phone's lock screen, she understood why.

4:17 a.m.

The water helped, but she still felt like she'd been standing under a cottonwood tree on a breezy day with her mouth open.

She padded to the bathroom, tumbler in hand, her eyes thankfully adjusting to the dark so she didn't have to accost her senses by flipping the light on. She brushed her teeth, remembering that the few times she'd been hung over in her life, a minty-clean mouth helped. Once again, it did. Then she refilled her tumbler from the tap and spun to collapse back into bed.

She gasped, raising the metal cup above her head, ready to strike, until—on further scrutiny—she realized the fully clothed stranger in her bed was Ash.

"Oh my god," she mouthed. She could have actually killed him this time.

Hand to her chest, she breathed in and out… in and out…until she wasn't shaking anymore. And then it came back to her, the one word she'd said—tipsy, pre-midnight—that put her in this predicament.

Stay.

And now Ash Murphy was sleeping in her bed. Her chest tightened, and her stomach protested for an entirely different reason than when she'd woken up. Or was that…butterflies? Her head swam with the memory of what she'd told her brother about forgiving Ash, with Ash telling her that he regretted what happened every day for four years. Realizing she was barely clothed, she set her cup on the dresser, scurried back into the bathroom and yanked down the shirt she'd hung from the hook on the back of the door. *Ash's* shirt. On instinct she buried her face in it and inhaled the mixture of her familiar tropical-scented body wash mixed with fresh grass and something inherently Ash.

Goose bumps suddenly peppered her flesh, and Willow found herself sliding her arms into the sleeves and pulling the shirt closed over her torso as if she were hugging herself.

She needed to get back to sleep if she wanted to feel remotely human by the time the alarm went off for her to head to the farmers market. She needed to get Ash Murphy out of her bed and onto the couch where he belonged.

Willow climbed tentatively onto her side and slid back under the covers. Ash lay on top of the duvet and top sheet.

"Hey!" she whispered, poking him in the shoulder. "Ash! You fell asleep in the wrong bed." He didn't budge. So she grabbed his biceps and gave him a soft yet insistent shake. "Come on, Ash. Time to go nighty night on the couchy couch." Still nothing.

If this had been anyone else, Willow would have accused him of faking it. But Ash Murphy slept like the dead...and sometimes talked in his sleep. She knew this not because she'd read it in a gossip magazine or seen it posted on social media. She knew he was a deep sleeper because one night four years ago, the side of the bed where he slept now was the side of the bed he shared with *her*.

She slid her hand from his arm, wondering how to regroup, but he grabbed her wrist midair. Willow gasped, and Ash pulled her arm to his chest, his hand now wrapped around hers.

"Don't you sneak out on me, Wills," he teased softly. "I just need five more minutes with my girl."

She couldn't breathe. This wasn't Ash Murphy talking to Willow Morgan *today*. It was Ash Murphy four years ago in his tour bus bed. Instead of a tank, shorts, and now his plaid shirt, Willow had been in that bed too, and she'd been wearing nothing. Neither of them had. And it wasn't just any morning either. Those were some of the last words Ash had spoken to her before she became a tabloid headline and some other woman became Ash Murphy's wife.

He dipped his head, eyes still closed, and brushed his lips across her knuckles.

"Please," he whispered against her skin. "I'm not ready to let you go." Even in his sleep-addled speech, she swore she heard a crack in his voice.

"Ash!" she finally barked, full volume now, and his eyes flew open.

He blinked several times as his vision seemed to focus on her. Then they dipped down to the hand gripped in his.

"Shit!" he hissed, letting go of her like she'd suddenly caught fire and he didn't want to get burned. "I'm sorry! I don't know what…" He scrambled out of the bed. "It was an accident, Willow. I swear. I know what this looks like, but you weren't feeling well, and I—"

"It's okay!" Willow blurted out. "It's okay," she said again, gentler this time. "I remember asking you to stay until I fell asleep. I was too tipsy to consider that you might have been tired too."

She was sitting up now, holding a pillow against her chest as what…protection? He couldn't be farther from her unless he made an Ash-shaped hole in the wall and ran straight for the barn.

He let out a shaky breath. "Dammit," he whispered. "We were doing better, right? Did I just set us back to square one?"

"No," Willow assured him. "We're fine. We're… exactly where we were prior to me and the endless flow of wine."

He let his head fall against the wall behind him with a thud. "Okay," he said softly. "Okay." He ran a hand through his hair and then strode toward the door. "I'll head back to the couch where I belong." His voice was rough, and he was moving so fast, Willow thought he wasn't even going to give her a backward glance. But he paused two steps out the door, one hand on the frame, and pivoted back to face her. "Where exactly are we, Willow?" he asked. "Because Colt said…" But his voice trailed off and he shook his head. "Forget it. I don't know what I'm talking about. I'm clearly still exhausted.

Or something." He tapped the doorframe twice. "Good night, Willow. Or…good morning, I guess." Then he pulled her door closed.

She hugged the pillow tight and exhaled a shaky breath.

What had Colt told him? It didn't matter because Willow had no idea where she and Ash were. All she knew was that he had just said all of that while staring at her once again wearing his shirt and that part of her wished she hadn't succeeded in waking him. Because then she could have used his sleep-addled death grip on her hand as an excuse to snuggle close to him, to breathe him in and revisit what it had been like—once upon a time—when she was, in fact, his girl.

"Five more minutes," she heard herself whisper. "Why couldn't you have stayed asleep for five more minutes?"

Willow swung her legs over the side of the bed and stood, hastily pulling her arms from the sleeves of the shirt she should not have put back on. She was clearly under the influence of…of…of the Ash Murphy scent. Or something. She needed it off her body and out of her room so she could get her head on straight.

She balled the shirt up in one hand and carefully turned the door handle so as to hopefully pull it open without making a sound. But something about the door felt heavier than usual.

She waited a beat but heard nothing.

"Ash?"

"Yeah," he replied from the other side of the door, his voice pained.

Willow opened the door, and there he was, still in his T-shirt and jeans as if he hadn't moved any farther from her room since exiting it.

"What are you doing out here?" she asked, a tremble in her words.

"I don't know," Ash replied through gritted teeth. "No," he amended. "That was a lie, and I don't want to lie to you, Willow."

She nodded slowly, then asked again. "What are you doing out here, Ash?"

He let out a mirthless laugh. "I'm wondering how we got to a place where I only get to lie beside you when you're afraid you're going to vomit and you might need me to hold your hair back."

Willow shrugged and sniffed back the threat of tears. "You married someone else." Why now, though, did it feel like she was missing part of the story?

He nodded, and in the pale moonlight that would soon turn to sun, she saw a muscle pulse in his jaw, like he was barely holding on anymore.

"Colt said you forgave me," he told her. "I'm not asking you for anything else, Willow. I swear to god. But I just need to know if what he said was true, and then I will march back over to that couch and won't bother you again." He blew out a breath. "Do you, Wills? Do you forgive me?"

She should have been furious at him using her nickname after he'd promised not to. She should have been pissed at her brother for telling Ash something that was never meant for his ears. But the should-haves were just as exhausting as the hate, and Willow needed to let go of all of it if she was going to forge a path out of the woods she'd been lost in for too long.

"I think I do," she admitted, and the wave of emotion that swelled in Ash's eyes was her complete and utter undoing.

He swallowed. "Thank you," he whispered. Then he nodded once and began to pivot toward the couch.

"Wait!" Willow cried, grabbing his wrist this time. Ash's hand clenched into a fist.

"Willow," he pleaded, unable to meet her gaze. "You don't want—"

"I do," she interrupted. "Just... Tell me the truth." His eyes finally met hers. "Were they really all for me? Your songs?"

Ash nodded. "Since I've known you. Every. Last. One."

Correction. *That* was her complete undoing.

She threw her arms around his neck, his balled-up shirt still clutched in her hand. And then his mouth was on hers, hot and wild and filled with years of need…of regret…of whatever he was feeling that made him claim her and reclaim her with every brush of his lips, every sweep of his tongue.

He hiked her onto his hips and strode toward the bed, but even when she felt him knock against the bed frame, he didn't put her down.

"I'm afraid to let go," he said against her, his voice rough.

"I'll still be here," she assured him.

"Promise?" he asked, squeezing her tight. "Because I don't think I'll survive it if you leave me again."

She sucked in a breath at how familiar and yet how terrifying it was to hear those words from him now. "I've got nowhere to run this time," she admitted. God, she hoped those words were true.

He kissed her one more time, this one gentle, and then laid her down with so much care it made her ache with a longing she swore she'd locked away and buried the key.

═══════════

Four years earlier, Willow had woken to lips softly brushing her cheeks, to the scratch of morning scruff she'd grown to adore.

"What time is it?" she asked dreamily, eyes still closed in the hopes of prolonging the night a few minutes—or if they were lucky—a few hours more before they had to get on the road to the next stop on the tour.

"I don't know, and I don't care," Ash replied. "I don't want to waste another second sleeping when I could be awake and doing this." He kissed her temple. "And also this…" He kissed the tip of her nose. "And—"

"NO!" she yelped, eyes wide open now as she threw a hand over her mouth. "Morning mouth!"

Ash groaned. "You're killing me, Wills…" He sighed as she slipped out of the bed—still naked—and ran quickly to the small bathroom included in the bus's master suite.

"Suite" was, of course, a relative term. It was a bus, after all, which meant the queen-sized bed *was* the room, and the toilet/shower/sink sort of closet was the bathroom. But to Willow it was her favorite place in the world because it was the place where she got to wake up to a man who—even after months on the road together—couldn't seem to get enough of her.

She brushed her teeth and hurried back into bed in minutes to find Ash feigning sleep.

"Hmph," she said, propping herself on her elbow to stare at a man who was adored by thousands yet walked offstage every night searching for her. "Guess I'll get dressed and head out for coffee before we hit the road."

She rolled toward her side of the bed again and

threw off the blanket but never made it any further before he called her bluff.

"Don't you dare leave me again, Willow Morgan. I won't survive it." Ash slid a hand over her hip, pressing his palm to her abdomen and pulling her to him. As he leaned over to kiss her jaw, she rolled her eyes.

"*You* smell minty fresh!" she exclaimed. "Which means *you* left *me* for the exact same reason."

He laughed. "Yeah, but you were still snoring away and had no idea I was gone."

Willow scoffed. "I do *not* snore."

"I'd still love you if you did," he told her, sliding his hand between her legs.

She gasped.

"Is that because of what I said or what I did?" he asked.

Because they hadn't done that yet...said that four-letter word that starts with *L*.

"Both," Willow replied, squirming as he teased her with his finger. "You can't just... I mean, we haven't..."

But when he dipped that teasing finger inside, Willow lost all ability to speak, let alone reason whether or not it was too soon to say the thing that he'd just said.

He rolled her onto her back and brought his lips to hers. "I don't say things I don't mean, Wills," he whispered against her. "And I don't hold back when I'm so goddamn sure about something...or some*one*."

He slid out of her, so achingly slowly against her sensitive skin that Willow thought she might break into a million tiny pieces.

"Ash," she whimpered, grabbing his wrist.

He always drove her blissfully mad, but this was different. The combination of his words mixed with his touch held a potency she wasn't prepared to handle.

He had to have known it, too, because instead of stopping, he swirled his finger over her swollen center, and Willow bucked against him, gasping for air as her throat tightened and she wasn't sure if she was about to have the quickest and greatest orgasm of her life or if she was going to burst into tears.

The former came first, and as the final wave of ecstasy rocked through her, the bedroom door flew open without so much as a warning knock.

"One hour until the missus arrives, Mr. Murphy!" Sloane announced. "Time to clean up your...mess and get yourself presentable so we can make the official announcement with a photo."

Ash flew out of the bed, stark naked with a full erection, and crossed his arms as he stared at his manager/publicist. "What the hell are you talking about, Sloane?" he asked, and to his credit, he sounded almost as gobsmacked as Willow felt.

Sloane laughed, unfazed by her naked and

still-aroused client. "Come on, honey. I appreciate the show you're putting on for your little groupie, but you signed off on this last week—your ticket to a UK fandom."

Something clicked in the recesses of Willow's memory, a conversation she'd had with Ash early on before she'd even let him kiss her, let alone do the things he'd done to her last night and had begun to do again this morning.

"How do you put up with that?" she'd asked him once after Sloane had whisked him out of a local bar where their two bands had been unwinding after a show. She'd needed him for some international conference call that was supposed to garner him a sponsorship deal with an up-and-coming whiskey brand. Or maybe it was a sports drink. The product hadn't mattered, but Ash's take on it had.

"I learned quickly that everything I do is some sort of transaction," he'd told her. "Everyone wants something from me, and Sloane makes sure I get something in return." He'd shrugged the whole situation off at the time, and so had Willow. Now, though, she suddenly realized that *she* had been his something in return. For what, though? Willow opening for him on the summer leg of his tour?

"Oh god," Willow said out loud, realization hitting her like a fist to the gut. "I'm one of them," she added, stumbling out of the bed and wrapping herself in the bed's top sheet.

"One of what?" Ash asked, and she could hear the panic in his voice, but the only sense her brain could make of it was that Sloane had beaten him to the punch in telling Willow that she'd served her purpose, on the tour and in his bed, and he was trying to save face.

"Good, good," Sloane replied, all smiles. "We're all on the same page. Willow, I'll make sure you get back to *your* bus discreetly while Ash gets ready to greet his wife, and then we can finish our last few summer dates as one big, happy family."

"Willow, wait!" Ash pleaded as she swallowed her pride and mermaid walked toward the smiling Sloane who would lead the way.

She gave him one backward glance and almost broke when she saw him scrambling back into his jeans as if he was going to chase after her and noticed what looked like genuine fear in his deep-blue eyes. But then she remembered that Ash Murphy had been a professional performer since his early teens, and she—apparently—had just been part of the show.

"For what?" she asked him, and for one tiny second she hoped he might actually have something to say that would change her mind.

But he just stared at her, speechless, the man of a thousand beautiful words that fans across the country—and now, she guessed, across the Atlantic—stood in line to hear.

"That's what I thought," Willow replied, answering her own question.

And then she turned back to Sloane, letting the other woman lead her out of Ash Murphy's sight, her only saving grace that she hadn't told him she loved him too. She knew better than to say those words out loud because she knew all too well the damage they could do.

She loved her mother, and her mother died.

She loved her brother, and the State of California separated them for seven years.

She dared to think she could possibly love a man who was already in love with a career and fandom with which she couldn't compete, and in the span of seconds, it had destroyed her heart.

Willow did not finish the tour. And she never heard from Ash Murphy again.

The memory crashed over her like a wave, and she was suddenly caught in the undertow. "Wait!" Willow cried, and Ash froze where he knelt before her, where his lips had been kissing a trail from her breasts down the length of her torso.

Ash pushed himself up to standing and immediately backed away, his hands raised. "I'm sorry, Wills," he told her, and she heard a crack in his deep voice.

She sat up, pulling her tank top down from

where he'd pushed it up to her collarbone so he could cover her with kisses like he used to do all those years ago.

"You *don't* really forgive me, do you?" he asked.

Willow grabbed a pillow and hugged it against her torso as she shook her head.

"I thought I did," she told him. "I really thought I was past it but, Ash, you didn't just hurt me. You humiliated me…and you *broke* my heart."

He nodded. "I know. But…." He cleared his throat. "Did you ever once think of unblocking my number and reading my texts? Or replying to even one of my emails to at least let me know you were okay? Did it really mean nothing to know that everything that happened that day broke my heart too?"

She furrowed her brows and stared at him.

"Ash, I didn't—"

"It doesn't matter," he added before she could finish. "I realize the bulk of the blame is on me and that I probably don't deserve credit for trying to fix what I never meant to break. But I did try, Willow. And I did love you."

She shook her head, too stunned to speak. Only after Ash had backed out of her door and closed it behind him did she hear herself whisper, "What texts? What emails?"

She didn't sleep the rest of the night, and when daylight finally broke, she called Colt.

"I need to borrow your truck," she told him.

"And I need you to apologize to Jenna for me for missing her at the market today. I promise I'll be there next week, but something came up that I have to take care of today."

"You can have the truck, Wills, but you're kind of freaking me out. Do you need me to come with you wherever you're going?"

"No," she assured him. "I promise I'm okay, but I need to deal with this on my own."

"Okay," he told her. "I'll have one of the ranch hands on duty meet me at your place and drive me back home after I drop the truck. And whatever it is, Jenna will understand. How long will you be gone?"

She opened the map app on her phone to double-check the distance. "I'll be back by early afternoon," she assured him. "Thank you, big bro," she added. "You are the best."

He let out a short laugh. "I know, but I still like to hear you say it."

Willow smiled, grateful for the levity. Because however today went, her heart was bound to break all over again, but at least she'd have some semblance of the truth. Then, hopefully, she'd finally be able to move on.

Chapter 11

Ash jumped barrel after barrel, he and Midnight leaving Boone in the dust every time. He wanted to jump the fence and ride as far and as fast from here as possible, but at the same time, he was afraid to leave the property in case Willow came back.

He brought Midnight to a halt after two more laps, finding Boone and Cirrus already resting near the place where the gate opened back toward the barn.

"Are we racing each other?" Boone asked. "Or are you trying to turn back time Superman style?"

Ash was sweating, his heart pounding even after he and Midnight stopped.

"I don't know," he admitted. "I..." He blew out a breath. "Have you ever wondered if maybe you made the biggest mistake of your life, and even though you regretted every second of it, you still didn't know how to fix it or if you ever even could?"

Boone let out a soft laugh. "You want to be a little more specific about that?" he asked. "Because it's really hard to help with hypotheticals."

Ash sighed. "I don't know if it even matters

anymore." But it did matter. To him, at least. He could still feel Willow's soft skin against his lips. Even now, the thrum of his heart had nothing to do with how hard he'd been riding. It was her. *All* her. But he'd been foolish enough to believe that Colt was right and she had actually forgiven him.

Both brothers pulled their phones out of their pockets at the same time.

"It's Eli," Boone said, and Ash nodded, opening the group text.

Eli: Get your asses down to the farmers market. Willow's performing at Jenna's tent.

Ash looked at his brother and then back down at his phone. It was a few minutes past noon, and the market closed at 1:00 p.m.

"I'm a mess," Ash admitted, figuring that would be reason enough for him not to go. It wasn't like Willow wanted him there after what happened the night before.

Boone nodded. "I can smell you from here. Guess you better get your ass in the shower, and I'll give you a ride to the market."

Ash's mouth opened to respond, but no words came out.

"Come on, little brother. Why do you think Eli even texted? We knew you were in love with her four years ago, and based on the way you were looking at her last night and how you've been riding yourself ragged this morning, I'm guessing not much has changed."

Ash sighed. "That's just it. What if I haven't changed? What if I'm still the asshole who broke her heart and she can't ever forgive or trust me again?"

Boone shoved his phone back in his pocket and tilted his hat up so Ash could see his brother's assessing gaze. "Are you really the asshole she thinks you are? Because from where I'm sitting, I think I'm looking at a guy who'd do what he could to make things right if given the chance."

Ash's throat tightened, and he felt the weight pressing down on his chest that had been there for four long years. "What if I don't get that chance?"

Boone shrugged. "What if you do?"

———————

Boone's bike rolled to a stop just outside the barricaded Meadow Valley town square. Ash was off and unfastening his helmet before his brother even killed the engine.

"Go get her," Boone called after him as Ash strode toward the soft sounds of a guitar strumming and his favorite voice singing the same lines she'd caught him singing in the shower just a week ago.

"'This time I'll pick myself up when I fall... This

time I'll block your number before you call. This time I'll hold the needle and thread. Jagged stitches 'cross my heart…cold sheets on your side of the bed.'"

Ash pulled out his phone and pushed his way through the crowd until he was close enough to get a clear shot. He zoomed in so all he could see was Willow sitting on a stool under the awning of Jenna's tent, her guitar in her lap. No band. No microphone. No *anything* other than her music and her words.

She wore a white tank, jeans, and the boots he'd pulled off her feet the night before. Her loose brunette waves hung over her shoulders as she parted her lips in a smile and sang.

It felt like the first time he'd seen her at a venue not much different than this. She hadn't even made it through one song before he called Sloane and told her he'd found the opening act for the summer leg of his tour.

"She's perfect, Sloane. We need her on this tour."

Sloane had laughed. "Are you sure you're talking about her *talent*? I've seen her, Murphy."

"Then you know she's better than I'll ever be," he'd replied. "Find out who her manager is and make the call."

Sloane sighed. "If she's better than you, Murphy, why does she need *your* audience?"

"She doesn't," he admitted. "I just want to be a part of her story."

Except now Ash was the chapter she wanted to rip from the book. So why was he here now? Why was Boone telling him to keep hanging on?

He snapped a couple of photos and recorded a short snippet of her next song. He couldn't bring himself to share "This Time" with anyone other than the local audience surrounding them both right now.

His phone buzzed with a text message as he was lowering it to slip it back in his pocket. It was from Sloane.

Sloane: More of this, Murphy.

He tapped on the link she shared with the text, and it opened to Willow's Instagram account and a photo she'd posted the night before.

Family reunion was all the caption said, but the photo contained none of Willow's family. No Colt or Jenna or *anyone* really...except an obscured glimpse of a man through the flicker of a firepit's flames. *Ash.*

Unless you *knew* it was him—like Sloane—there was no way to *know* it was him.

But the comments were full of speculation about who the mystery man was: a blood relative or someone new to Willow's *family*.

cntrylvr: awww...glad you're getting some downtime before the next big show!

morgansminions: it's her brother, right? Have u seen him? Soooo sad he's married.

wmstanfan: but what if it ISN'T her bro? announcement? Easter egg?

morphy4eva: never over her and @ashmurphofficial not being a real thing. at least not for the long haul. can someone tell her he's back on the market and make this thing happen on AND off stage?

morgansminions: no way. she's too smart to forgive him. you've seen the speculation surrounding the marriage announcement, right? if not, google it. #teammorgan is NOT reposting that garbage. WM deserves better.

Ash flinched.

He knew there was plenty of bullshit written about him online, some true and some not so true. It was all part of the gig. But this one stung, not because of how true it may or may not have been but because if this was how one of Willow's fans felt about her forgiving him, then how the hell could Willow herself do it?

Yet that previous comment—not the disparaging reply—had over two thousand likes already since she'd posted it late last night. Wait…no. He looked at the time stamp from the post, which said the post went live only six hours ago. *After* he'd left Willow's room.

Logically he knew Willow was just doing what she promised Sloane she'd do, but if it wasn't an Easter egg, was it at the very least a bread crumb?

What if I don't get a chance?

What if you do?

Willow finished the song, and the entire crowd at the farmers market erupted into applause. She stood and bowed, then blew a kiss to no one in particular before cupping her hands over her mouth and calling, "I'm Willow Morgan. This is my sister, Jenna, and she has the *best* eggs in Plumas County, so you better grab them before the market closes!"

And then she disappeared behind the tent as customers lined up for last-minute purchases.

Ash ducked his head as he weaved through the crowd, laughing to himself as he heard nothing more than, "Hey there, Ash," or "Welcome home, Murphy." Everywhere else he went, someone wanted a photo, autograph, or recorded message to a girlfriend. Here, no one wanted anything more than a "Hey there" or "Hi" in return.

"Hey there," he said as he rounded the corner of the tent to where Willow was packing up her guitar.

Willow straightened and met his gaze.

"Hey there yourself," she replied, her expression unreadable. She wasn't smiling but wasn't *not*.

"Did I mess this whole thing up, Wills…?" He cleared his throat. "*Willow*. Sorry. Old habits."

Willow shook her head. "I asked you to stay last night, Murphy." She sighed. "And *I* initiated the kiss."

He nodded once. "But you also put a stop to it once you came to your senses, and then when I woke up this morning, you were gone. I can pack up my shit and crash on Boone or Eli's couch." He shrugged. "A couch is a couch at this point, right? And if you want to call off the duet, that's okay too. You can have whatever we've written so far and—"

"Stop it, Ash!" she cried, fisting her hands at her sides. "Stop trying to bend over backward for me like…like…"

"Like it's going to make a difference when I know it won't?" he asked.

She blew out a breath and shook her head. "Colt wasn't wrong about what he told you, even if he had no right telling you what I'd told him in confidence."

Ash cleared his throat. "About…forgiving me?"

Willow pressed her lips together and nodded back at him. "But last night brought *so* much back, and then what you said…about blocking your number?" She let out a bitter laugh. "I did more than block your number, Ash. I got a new phone, a new number. I didn't trust myself not to go back over every other word you'd ever texted me trying to figure out what was real and what—"

"All of it," he interrupted. "All of it was real, Willow. I swear. I *loved* you."

She sucked in a breath through her nose, and the way the sun reflected in her eyes made them look like dark, glassy pools about to overflow.

"I borrowed my brother's truck this morning to head out to the nearest store I could find for my cell phone provider to see if they could retrieve blocked texts from my old number."

Ash's eyes widened. "Did they find them? Did you read them? Do you believe me now that I never wanted...that the marriage was..."

His voice trailed off as she took the few steps toward him to close the distance.

"It's not as quick a job as I thought it would be, but they're working on it." She fidgeted with the hem of her shirt.

"But you believe me that I tried to get ahold of you, right? If that's as far as this ever goes..." He motioned between them. "I need you to at least believe that I tried, even if I failed."

His hands opened and closed where they hung at his sides as he itched to touch her but didn't dare to make the first move.

"You said something about emails too. Ash... I never got any emails."

He closed his eyes and gritted his teeth. "I know I sound like I'm making all of this up, and I don't know. Maybe I am. I drank a lot after you left, and what I swear I wrote in those early days...? I can't find anything in my sent folder or in my sent texts.

But it felt real. It still *feels* real, all those things I said to you to try to explain…to try to create the outcome where I didn't lose you." He opened his eyes and sighed. "I don't believe myself when I hear it out loud. So I don't blame you if you don't believe me either. But—"

"You *loved* me," she said, realization in her tone. Ash could see now that her lashes were wet.

He shook his head. If he had any chance at all of getting her back, then he had to tell her the whole truth, as much as she was willing to hear.

"Not past tense, Willow," Ash admitted, his voice rough.

She sniffled again, and this time a tear leaked out of the corner of each eye. "Call me Wills," she whispered.

He cupped her cheek in his palm and swiped at another falling tear with his thumb.

"I still love you, Wills. I always have. And if there is even the slightest chance that you could trust—"

She pressed her hands to his chest, and her lips brushed against his.

"Are you sure?" he whispered, still afraid to give in to what he'd wanted every single day for four goddamn years.

"No," she whispered back, her mouth parted against his. "I'm not sure about anything other than being terrified of how much I can still want you after everything that's happened. But I want to trust what you're saying. I want to trust that this is real."

"It's real," he ground out. "It's always been real, Wills."

"It's always been real for me too," she admitted. "But if you hurt me again—"

"I *won't*." He kissed her. "I'd trade my career before I hurt you again."

She nodded, and not another word was spoken as he held her closer, kissed her harder, and hoped to hell she knew he was telling the truth. Ash Murphy would burn it all down before he'd ever break her heart again.

Chapter 12

EVEN THOUGH THE RIDE BACK FROM THE FARM-
ers market was less than five minutes, the silence
in Colt's truck—despite the four people sitting in
it—felt interminable.

Willow leaned forward and placed a gentle hand
on her brother's shoulder as he slowed to a stop in
front of the guesthouse.

"What are the odds we make it out of this truck
and back inside without you doing the big brother
thing I already know you did last night?" she asked
with what she hoped was a mollifying tone.

To her sister-in-law's credit, Jenna did grab her husband's hand and gave it a reassuring squeeze. Willow
had at least half her immediate family's support.

"Slim to none after what I saw behind that tent,"
Colt replied through gritted teeth.

"It's okay, Wills," Ash remarked from where he
sat in the back of the cab beside her. "Whatever
Colt wanted to happen last night needs to happen
now. Then we move forward."

Willow sighed, kissed her brother on the cheek,
and then pivoted to face Ash. She thought better of
putting on any sort of public display in her brother's

truck. So she offered him a tentative smile, still not sure herself what to make of everything Ash had said…and the words she'd still been unable to say back.

"Come with me to check on the hens?" Jenna suggested, and Willow nodded with a sigh.

She hopped out of the cab and retrieved her guitar case from the bed, carrying it to the front porch of the guesthouse before following Jenna across the field to the chicken coop.

"I don't really need to check on the hens," Jenna admitted once they were far enough away from the truck that they could no longer see or hear what might be taking place between Colt and Ash. "I was already here before dawn collecting eggs for the market."

"I know," Willow replied. "But can we… I mean, if you're going to tell me how stupid I am or what a huge mistake I'm making, can you just not? It's not any different from the conversation I've already had a hundred times in my head, and it's not going to keep me from worrying that the two men I care about most might be a hundred yards away kicking the shit out of each other because of me."

Jenna cupped Willow's cheek in her palm and smiled sweetly. "You know that the reason your brother and I do what we do—fostering kids, especially siblings others deem too old to adopt—is because of what happened to you and him."

Willow nodded, her throat growing tight as her eyes burned. "They were good people," Willow admitted, unable to keep the tears from falling. "They loved me and treated me like their own, but a part of me never forgave them for splitting up Colt and me. All those years apart when he was bouncing in and out of Child Services." She shook her head. "He won't even tell me about it, which means it's probably worse than I imagine." Willow sniffled. "I don't know if I'll ever get over that."

Jenna nodded, then pulled a pack of tissues out of the tote bag slung over her shoulder.

"Thank you." Willow let loose a soft sob as she accepted the offering.

"The hurt that you will always feel for your brother is not unlike the hurt he'll always feel for you after what happened with Ash four years ago."

"But he doesn't know..." Willow began but then let her voice trail off. Colt didn't know the whole story. He didn't know that Ash tried—at least, Willow wanted to believe he tried—to make things right. But that didn't matter. He was her brother, and he loved her and would do anything to protect her from getting hurt like that again. "Right," she continued. "I get it."

Jenna grabbed Willow's hand and gave her a soft squeeze. "If there is one thing you can rest your heart on, it's that one of Colt Morgan's missions in life is to make sure you never hurt like that again...

even if that means bitin' his tongue and grittin' his teeth while he watches you fall for a man he neither likes nor trusts...*yet*."

A hen squawked inside the coop, and Jenna grinned. "Attagirl," she said with a grin. Then she slipped inside the coop and returned with one of the hens under her arm. She set the chicken down in the grass and watched as she circled Willow's feet, pecking a trail around them.

Willow laughed. "Lucy, right?" she asked, remembering the hen from the last time she'd visited her brother and sister-in-law. Though Willow hadn't received such a greeting from the feathered friend back then.

"That's right," Jenna replied. "And that's all I need to see to know that my girl hasn't lost her touch and that this thing with you and Ash is the real deal."

Willow's brows furrowed. "I don't follow."

Jenna picked the hen back up and cooed at her like they were speaking their own language. "Lucy here is an expert at matters of the heart." She held up a hand to ward off any protest, not that Willow could think of one at the moment. "I don't like to share when it comes to Lucy's...*abilities*...unless she's in the midst of...ability-*ing*. Otherwise I might have people making demands of my girl to predict things she cannot predict. She can only call it when she sees it."

Willow took a step back, suddenly yet inexplicably on the defense. "What does she see?" she asked, not sure why she heard a tremor in her own voice.

Jenna waved her off with a grin. "That you're in *love*, sweetheart."

Willow swallowed. "I'm not… I mean, I never said…"

Jenna kissed the feathers on top of Lucy's head and then put her back in the coop.

"It's okay," Jenna assured her. "Even if you don't know it yet, Lucy does."

Except Willow had never said the word *love* to anyone other than her birth mother and Colt. Just because she was letting Ash back into her life didn't mean that would—or could—change, not after her heart had been clobbered just for having the audacity to *think* it.

"She could be wrong, couldn't she?" Willow asked. "I mean, she's a goddamn chicken, Jenna. Just because she pecks at my feet doesn't mean—"

"Hey…" Jenna interrupted, hands held up in defense. "I didn't mean to upset you. I just thought it would help you to know it was real."

"I'm sorry." Willow cleared her throat. "I know you're trying to help. But I need to be able to trust Ash on my own." She held her arms out, spinning slowly to take in not just the Murphy Ranch but all that Meadow Valley had become for Jenna and Colt. "I'm so happy that you and my brother got the fairy tale. I really am. But that doesn't mean it exists for all of us."

Jenna sighed. "You're right," she told her.

Willow's eyes widened. "Wait... I am?"

Jenna took a step forward and placed her hands on her sister-in-law's shoulders.

"Darlin', if you are always waiting for the other shoe to drop, you'll find a way to make sure it does." She shrugged. "Lucy might be able to spot the real deal, but she can't do your part of the job."

Willow scoffed. "Which is what, exactly?"

"Letting yourself believe that you deserve the fairy tale just as much as the rest of us do." Jenna nodded back toward the guesthouse. "Come on. If they were going to kill each other, they ought to be done by now."

Jenna dropped her hands, turned toward the guesthouse, and started walking without giving Willow a backward glance.

What the hell did Jenna mean...believe she deserved the fairy tale? Of course Willow believed she deserved it. Why wouldn't she? She was a good person, right? And good people deserved good things. So why were Jenna's words crawling beneath her skin and seeping into her blood like a slow-acting poison?

Willow shook off the thought. Whatever happened between her and Ash was about *Ash* proving that they were the real deal, regardless of whether a hen agreed with them or not.

When she got back to the guesthouse, Colt and

Jenna were gone, and she found Ash waiting for her on the porch swing, beside which she'd rested her guitar.

He patted the spot next to him, and Willow was relieved to see no evidence of violence having ensued between him and her brother. She lowered herself beside him and felt her pulse quicken not only at his nearness but also at what she recognized was her fight-or-flight instinct kicking in.

They rocked back and forth for several seconds in silence. Finally, Willow broke the ice.

"I'm terrified," she admitted.

Ash slid an arm behind her and pulled her to him, and she rested her head on his shoulder.

"I know," he replied. Then he pressed a kiss to the top of her head, lingering to inhale with his nose buried in her hair.

The realization sent a shiver down the back of Willow's neck all the way to her toes.

"Your brother wanted to hit me, you know," Ash added with a laugh. "You want to know how I changed his mind?"

She tilted her head to look at him and nodded.

"Same thing I told you, except I put it in writing." He pulled a folded-up napkin out of his pocket and handed it to her. In his smeared, left-handed scrawl, the words on the napkin read:

I, Ashton Murphy, hereby certify that from this day forward, the day I broke Willow Morgan's heart, I am retiring from the music industry as a singer, song-writer, performer, and any other entity whereby I profit from being a musician. Additionally, the witness to this contract is permitted to enact Article A should the former come to pass.

It was signed both by Ash and by her brother as a witness.

"All we have to do is take it to the library in the morning and get it notarized. Then it'll be official," he added.

"Ash..." she started, shaking her head. "I would never ask that of you. To say it is one thing. But you can't put your career on the line to get me to trust you."

He shrugged. "I didn't. I put my career on the line to get your brother to trust me." He flipped the napkin over and handed it back to her. "Article A was his idea."

Willow gasped.

Should the former come to pass, the witness and promisor will face each other in the firehouse ring, gloves off.

"Absolutely not!" she exclaimed. "Honestly, what is the matter with men? Violence solves *nothing*."

"Says the woman who knocked me out on first greeting."

Willow groaned. "How long are you going to

keep throwing that in my face when *I thought someone had broken into my house and bedroom*?"

Ash laughed. "Okay! Okay! Last mention. I promise. But this?" He waved the napkin between them. "I need the people who matter to know that I am prepared to put my money—and your brother's fists—where my mouth is."

Willow hated the contract. She really did. But she couldn't help the way it forced a crack into the armor she was still wearing.

"What if I put something *else* where your mouth is?" she teased. Because even if the prospect of love terrified her, the prospect of want was something else entirely.

He hooked a finger under her chin and tilted her head toward his. Willow closed her eyes and skimmed her teeth over her bottom lip, waiting for Ash to take her up on her offer.

"Willow Morgan, there is nothing I want more than to scoop you up off this swing and take you straight to bed. But I have something else I want to do first."

He spoke so close to her mouth that she could feel the vibration of his words in his breath. But he didn't kiss her. When she opened her eyes, ready to protest, he was grinning at her with the kind of mischief she would never trust on another man's face, but she decided if they were going to give this thing a real chance, she had to start somewhere.

"This better be good, Murphy."

"Oh, it will be," he assured her with his patented Ash Murphy wink. And then he hopped off the swing and held his hand out for Willow to take. "Follow me."

———————

"Riding?" she asked after Ash directed her to put on boots suitable for riding and walking and pack a few overnight essentials. Then he led her to the barn. "I basically throw myself at you, and you want to go riding?" He already had Midnight tacked and ready to go with more substantial gear than Willow had shown up with. "Why do I get the feeling we aren't heading out to the clearing?"

Ash answered her first with a grin. "Because we're not heading out to the clearing," he added.

"We're taking the horses overnight?" she asked as Ash grabbed her small backpack and hiked it onto his shoulders. "Hey... I can carry my own pack," she added.

He nodded toward Holiday where she stood tacked and ready to go as well. "I talked to Eli, and we both agreed that Holiday is good to go for the trip, but we don't want her bearing any more weight than her rider for at least another six months, so the pack's all mine."

Willow crossed her arms and narrowed her eyes

at him. "You talked to Eli, figured this whole trip out, and tacked up both horses while I was throwing together a 'few overnight essentials'?" She made air quotes around the last three words, and Ash nodded.

"Fine," he relented. "I talked to him and Boone about it last night before you showed up. And before you think I was getting ahead of myself and assuming you would actually agree to come with me on a trip like this, I put it all out there as a hypothetical. I just…" He blew out a shaky breath. "The thought of having you in my hometown and not being able to show you some of my favorite places?" Ash shrugged. "I wanted to be prepared on the off chance you decided you didn't hate me anymore."

He winced when he said the word *hate*, and Willow found herself doing the same.

"I never actually *said* I hated you," Willow mumbled.

He huffed out a laugh. "Maybe not, but when I asked if you were going to hate me forever, I remember you saying something about checking back at forever o'clock."

"Yikes." She grimaced. "So that's what I sound like after four years of buried—"

"*Hate*," Ash interrupted, finishing the sentence for her.

But Willow shook her head. "*Hurt*," she corrected.

"Four years of buried hurt can sound an awful lot like hate."

Ash nodded slowly. "And now?" he asked.

She glanced from him to Holiday, and the mare whinnied and snorted at her in response.

"Now," she started, "I think you should show me one of your favorite places."

He grinned, and they both mounted their horses and rode with Ash leading the way.

Chapter 13

"OH MY GOD," WILLOW REMARKED AS SHE climbed onto the wooden platform to explore their accommodations.

"It's just a tent," Ash called over his shoulder as he added her backpack to the small pile of gear he'd unloaded when they boarded the horses.

She spun around and greeted him with a smile he swore would illuminate the night.

"I know!" she exclaimed. "But look at this view!"

He abandoned their gear and joined her on the covered platform that looked out over a small lake framed by mountain hemlock and foxtail pines, beyond which they could see the rolling hills that eventually turned into mountains. Directly in front of their platform sat a firepit and two Adirondack chairs. Ash felt like everything he needed in the entire world was right here within his reach.

"You're right," he told her. "It's beautiful." But Ash didn't mean the view. "Should we unpack?" he asked. "Get a fire going so I can cook you dinner?"

She turned to him, still beaming, and nodded. "I still can't believe you did all this. How was this place even available on such short notice?"

At this, Ash had the decency to look a tad bit chagrined. "I maybe, possibly got the reservations clerk to offer the original renter a week's stay on me if they let me have the tent for tonight."

Willow raised her brows. "Ah, yes. The man who always gets what he wants *gets* what he wants."

"Ouch," Ash replied, pressing a hand to his wounded heart.

"Sorry!" Willow threw a hand over her mouth. "Hard habit to break…throwing barbs your way."

He swooped in and kissed her on the cheek, and she gasped. "Hard habit to break," he parroted. "Wanting to do that every time you're within range."

———

Ash crossed his arms and smiled nervously when they'd finished unpacking. The empty tent on a raised platform might have seemed luxurious when they first arrived, but his minimalist floor mats and sleeping bags were anything but.

"I didn't think of pillows," he admitted with a wince.

Willow dropped to a squat and pressed her palm against the padded headrests inside the sleeping bags. "No need," she replied with a grin. "They're included." She straightened, strode over to where he was rummaging through his pack, and tried to peek inside. "Is that dinner?" she asked, and he heard her stomach growl.

He produced a small pot and a box of mac and cheese, the kind with the "cheese" already in liquid form.

"Ta-da!" he proclaimed, waiting for her expression to fall, but instead she gave him an even bigger smile, if that was possible.

"My favorite," she told him.

"You're a terrible liar," he replied, but she shook her head and stepped toward him, sliding her arms around his waist.

"You've never cooked for me before," she said softly.

Ash sighed. "There's a lot that I never did but should have." Turned out he was the one having trouble maintaining a smile.

She leaned up and kissed the bottom of his chin. "Can we exist here tonight without any of our messy past joining us?"

He leaned his forehead against hers. "Are you sure? Because I feel like there is so much left to tell you or to explain about…"

He felt her clasp her hands against his back. "Did you love her?" she whispered, and he knew she meant his ex-wife.

"It's complicated," he admitted, his voice rough. Because even after the way things went down, he wouldn't betray his ex-wife's trust. "She's a good friend."

"You know what?" Willow shook her head. "Don't tell me any more, okay? I don't want to know more about that part of your life. Not tonight."

"Okay," he agreed. But someday he needed to tell her everything he'd tried to convey over the past four years. "There's wine and water in the cooler pack," he added, nodding toward a backpack that still hadn't been opened. "You do drinks, and I'll do food?"

"Deal," she told him, and they got to work putting together their minimalist meal.

"Cheers," Willow said afterward, holding up her plastic cup filled with the sparkling wine he'd remembered that she loved. "This was the best meal I've had in years."

"You're still a terrible liar," he told her. The mac and cheese was gummy and awful, but at least they had something in their bellies to sustain them until morning.

Willow inched her chair closer to his than it already was and draped the flannel blanket over both of them. "You have goose bumps on your arms," she added.

He clinked the bottom of his cup against hers and smiled. "Maybe it was just a ploy to get you closer to me."

She leaned her head on his shoulder and sighed. "Then it was a very successful ploy," she replied. "But for future reference, you can just tell me you want me closer to you."

He kissed the top of her head and inhaled the scent of her shampoo. He needed to continually fill his senses with her presence. It was the only way he could prove to himself that any of this was real, that Willow was here with him not because she had to be but because she wanted it.

"I've missed you, Wills," he told her, his voice tentative. "Am I allowed to say that?"

She nodded against his shoulder. "I'll allow it."

He switched his cup to his right hand and slid his left one under the blanket to find hers. As soon as the tips of their fingers touched, Willow linked her fingers through his so they were completely intertwined and locked together until one of them decided to let go.

"You know I always felt like Meadow Valley was too small for me. Too intimate," he continued. "Like I couldn't have this big life if I was stuck in the place where I'd been since the day I was born."

She squeezed his hand, but both of them gazed at the fire as they spoke.

"And now?" she asked.

He squeezed her back. "Now... I'm not so sure. Meadow Valley feels different with you in it."

Willow bent her arm and brought his knuckles to her lips, pressing soft kisses to each one individually. "You know I'm only here through the festival, right? I have a few more tour stops and a record to launch before the season ends. And then, depending on sales…" She shrugged. "I don't know what's next after that."

He understood what that meant. She didn't know what would be next for them. Regardless of what happened at the end of their two months together, they had lives outside of Meadow Valley that would likely be traveling in entirely different directions.

"You know what?" she continued. "I'd like to amend my further decree about not letting our messy pasts invade our evening."

"No futures either?" he asked.

She turned her head to glance up at him, and he found the fire's reflection dancing in her dark eyes. "Is that okay? I know we have to deal with reality eventually, but tonight feels like a fairy tale, and for one night, I want the happily ever after."

He wanted to ask her if she believed that happily ever after could extend past tonight, but he also didn't want to break this spell of complete and utter perfection. It was the happiest Ash had been in four years…or maybe ever. He had no problem making it last as long as he could.

"No past and no future until we turn into pumpkins or whatever at midnight," he told her.

She backhanded him on the shoulder with a laugh. "It's Cinderella's coach that turns back into a pumpkin, not *her*. And this spell better last later than midnight!"

Ash laughed too, and—noticing her plastic glass

was empty—topped off her bubbly and then his own.

She grinned. "You know… I haven't had sparkling almond wine in years," she told him. "I forgot how much I like it."

"I didn't," he told her once they were snuggled under the shared blanket again. He leaned back against the chair and tilted his head toward the sky, marveling at the stars twinkling like fairy lights strung from the tallest trees.

He could feel her looking at him, but he kept his eyes trained on the stars.

"What else about me do you remember?" she asked.

One corner of his mouth quirked up. "Changing the rules, are we?" He rolled his head to meet her gaze. "Doesn't this line of questioning fall under *past* us?"

Willow shrugged. "My rules. Means I can bend them. Besides, my likes and dislikes don't necessarily fall under *messy past*. Especially if they still describe present me."

Ash laughed and turned back to the sky. "You love sparkling wine but hate soda. Banana bread or muffins are a yes, but an actual banana—and these are *your* words—is like eating food that has already been chewed."

She snorted, then covered her mouth with her hand.

"Favorite movie is *Ferris Bueller's Day Off*. Favorite song to cover—and you sing it at every show—is "To Make You Feel My Love." Favorite person is your brother, Colt. And though you've never had a pet, you love animals and plan to buy a farm someday once you decide to stay put more and tour less." He cleared his throat. "Though… maybe you've already bought a place that I don't know about, which I guess would be great because it would mean you achieved something you've always wanted." Why, then, did it feel like a punch to the gut when he considered that she might have gone and done this amazing thing on her own? Without him?

Willow was silent for several long moments before he even heard her stir. When he finally had the nerve to look at her, he found her wiping tears from the corners of her eyes.

"Shit," he hissed. "Wills. I'm sorry. What did I say?" He quickly racked his brain, trying to locate the misstep so he could make it right. But Willow shook her head.

"You didn't say anything wrong," she told him, then sniffled.

He straightened in his chair. "Why am I not convinced?"

She let out a tearful laugh. "I just can't believe you remember all those things about me. You rattled it all off like it was stuff I told you yesterday, but it's been four years, Ash. *Four* years. You had a life and a career and a marriage, and—"

"And it all paled in comparison to the life I had with you."

"We didn't have a life, Murphy. We had make-out sessions backstage and sex in your tour bus bedroom. What if...? What if all we really had was a shared love of music and a dream of making it big?"

He downed the rest of his bubbly and set his cup on the ground. Then he patted the blanket on his lap. "Come here."

Willow's eyes widened. She glanced at her still-full cup and then drained it in a few swift gulps. "Liquid courage," she remarked with a nervous laugh. Then she maneuvered out of her chair, somehow staying under the blanket, and climbed into his lap.

Ash pulled the blanket tight over her shoulders and then wrapped his arms around her waist. "It was the only life I knew," he told her. "And you were the best part of it." He slid a hand up to her cheek and brushed his thumb across the damp skin beneath her eye. "There's no stage," he whispered. "No tour bus."

Willow nodded slowly. "I noticed you didn't pack any guitars. Does that mean we're off the clock?"

"That's exactly what it means." He leaned up and brushed his lips across hers. "I know you're looking for any reason to logic your way out of thinking this could work. But this?" He motioned between them. "Us? It has nothing to do with the business part of our relationship and everything to do with the fact that *you*, Willow Morgan, do this thing to my heart that thousands of fans singing my own words back to me could never do."

She gave him a teary smile. "What's that?" she asked, thankfully taking the bait.

He pressed his lips together and swallowed the knot in his throat. "You fill it up, Wills. You fill it up."

She sucked in a sharp breath and then cupped his cold cheeks in her warm palms.

"Take me to bed," she whispered.

"Are you sure?" he asked.

"Yes."

So he stood from the chair, lifting her and the blanket and piloting them onto the platform and into the tent. He knew he'd have to tend to the smoldering embers of the firepit when all was said and done and he'd be physically and emotionally spent, but it would all be worth it. Because after four years—four goddamn long years—Willow Morgan was his again. And whether it was for this single night or the possibility of many more to come, he would not squander a second of it.

He laid her down on one of the opened sleeping bags and then untied the flaps of the tent so they fell closed. Then he climbed over her, pulling the blanket with him, covering her body with his own.

Chapter 14

"ARE YOU SURE NO ONE KNOWS YOU'RE HERE?" Willow asked him, and the man had the audacity to laugh.

"Yes, Wills. I'm sure." He kneeled above her and peeled off his T-shirt. "We're on a private site, inaccessible by car. I paid cash and used my brother's name. We are in middle-of-nowhere Plumas County, which means middle-of-no-one-gives-a-flying—"

She reached up and clamped a hand over his mouth. "What if there are *kids*?" she whisper-shouted.

He laughed. *Again.* "Should I continue undressing, or do you want to park this"—he waggled his brows—"intimacy idea until I give you a tour of our very secluded surroundings?"

Willow blinked at him absently. She knew there were more words that came *after* he mentioned undressing, but for the life of her, she couldn't remember what they were because Ash had already pulled *her* shirt over her head and had peppered her neck and shoulders with sweet, delicious kisses. And then she'd gone and gotten all in her head about where they were and who might find them and… She was doing it again.

"Wills?" Ash inquired, and she had the distinct feeling that it wasn't the first time he'd tried to get her attention.

She stared at his lean, muscled torso that looked more defined, more *man* that it had four years ago. Who knew there could be such...changes between twenty-five and twenty-nine?

"What?" she asked, then shook her head. "Sorry. I was just...um...admiring the view." Her cheeks flamed, which only made him grin wider. Then she remembered the reason for her hesitation in the first place, and she exhaled a steadying breath. "If someone did recognize us, and my picture got splashed all over social media in the morning as the homewrecker who came between country music's bad boy and Scotland's tennis darling..."

Ash lowered himself onto his heels and cradled her head in his hands. "You're safe," he whispered, all traces of his devil-may-care grin now gone. "I would never knowingly put you in that kind of situation, Willow. You believe me, right?"

She closed her eyes and nodded even as the entertainment news outlets' posts and tweets replayed themselves on the backs of her eyelids.

Ash Murphy's opening act attempts an encore but gets booed off the stage...or out of the bedroom.

Willow Morgan tries sleeping her way to headliner, but it's love-forty in the game of Morgan vs. Calder-Payne.

She squeezed her eyes shut even tighter, but though she couldn't *see* the posts, she still remembered.

"What happened to leaving the past out of tonight?" Ash asked softly.

Willow heard no anger or malice in his voice. He was simply calling her on her own rule that she was clearly breaking.

She opened her eyes and painted on a sad smile. "Memories are assholes," Willow told him. "They don't care about rules."

Ash nodded. "Then I guess we have a choice to make," he explained.

"What's that?"

He kissed her forehead and then the tip of her nose, and Willow couldn't help but smile for real this time.

He sat back on his heels and shrugged. "Hold on to the old memories or replace them with new ones?"

Willow wrapped her hands around his wrists and lowered his hands until each palmed the demi cups of her bra. "New ones," she whispered, still terrified that someone might be waiting close by to blow their cover or that another camper might stumble upon their campsite.

Or what if she trusted the man who assured her they were safe? What if she seized the opportunity to replace the movie that played behind her closed eyes with something great? What if she allowed herself to see just how much he'd grown *elsewhere* in the years since she'd seen him last?

Ash flicked open the front clasp of her bra, and Willow gasped as he slid a palm over each of her now-exposed breasts.

"*Wow*," she exclaimed. "You just changed the documentary that plays in my head to a super-sexy fantasy."

He lowered himself to all fours and kissed each of her taut, sensitive nipples. "Who says fantasy can't also be a documentary?" he asked, his voice rough and aching with a need Willow guessed matched her own.

She reached up and unbuttoned his jeans, then carefully lowered the zipper over his thick, hard length and pulled the pants down to his thighs.

"I think you have your genre wires crossed," she finally replied, her breath coming in short pants as he nipped gently at her hardened peaks.

He unbuttoned, unzipped, and helped her shimmy out of her own denim. Then she stared at his half-removed pants and raised her brows. "If I can't wear anything but my undergarments, then the same goes for you."

"I was hoping in a minute or two that you wouldn't be wearing *anything*," he replied, letting loose a soft growl that made Willow's body hum.

He stood and let his jeans fall the rest of the way

to the floor. Then he raised his brows and hooked his thumbs behind the band of his black boxer briefs.

"Wait!" Willow cried, then scrambled to her feet, letting her unhooked bra fall where she lay. "I want to do it," she told him.

Ash grinned and dropped his hands, but Willow stayed frozen where she stood.

"What's wrong?" he asked, and she felt her smile fall.

She brushed her fingers over the fading yellow bruise covering his ribs, the one she'd failed to notice when he'd been looming over her looking like he wanted to devour her and she'd been all too willing to let him.

Ash flinched.

"Sorry!" she told him. "Does it still hurt?"

He shook his head. "You just surprised me."

Willow tilted her head up to meet his inscrutable blue eyes. "Admit that it hurts," she said.

His brows furrowed. "What?"

"Bruises hurt, Ash, and that one's a doozy. So why won't you admit it?"

He laughed, but she could hear the bitterness in his voice. "Uh…you're kind of killing the mood, Morgan."

Willow's throat tightened, and she nodded. "I know. But if we're going to really do this, I want *all* of you, Ash. I don't think that's something I ever had before." She realized now that despite the sweet things he might have said to her when they were together, she only knew Ash the performer, the guy who was always a little bit still *on* even off the stage. "I want…" she continued, blowing out a long breath. "I want whatever is going on in your head… and…whatever you're feeling in your heart." She slid her arms around his waist and pulled his bare torso to hers. "Please?" she added.

Ash rested his chin on top of her head and exhaled. "I already told you I still loved you, and I meant it. What else do you need from me?"

"Everything," she replied matter-of-factly. And Willow realized she wouldn't settle for anything less. "But tonight…just two more things."

He pulled back enough to look her in the eyes. "Name 'em. I've got nothing to hide from you."

Willow both shivered from the breeze sneaking in from outside and crackled with electricity at being so close to Ash Murphy after all this time.

"Does the bruise hurt?" she whispered.

He nodded. "But only a little now that it's had time to heal."

"Do you think you deserve to be hurt by those who are supposed to love you?"

A muscle in his jaw pulsed. "Willow…" he whispered through gritted teeth. "I've seen what people say…about you being too smart to…" But his voice trailed off, and she could tell he was too scared to finish the thought, scared that he might be right.

"I don't care what other people say." Willow wanted to believe that was true, that she was stronger now than she was before. That her life was *her* life despite so much of it being lived in the fishbowl of the public eye. She leaned up and pressed her lips to his—and felt him inhale a stuttering breath. "I forgive you," she said softly, then kissed him again. "Your brothers are *happy* you're home." Another kiss. "Maybe it's time you let yourself off the hook too." She kissed his cheek, his mouth, his neck.

She felt him tremble beneath her touch, this big, strong man who was the boy she fell for one summer four years ago. Then she lowered his boxer briefs as he stepped out of both them and his jeans, and she took him into her hand, stroking him from root to tip.

Ash stumbled back a step before righting himself again.

"You okay?" she asked.

He nodded and finally gave her what she wanted to see, his smile.

"I guess you make me weak in the knees, Morgan," he admitted.

Willow did a victory dance in her head.

It was real.

This was real.

They were real.

She stepped out of her underwear, and there was nothing left between them. Then she spun him so he stood where she had been and nodded toward the sleeping bag.

"Lie down, cowboy, and let me have my way with you."

"That sounds like a lyric from a song," he replied.

Maybe someday it would be. But tonight those words were only for them.

"You gonna do as you're told, handsome?" Willow added, emboldened with a confidence she hadn't known she'd possessed before tonight.

Ash grinned, then lowered his exquisite naked body to the floor beneath her.

Willow climbed over him, lowering herself to her knees, one on either side of him.

"I'm still on the pill," she told him. "And I haven't… I mean, it's been a while since…"

"Me either," Ash replied, and though her eyes widened in question, she didn't want to know how long it had been since he'd slept with another woman. She didn't want to think about him sleeping with anyone other than her. Period. And she wanted to make him forget that he ever had. So she glided over him, already slick and ready to obliterate his memory of any woman who came before.

"You're so beautiful, Wills," he whispered. "Wherever you go, always the prettiest damned woman in the room."

Willow's cheeks flamed, and a fire ignited in her core. She tilted her head forward, her hair falling like a curtain around their heads, and gave him one final chaste brush of her lips before sinking over him, burying him deep inside.

Something feral and animal tore from Ash's lips as he rolled them both onto their sides, hooking her leg over his hip as he slowly slid out and then filled her again, making her cry out as she tried to pull him closer, tighter, deeper. The only thing Willow loved more than making the first move and reducing Ash Murphy to his basest form was Ash Murphy stealing the control right back from her and making her see stars.

He rocked inside her, and when she grabbed his ass and he slipped a hand between them, rubbing a finger over her sensitive, swollen clit, she arched against him, biting his bottom lip, and they both lost the ability to form intelligible speech.

The temperature had dropped outside their tent, but inside they were a tangle of sweaty limbs, of hot lips rubbed raw from deep, hungry kisses that refused to cease.

Who was this man who hadn't known her in years yet knew without fail when to roll her onto her back and hike her leg higher, when to plunge deeper, and when, exactly, to swirl his thumb between them right when she thought she couldn't hang on any longer?

Willow cried out Ash's name as he shuddered inside her with one final growl. His arms gave, and he collapsed onto his elbows, still shaking, his face buried against her shoulder.

"It's okay," she whispered when she found her voice again. "You don't need to hold yourself up anymore."

He was quiet for several seconds, still trembling above her, but then he ground out a single word, "Okay," and let the full weight of his torso fall against hers.

She held him tight, combing her fingers through his sweaty hair, and kissed his temple.

"Don't you dare leave me again, Willow Morgan," he pleaded with a shaky whisper. "I won't survive it." And now she knew that he remembered the words he'd spoken the morning when he thought the farthest she'd go was the bathroom to brush her teeth.

"Neither will I," she admitted.

Because there was no getting over Ash Murphy. It took her until now to realize that she never had.

Chapter 15

ASH WOKE UP COLD ON A HARD FLOOR IN THE middle-of-nowhere Plumas County, yet he couldn't stop smiling. Why did no one tell him that being this happy could obliterate a cold, damp morning or a wooden slab for a bed? Why was there no guidebook that spelled it all out for you, letting you in on the best-kept secret that being ass over elbow in love fixed everything? Except both his ass and his elbow realized that he was in bed—or in a sleeping bag—alone. Warning alarms should have fired off inside his overactive imagination, but instead he just kept on smiling, confident that after what happened between him and Willow last night, there was no way she'd bolted, even if it had freaked her out.

Then he smelled the most glorious scent next to Willow Morgan's shampoo...*coffee.* Ash pushed himself up to sitting and was ready to scavenge the nearby floor for something resembling clothes when Willow emerged through the tent's flap with the French press he'd packed—a super-buff camping one, of course—along with two camping mugs.

"Good morning, sunshine," Willow announced

and then held out her hand that held the two empty mugs, offering one to him.

"What time is it?" he asked, his voice gravel after several hours of not being used…and an hour or three of using his voice in ways he hadn't known were possible… A deep growl emanating from somewhere in the depths of his soul? A string of curses as Willow sheathed him like a sword when he'd thought for sure she'd been ready to pass out? As the night before replayed in delicious, achingly slow motion, Ash began to ache—and stiffen—in the present.

"Almost eight," she told him, dropping down to a crisscross-applesauce position as she *pressed* the French press and then poured them each a steaming mug.

"Almost *eight*?" Ash said. "Who is up and boiling water for coffee at almost eight in the morning when we have this whole portion of the campsite to ourselves, which means sleeping in?"

Willow raised her brows, then dipped her gaze to where the flannel blanket had slid off his lap to expose his unhideable erection.

"You look pretty awake to me," she teased.

"And you look like you're wearing entirely too many clothes." He set his coffee mug down and then did the same with hers. "Coffee can wait." He tugged on the string to her hoodie and then took the liberty of unzipping it.

She laughed. "The coffee will get cold."

"I'll drink it cold."

Willow groaned with mock exasperation but then climbed over him, sliding her yoga-pants-clad pelvis over his hardened length. She groaned again for a whole other reason and then pushed a grinning Ash onto his back.

That morning they did, in fact, drink their coffee cold.

———

It was well after ten when they'd tacked up Midnight and Holiday and taken to the trail. The morning chill was already gone, and the sun shone brightly overhead.

"How long did you rent that camping site for?" Willow asked as their two mares walked leisurely side by side.

"As long as we want it," he told her. "Another night. A week. A month…"

She laughed. "We can't just avoid the real world indefinitely. And you only told me to pack essentials."

"There's a general store at the check-in lodge." Ash glanced in her direction. "Why can't we avoid the real world indefinitely?" Hell, he could live in that tent and eat nothing but shitty mac and cheese until the end of time if Willow stayed with him.

She eyed him warily. "Because we have work to do," Willow reminded him. "We have a song to write, record, and get approved by both of our labels. And don't forget that Sloane has you in damage-control mode right now. I know you said you wanted to keep a low profile as far as *my* socials are concerned, but shouldn't you be making some sort of public statement about the…you know…"

"Arrest?" he asked with a laugh. "I know the song is important to you. It is to me too, but not because I'm looking to use it to boost my image. I don't give a shit about my image."

She stared at him for a few seconds, then shook her head and laughed, turning her attention back to the trail.

God, he loved seeing her in that straw hat and boots. But regardless of what Willow was wearing, she fit so well into Holiday's saddle.

"You were made for riding," he told her. "You took lessons as a kid, right?"

She glanced at him and nodded, then pivoted back to the direction they were riding. "In that first year, my adoptive parents tried anything and everything to get me 'involved' in my new life." She let go of the reins with one hand to make air quotes. "I was so determined to resist. Dance classes?" She wrinkled her nose. "Gymnastics? No thanks." She shrugged. "Then one day they took me to this horse farm, and something clicked. My mom…"

She cleared her throat. "My *birth* mom…thought I was too young to ride when Colt started taking lessons. Guess when I finally got to do it, it made me feel closer to my brother."

He knew enough of the rest not to push her any further. Colt, five years her senior, did not do well in foster care after he and Willow lost their mom, even landing himself in juvie for a short stint. Willow's adoptive parents didn't want to take in a troubled and supposedly violent teen and thought they were giving her a fresh start by separating her from her only living relative.

Ash gently brought Midnight to a halt as they reached their destination. He hopped down, grabbed his day pack, and tied her to the grazing post as Willow did the same with Holiday. When they were free and clear of the horses, he pulled her to him and simply hugged her while she held on tight.

"You okay?" he asked after she took several long inhales and exhales. "I didn't mean to break the rules by bringing up the past." He'd just wanted her to know how much he appreciated her riding, one of many in a long list of talents Willow Morgan possessed.

She gave him one final squeeze and then took a small step back so she could look up at him. "It's okay," she assured him with a bittersweet smile. "I lost a lot, but I have everything I want now…short of having my mom back." She flicked the brim of his hat and let out a soft laugh, her small attempt at the levity he knew she needed now.

"*Everything*?" Ash asked.

She nodded, and her sad smile turned into something that looked a little more hopeful.

"I'm not assuming that I'm on that list of *everything*," he began. "But I thought you should know that whether you want me or not, you have me, Wills. All of me."

She rose onto her toes and rewarded him with a soft kiss. "You're on the list," she whispered. "And I really missed you calling me *Wills*."

Ash grinned. He was pretty sure he'd smiled more since waking up this morning than he had in years. It still felt a little surreal.

"Come on," he told her, holding out a hand. "We don't have too far to go, but the terrain might be a little rough. I promise it will be worth it."

Willow eyed him skeptically but took his hand. She trusted him at the very least to get her from point A to point B safely, but the point was…she found him worthy of her trust, and that meant everything.

The rocky path was no longer slick with morning dew, so they were able to maneuver their way from the grazing post and through the trees with ease. There wasn't an actual need for him to hold her hand, yet neither of them made any move to let go.

The trees began to part, and they both slowed as they came to an outcropping of rock, one that overlooked a large swimming hole and across the way...a waterfall.

"Shut the front door," Willow said softly, but he could hear the wonder in her voice.

"It's not the biggest waterfall around," Ash replied. "But it's one of the prettiest. And we can swim in it too...if you want."

She let go of his hand and then used hers to backhand him on the shoulder. "Ash Murphy...you did *not* tell me to pack a bathing suit."

He waggled his brows at her and grinned. "Who said we need bathing suits when we both came equipped with our birthday suits?"

Willow's mouth fell open. "It's a *public* swimming hole."

He held out his arms and pivoted right and then left. "And yet I don't see another soul other than you and me."

She narrowed her eyes. "You can't rent a public swimming hole and waterfall."

"Maybe not..." He sighed. Then he pulled off the backpack he'd brought with for the day and opened it up so he could reach inside and produce the green two-piece swimsuit. "But I have this." He smiled sheepishly as her mouth fell open yet again.

"That's my swimsuit," she told him.

Ash nodded. "I can't tell if you're the happy kind

of surprised or the pissed-off kind of surprised, but I'm really hoping it's the former."

Willow glanced from Ash to the waterfall and back to Ash again, her jaw set. "You went through my stuff."

It was a statement, not a question, but Ash answered it anyway. "I didn't, actually. But Jenna maybe did. On my behalf. I just… The second I realized Colt and I weren't going to settle our differences caveman style, I knew I wanted to take you somewhere and give us a chance to just be. I wanted to take you here. So when Jenna made it back to the house before you did, I asked her if she had a suit you could borrow, and she told me that if you brought one, it'd be in your underwear drawer and that any woman could find another woman's underwear drawer with an error count of one or less. Is that true? Because she was in and out of the house in, like, thirty seconds, and she brought me this."

Willow's expression softened, and he watched the corner of her mouth begin to curl into the beginning of a grin.

"It's always a top drawer," she told him. "Not every woman keeps her swimsuit in the underwear drawer, but if she's staying somewhere that's not home and only has some of her belongings…"

"Looks like your sister-in-law knows you well," Ash remarked.

This made her smile, which made him smile. Had he mentioned how much smiling he was doing today? His cheeks were starting to hurt. No. That was a lie. Nothing hurt when Willow Morgan was nearby. Not his cheeks. Not the bruise on his ribs. Not the ache in his chest he'd been nursing since the moment she walked off his tour bus and out of his life.

"Jenna is the kind of person who makes you feel like she's known and loved you all your life. My brother is a lucky man, and I guess that makes me lucky by proxy." She laughed. "They're proof that it works. The whole love thing." She shrugged. "At least for some people, right?"

She snatched the suit from his hand before he could respond. "I guess I better find a secluded spot to change. Meet you in the water?"

She headed back toward the trees and left Ash standing there to overthink her assessment of Colt and Jenna's relationship. *At least for some people.* Did that mean Willow didn't see *the whole love thing* working for her? For *them*?

Ash shook his head, effectively shaking away the thought…for now. They were still stretching the bubble of the fairy tale. As far as he knew, Cinderella or her coach or whatever still hadn't seen the stroke of midnight, which meant Ash wasn't going to waste time worrying about the real world. Not when Willow was somewhere in the trees shedding her clothes and putting on a swimsuit to dive into a waterfall…with him.

Ash climbed down to the small beach area that was surprisingly still empty and stripped down right there. After all, he'd snuck on his swim shorts beneath his jeans while Willow had made the hike to the campsite's *not entirely horrible*—her words— public restroom to freshen up after their prolonged morning coffee.

He kicked his clothes and boots into a pile next to the backpack and stretched his arms overhead, tilting his head up and closing his eyes as he basked in the warmth of the sun.

"Pink-flamingo swim trunks," he heard in Willow's familiar teasing lilt.

"Are you surprised at my need for atten—" Ash teased back as he opened his eyes. But then his mouth went dry, and he couldn't even finish his last syllable. Hell, he'd lost all ability to form words, let alone string them together into coherent sentences because Willow wasn't simply standing there, teasing him about his pink flamingos. She was standing there in an emerald-green bikini top that covered her breasts with nothing more than two well-placed triangles of fabric. And the bottoms were more of a tiny pair of shorts that he knew—once she turned around—he'd see hugging her ass in the best possible way.

"What's the matter, cowboy?" she asked, striding closer so she could toss her clothes on the pile with his. Then she tugged on the tied drawstring of the aforementioned pink-flamingo trunks. "Cat got your tongue?"

Ash nodded because…words. What were words again?

"You're probably wondering why I even had a suit with me if I was going to be holed up at a horse ranch writing a song."

He cleared his throat. "No," he managed, but the word sounded more like a growl. "Not wondering. Just. Enjoying."

Willow laughed, then ran her index finger along the waistband of his swimsuit, and Ash sucked in a breath. "The songwriter at a loss for words," she mused. "This is fun. And because I want you to know how wowed I am by this place, the reason I brought a suit was because Colt told me about a swimming hole a short ride from his guest ranch that they take guests to for a day trip. But I've seen photos on the ranch's website. The place is cute, but…"

"Mine is better?" he asked, his voice low and rough as his ability to speak finally returned.

She bit down on her bottom lip and nodded.

"Just so you know," Ash added. "We're never leaving this place. We live here now. And I'm burning the rest of your clothes so that all you have left is that green work of art." And because two could play her daring little game, he took it one step further and dipped his finger just beneath the hip-hugging band of her tiny green shorts, gliding it across her soft, pale flesh. Her breath hitched, and Ash gave himself a mental pat on the back. He leaned in, his lips and stubble trailing across her cheek until his mouth reached her ear. "I'm not sure why this place isn't overrun with tourists yet, but I'm going to take our lack of audience as a sign that I should probably kiss you senseless right here on this beach before our little bubble of privacy is broken." Her whole body shivered, but just to double-check, he asked, "Is that your way of giving me permission?"

"Yes," Willow whispered.

So he snaked his fingers into her hair, cradling her head in his palm as he dragged his lips back across her jaw until they found her mouth.

She parted her lips and moaned as his other hand reached around her backside to see—or at least feel—just how good those tiny emerald shorts hugged her soft yet toned behind. In the distance he heard what sounded like children shouting, and he knew their bubble was about to burst.

"Grab on," Ash told her, and as if she knew exactly what he intended, Willow hooked her arms round his neck, and he grabbed her by the thighs, lifting her onto his hips, her pelvis gliding over his erection. He swore, knowing that there would be no satisfaction as far as the things Willow Morgan did to him. At least not here. So he kissed her hard and deep, their lips making a promise to finish what they started when they got back to the campsite.

For now, a plunge into a cold swimming hole should do the trick.

Willow yelped, and Ash swore as the water hit their skin. Soon they were soaked and laughing, the kiss and their arousal giving way to something more playful and definitely more G-rated as the first of what would be many tourists emerged onto the sand where they'd just stood.

Chapter 16

WILLOW COVERED HER EYES AS ASH NEARED THE edge of the cliff over the falls. They'd already watched several others—mostly teens—jump from the same spot and land safely in the water below, but something about seeing Ash up there made Willow feel like she was nearing the edge of the cliff herself rather than wading in the water below.

She held her breath as he took a couple of deliberate steps back, enough to give him a running start. And just like that, after a short sprint, his feet left the ground, and Ash Murphy was airborne. He whooped and hollered with unbridled joy as he soared out and then down toward the water, finally landing with a thunderous splash.

When he popped back up through the surface wearing an exuberant, boyish grin, Willow finally exhaled. Ash swam toward her as she waded in his direction until they finally met where the water was up to her shoulders and just below his chest.

"That was—" he started, but Willow cut him off.

"*Terrifying!*" She pressed her palms against his chest and gave him a gentle yet, she hoped, meaningful shove.

Ash laughed. "I was going to say *unbelievable*, but do we need to unpack your reaction first?"

Willow splashed him this time. "*No*," she replied petulantly.

He had the audacity to wrap his arms around her and pick her up, and only because she didn't want to be rude did she drape her arms over his shoulders and hook her legs over his hips.

"Wills…?"

"What?" she replied with a sigh.

"Were you worried about me?"

"No," she insisted again, but the response sounded even less convincing than the first time.

Ash laughed as they slowly bobbed up and down in the water surrounded by other campers and tourists who hadn't noticed that country's biggest bad boy had just cannonballed off the cliff. Willow's star might have been on the rise, but she'd learned how to move about in public places and stay under the radar.

"Wills…" he said again, but this time her name was a declaration. "If you didn't want me to do it, you could have said something."

She scoffed. "Right…like I'm going to be the kind of girl who tells her guy not to do something that he wants to do and that is well within his right to do."

If it was possible for Ash Murphy's smile to grow any bigger or brighter or more knock-her-off-her-feet gorgeous, it just had. Luckily, her feet were already off the sandy bottom of the swimming hole.

"What now?" Willow asked, worried he was about to ask her if it was okay if he went and risked life and limb again while she watched.

"Willow Morgan…did you just call me your *guy*?"

Her mouth fell open. Then she threw a hand over it as if something else incriminating might leak out.

"Holy shit," Ash remarked. "I'm Willow Morgan's guy!"

"Shh!" she hissed. She might fly under the radar, but if someone nearby recognized her name, their whole fairy tale would end, and they'd have to go back to the real world.

He tilted his forehead against hers. "You *like* me," he teased.

"Shut up," Willow mumbled.

"You *care* about me," Ash added.

"Seriously, Murphy…" she warned this time. "You better shut that stupid mouth and throw away the key."

"You were *so* worried about me on that cliff, and now that you know I survived what a bunch of teens and preteens have been doing since they got here, you want to kiss the hell out of my stupid mouth."

He grabbed her thighs and hiked her higher and a little closer so that now they were practically mouth to mouth.

Of course she wanted to kiss the hell out of his stupid mouth. In barely more than a week she'd gone from hating him, to trying (accidentally) to kill him, to tolerating him, to forgiving him, and now to what? Caring about him so much that she couldn't breathe when he did exactly what a middle schooler was doing right then and there?

"I don't want to care this much yet," Willow finally admitted.

"I know," Ash replied.

"This is supposed to be the fun, easy, fantasy getaway where we don't think about the after." But Willow was thinking about the after, things like... What if he'd hurt himself jumping off that cliff? What if he'd done something worse? How much would it hurt to lose him a second time? Yeah, those were not questions she wanted to be asking or answering on an impromptu trip where the only thing on her mind should be how great the sex was and when they were going to do it again.

Ash nodded. "Then let's get back to fun and easy," he told her and dropped her back to her feet. "Last one to the waterfall has to make *and* clean up dinner tonight." And then he dove beneath the surface and popped up only when he was already a few yards away. "Better catch up, Morgan!" he called over his shoulder. "Not sure if I have any mac and cheese left, but I bet there's a fish or two swimming around your feet right now!"

He dove back under, and Willow yelped as she felt something touch her ankle. *Please let it be seaweed. Please let it be seaweed.* Willow wasn't going to wait around to find out. She dove after him, kicking and paddling like she was aiming for Olympic gold rather than simply trying to get out of dinner duty. Then she found herself smiling even as her arms, legs, and lungs worked overtime to not only catch up but overtake her daredevil of a guy just before the spray of the falls hit them.

Her guy, she thought again.

Hers.

She could admit it, right? At least to herself. Ash was different now. *They* were different. Maybe she didn't have to think about the after as far as this little getaway was concerned. Weren't her two months in Meadow Valley a getaway—albeit a working one— in and of itself? She treaded in water barely over her head, pumping one victorious fist into the air as Ash popped up beside her.

Because he could stand, he shook out his hair like a golden retriever and then scooped her into his arms.

Willow laughed as he spun her in a circle singing Queen's "We Are the Champions."

"We?" she cried. "What's this *we*, you cheater! I beat the pants off of you even after you gave yourself a head start!"

He flipped her over his shoulder caveman style

as she continued to laugh and pretend to beat at his back as if she were opposed to being taken prisoner. Ash strode through the waterfall toward a small patch of sand on the other side, a spot you could only reach by swimming, and a spot that—as of right now—was free of any other visitors.

Even when the water had made it to his knees and then his ankles, Ash held her tight, only relinquishing her when they finally reached shore.

He laid her down on the sand, cradling her neck with his hand as he hovered over her, dripping wet and smiling like he had when he'd leaped off the cliff—with complete and unmistakable joy.

"You look happy," Willow told him, still breathless after the race and her subsequent capture.

"That's because I'm happier than I've ever been, ever in my life…ever," he replied, staring down at her with his hypnotic blue eyes.

"That's a lot of 'evers,'" Willow informed him.

"It bore repeating," he said. "Now do you want to kiss the hell out of my stupid mouth or not?" he added, teasing her by lowering his head but keeping his lips just out of her reach.

Willow swallowed, her throat dry despite the two of them being soaked to the bone.

"Is that my reward for kicking your ass and leaving you in the dust?"

"Sure is," he said with a laugh. "But—spoiler alert—I'm a sure thing. You can kiss my stupid mouth anytime you want, whether you kick my ass or not."

She knocked the inside of his elbow, causing him to lose his balance and drop to his forearm so that his lips were now right where she wanted them. "Shut your stupid mouth, then, cowboy." And in case he didn't understand the request, she cupped his cheeks in her palms and pulled his mouth to hers.

"Permission to *not* keep my stupid mouth all the way shut?" he asked in a gravelly whisper that made Willow's whole body tingle.

"I'll allow it," she whispered back and then parted her own lips, inviting him to lick and taste and drive her absolutely mad with want. "I think I'm done swimming for the day," she managed to say through kiss after breathless, needy kiss.

"Me too," Ash growled.

They had to swim back to the actual beach, dry off, and then hike back to Holiday and Midnight. Then they had to follow the trail back to the campsite, where they both realized they were too sandy to simply hop back into the sleeping bag.

"I don't want mac and cheese," Willow admitted. "Or to shower in a public bathroom when there is a perfectly good shower and tub back at the guesthouse. And a *bed*," she added wistfully. "That big, giant, king-sized bed with all those pillows and blankets and…" Her voice trailed off and she ran her fingers up Ash's damp T-shirt until they reached those stupid lips again.

"Can we go home?" she asked. "And move you into the bedroom for the rest of our time in the house?"

Chapter 17

ASH HAD NEVER WANTED TO RIDE A HORSE faster, but you didn't send your new mare into an all-out gallop on woodsy terrain unless someone was chasing you, and the only thing chasing him at the moment was his need not only to explore all the amenities the master bedroom had to offer with its current inhabitant, but also to take Willow up on her offer of relocating him from the couch to the bedroom before she had time to change her mind.

Not that he had much in the way of possessions to relocate, but he figured once he occupied a drawer or two…took up residence on one side of the bed…it would be harder to evict him.

"I'll untack the horses if you want to head inside to…uh…de-sand yourself," he told Willow as they led the mares to their stalls, but they both stopped short when they found Cirrus's stall door open and Boone about to lead the horse out.

"Welcome home, li'l bro," Boone said in greeting. "You're just in time, though…" He looked his brother up and down and wrinkled his nose. "You might want to shower first."

Ash blinked twice, then looked from his brother to Willow and back to Boone again. "Just in time for *what*?" he asked.

Boone raised his brows. "I'm bringing Cirrus over to the grazing field to give him some outside time while we're gone. Beth will bring him back to the barn later."

"I'm gonna get Holiday untacked while you two hash out whatever this is," Willow informed the men as she motioned between them. Then she disappeared into Holiday's stall with the mare.

Ash opened Midnight's gate and nudged her inside, promising to get her situated in a minute. Then he stepped inside Cirrus's stall with his brother and whispered under his breath.

"I'm kind of in the middle of something important, *big bro*," he told Boone.

Boone nodded in the direction of Holiday's stall with a grin. "Sand-in-your-pants kind of important?" the older Murphy teased.

Ash instinctively gave his right leg a gentle kick and watched as sand sprinkled onto Cirrus's bedding. He cleared his throat. "*Important* important, okay? I don't need to justify my reasoning to you."

Cirrus nudged Ash's shoulder with his nose, and Boone laughed.

"Maybe not to *me*," Boone conceded. "But Cirrus here might not let you leave without an explanation." He patted the gelding on the nose, and Cirrus gave an approving snort. "Look…there's a rescue pair we need to grab over in Tahoe."

"A pair?" Ash asked. "Can't you and Eli take care of it?"

Boone scrubbed a hand across his jaw and sighed. "It's a pretty bad neglect case. The owners were taken into custody, and there's not a good equine vet in the vicinity. The one tending to them for the time being called Eli directly and asked for his help. Custody goes to the state if the owners are formally charged, which looks to be the case. But the doc in Tahoe can pull some strings and hope-fully get us on the short list. This is an all-Murphy hands-on-deck kind of situation." He crossed his arms. "We were just waiting for you to get home."

Ash's chest tightened as he clenched his jaw. The thought of someone harming a horse—or any animal for that matter—made him want to smash a fist into the wall…or a phone into another seventy-five-inch 4K television.

"Go," Willow told him, brushing off her hands as she appeared in the stall door. "I'll get Midnight untacked so you can run inside and shower."

Ash's mouth fell open, but he didn't know what to say. He was too afraid to slow the momentum of whatever was happening between them. What if—given time and distance—Willow came to her senses and realized he wasn't worth the risk after all?

"I'm gonna walk Cirrus over to Eli's," Boone

announced, effectively excusing himself and his horse. "Meet us in front of the clinic in thirty?" he asked his brother, though Ash knew there was only one answer to the question.

Soon, Boone and Cirrus were gone, leaving Ash and Willow to slow the momentum.

She pressed her hands to his chest and laughed. "You really do need a shower."

He smiled. "We both do…and I figured we might do that together," he lamented.

She shrugged. "We still can…"

But Ash sighed. "There is nothing I want to do more than climb into that shower stall with you. But if Boone says to meet in front of the clinic in thirty, I guarantee you Eli will be knocking on the door in fifteen. Hell, it's his place. He might not even knock."

They both laughed, though neither of them were smiling as much as they had been the entire ride back from the campgrounds.

"Go get cleaned up," she told him. "Sounds like an important job and probably some really good bonding time with your brothers. This is important."

He nodded and reached for the waistband of her pants, hooking a finger inside and tugging her toward him. "How do you feel about kissing my stupid mouth one more time before I go?"

She licked her lips, and hell if that one little movement didn't unravel him entirely.

"They're actually not so stupid," she admitted, rising up on her toes and brushing one sweet, chaste kiss across his lips before sliding her mouth up to his ear. "I know what you're thinking, cowboy, and you don't have to worry. I'm not going to change my mind."

He sighed and kissed her jaw, then buried his face in the crook of her neck. Despite their night outdoors, their swim in the falls, and their ride home, she still smelled like her coconut shampoo and the faintest hint of fresh-baked cookies.

"How do you already know me so well?" he asked, lips trailing up her neck.

She hummed a soft moan and then leaned back, pushing him to arm's length. "I might want you bad, Ash Murphy, but I draw the line at a horse's stall. No offense, Holiday and Midnight."

"Seriously, though, Wills…" Ash started. "If you do change your mind, it's okay. This is all happening kind of fast, so if you decide we need to slow down or hit the brakes, I'm not going to fight you on it."

"Oh," she replied, her smile falling. "Yeah. Okay." He furrowed his brows, but then she brightened and added, "I appreciate you giving me space…if I need it, I mean." She kissed him again, this time a quick peck, and then patted him on the ass. "Now go before you're late being fifteen minutes early!"

He laughed, kissed *her* one more time, and then

thanked her for taking care of the horses while he got ready and left.

When he got out of the shower, to absolutely no one's surprise, Eli was waiting at the breakfast bar.

"Nice outfit," his brother remarked, nodding at the one garment Ash wore, a towel wrapped around his hips.

"Where's Willow?" he asked. "She not back from the barn yet?"

"Colt came and picked her up a couple minutes ago," Eli informed him. "Said she can shower at his place and have dinner with him and Jenna."

Something sank in Ash's gut. Was she pulling away already? He tried to retrace his steps to figure out what could have flipped a switch in the short time since they'd raced home to tear each other's clothes off and essentially start living together as Ash and Willow instead of *Ash out here and Willow in there.*

He offered to slow down for her benefit. But that was it, wasn't it? When he said he wouldn't fight her if she pulled the brakes.

The truth was, he couldn't fight her. He didn't have it in him after he'd already fought for four whole years without so much as a word from her. He owned his part in messing up what they had, but how could he fix what he'd broken if he was doing it all by himself? If Ash fought now, and she hung him out to dry again? It would break him beyond repair.

"Oh," he finally replied. "Right. Yeah. Colt," he added, hoping to make it look like this was always the plan. "I'll be ready in a few. How long do you think we'll be gone?"

Eli shrugged. "Depends on what kind of shape the horses are in, if they're healthy enough to travel."

A muscle in Ash's jaw pulsed. "I know I got lucky with my—uh—law enforcement situation last week, but I'd sure love a few minutes alone with the assholes who thought starving a couple of horses was a good idea."

Eli shook his head and huffed out a bitter laugh. "Why don't you rein it in there, Rocky. From what I hear, you and Boone barely lasted ten minutes in the ring. The owners are in custody and being dealt with. Our job is the horses, a mare and a stallion I think they were trying to breed. I'm guessing their lack of success in that department is what contributed toward the neglect. Or maybe it was the other way around. Either way, we'll be gone a few days at least as we get the whole ownership thing sorted out. The rest depends on the horses."

Ash nodded. "Okay. I'll get dressed and pack up...again," he responded coolly.

Eli stood and headed toward the door, stopping briefly in front of his towel-clad brother.

"Just because she might be a little spooked about whatever happened on your little getaway doesn't mean you have to get spooked too. Call her. Text her. Do whatever you need to do to let her know you're all in if you are." He shrugged. "It's just a thought." He strode back out the door before Ash had a chance to respond.

Once back in the bedroom, he grabbed his phone from where it was charging on the dresser and then swore.

His phone was a loaner with exactly *zero* contacts aside from the two numbers he knew from memory—his brothers' and Sloane's. Okay, so he did remember one other, but Willow hadn't just blocked his number. She'd gotten a new one herself. And since they'd both been living under the same roof for the past ten days, they hadn't yet gotten around to exchanging numbers.

He hurried back out to the kitchen, opening and closing drawers and cabinets.

"Come on, Eli," he mumbled to himself. "Tell me there's a drawer full of junk somewhere around here. No man is *that* organized." He finally found it in the drawer next to the fridge. Amid random pens and pencils, a tape measure and *three* rulers, and so much loose change that Ash wished it was 1989 and there was an old-school arcade around the corner, he found an unopened package of sticky notes.

When his short nails were no match for the cellophane wrapping, he tore the package open with his teeth, grabbed one of the random pens, and scribbled what he would have sent in a text. Then he marched back into the bathroom and stuck it right in the center of the mirror where she wouldn't miss it.

After that, he threw on a clean T-shirt and jeans, tossed a few odds and ends into the camping pack he'd emptied straight into the washing machine, slid on his boots, and grabbed his hat. When he made it outside, his brothers already had the trailer hitched to Eli's truck and were ready to hit the road.

He laughed as he watched Eli hop into the driver's seat and Boone take the passenger side.

"Right," he mused, opening the cab's rear door. "The youngest has to sit in the back seat."

Boone reached back and ruffled Ash's hair like it was twenty years ago. "What…was the celebrity hoping for some sort of special treatment?"

Ash swatted his hand away and told his brother to piss off using a much more choice four-letter word. "I've been sleeping on a couch for over a week without complaint," he reminded them.

Eli laughed as he put the truck in gear and began rolling away from the property. "I think I'd file the mention of the couch as a complaint, wouldn't you, Boone?"

Boone shook his head. "Come on, Eli. Is that any way to treat our poor baby brother's martyrdom? The man has been suffering."

Ash groaned. "All right. I can see how this little trip is going to go. You two get to be assholes, and I get to take it." But a smile tugged at his lips. Before Eli's little family reunion, it had been years since the three Murphy brothers were in the same place, and even then it was at one of Ash's shows, so how much did that count? Before that? Ash was pretty much a kid. And though he'd never have admitted it then, he loved when his older brothers messed with him because it made him part of their world, a world for which he was always just a little too young or a little too naïve.

"Exactly," Boone replied. "I'm glad you understand the group dynamic."

They all sat in what felt like their first comfortable silence as they made their way out of their small hometown and toward the state highway. Then Eli turned on the radio, and the ribbing started all over again when they landed on a station playing none other than an Ash Murphy song.

"Nope," he declared, leaning forward and reaching for the station presets. "Not happening," he continued, then pressed button after button until he found an alternative rock station that had no chance of tossing one of his records on. From there on out, it didn't matter what song blared through the speakers because in his head he started to hear it—the melody for his and Willow's duet.

That was a good sign, right? It all was... Time with his brothers, bringing two more horses back to the ranch, and the song—no...his *life*—finally starting to take shape.

Chapter 18

COLT, JENNA, AND WILLOW HELD OUT THEIR flashlights to illuminate the trail that led from the Meadow Valley guest ranch out to the property's bonfire site where this morning—because technically 2:00 a.m. *was* morning, even if no one had actually slept yet—Colt was on duty with the ranch patrons who trailed behind them, all with flashlights of their own.

"I still can't believe this is your job," Willow told her brother as she glanced in his direction. His free hand was clasped in Jenna's, and she smiled wistfully at her brother for this life he'd created for himself. "You get to spend every waking moment doing exactly what you love," she added.

Colt smiled at his sister and then planted a kiss on top of his wife's head as they continued toward their destination. "Isn't it the same for you?" he asked.

Willow paused to think, which didn't feel like the right response. Shouldn't she have immediately replied with "Yes!" or "Of course!" Instead she found herself taking mental stock of the career she'd built over the past five years, the weight of the guitar case in her free hand.

"Wills?" Colt asked when she'd seemingly gotten lost in her head.

"How y'all doing?" Jenna called over her shoulder, letting go of Colt's hand and dropping back toward the trail of guests several feet behind them.

"She's not subtle, is she?" Willow asked with a laugh as her brother closed the gap between them so they were now walking side by side.

Colt laughed too. "Not even a little. Just one of the many, *many*, MANY things I love about her."

"I get it. You're in love, and your life is perfect, and the rest of us are all just here to cheer you on from the sidelines." Willow let out a breath "Sorry. That was a bit of an extreme reaction to you simply acknowledging that Jenna is amazing, which she is."

"She is," Colt agreed. "But our life isn't perfect, Wills. We have our good days and not-so-good days just like everyone else. Before you got here, we had a three-day stint of giving each other the silent treatment and me sleeping on the couch."

Willow's mouth fell open. "What? Why? What were you two fighting about?"

Her brother shrugged. Like…actually *shrugged*. "Whatever it was doesn't seem so important now."

"You forgot to clean the coop when I was gone all day picking up Biscuit with Delaney, drank too much at the bonfire, and then I had to do it at midnight after I got home!" Jenna called up to them.

Willow snorted. "Seems like it was a *little* important," she told him. "Also, who's Biscuit?"

"A hedgehog Delaney took in at the animal rescue." Colt sighed. "Love you, Babe!" He called back to Jenna.

"Love you too!" she singsonged in response.

Colt cleared his throat. "The point is, we're not perfect. *I'm* not perfect. We just tend to keep the not-so-good days behind closed doors. On the couch. Until she misses me enough to forgive me. I guess living life behind closed doors is a luxury you don't always have these days, huh?"

Willow shook her head. "I mean, I've been really good at keeping a low profile since…you know. But it's not that…" She let her voice trail off, thinking again. "When I first started this, like, before I got signed, I was making music on my own timeline, on my own terms." She laughed. "'Course, I wasn't getting paid a living wage, but the band and I almost always broke even after we had a gig and moved on to the next one. It was hard and simple at the same time. Does that make sense?"

Her brother glanced her way and nodded, then turned back to the trail. "Sorry, Wills," he told her, pushing through a small thicket of bushes. "Can we pick the chat up again once we get everyone situated?"

"I'm fine," she told him, which was mostly the truth. Nothing was actually *wrong*. She simply felt *off*.

They broke into a clearing containing a few picnic tables and a bonfire circle framed by thick logs that Willow assumed doubled as benches when everyone huddled around the fire. Tonight, however, there would be no fire other than in the sky.

"Welcome, everyone. Grab as comfortable a spot as you can find." Colt called out to the fifteen or so guests who signed up for the late-night pilgrimage to catch a meteor shower where there promised to be zero light pollution getting in the way of their view.

The men, women, and even a few school-aged kids spread out on the logs and at the picnic tables, one by one powering down their flashlights.

Colt shook out a big flannel blanket for Jenna, Willow, and himself, and Willow couldn't stop herself from smiling. It had only been a day since she and Ash had returned from the campsite, yet little things kept triggering memories of a day and night that still didn't feel real.

"You know what?" she told her brother and sister-in-law. "I think I'm going to grab a spot on that log over there." She nodded toward the bonfire circle and a still-unoccupied tree log that served as a bench. "I feel like this is something you two should do alone."

Jenna thrust her hands on her hips and cocked her head to the side. "Darlin', we get plenty of time with just the two of us. Tonight is for family." She held her arms out to include all the ranch guests who were apparently extended family for the night. "And I will not have *family* lying around on a fallen tree all by herself watching the sky produce the kind of magic that's meant to be shared."

Willow's cheeks warmed, and she was grateful for the dark.

Colt leaned forward and whispered conspiratorially. "She's pretty smart. I'd listen to her."

Willow sighed. "Okay, but the second I feel like a third wheel, I'm taking up residence on the first empty log I find." She winced. "I didn't hear how that sounded until it came out of my mouth, and I'd like to strike 'take up residence on a log' from the record for the rest of time."

Jenna dropped down onto one side of the blanket and patted the spot beside her. "Not a chance, honey. Now park your log-loving ass next to your sister so we can catch some shooting stars."

Willow did as she was told, and after Colt took a survey of the small clearing to make sure the guests were situated and ready for the event, he stretched out on his sister's other side.

"What if we don't see anything," Willow whispered.

Jenna nudged her with her shoulder and pointed up toward the sky. "Open your eyes and look," she whispered.

Willow stared up at the vastness above, at the pinprick speckle of the 100 billion stars in the galaxy, beautiful and ordinary all at the same time.

"If you keep waiting for the good part," Jenna continued, "you'll miss what's right in front of you, which is pretty great too."

Willow sighed. Was that what she'd been doing for the better part of her adult life, still waiting around for it to start?

Colt threaded his fingers through hers and squeezed. "See?" he told her. "*Smart*."

"Yeah, yeah," Willow admitted. "I guess what's going on up there is pretty damned spectacular all on its—" She gasped, and seeing as she wasn't alone with countless others doing the same, she already knew the answer to her question. "Did you see that?"

Jenna grabbed Willow's other hand and held tight as the late night/early morning sky went from pretty damned spectacular to complete and utter magic in seconds flat as streaks of light rained across the sky.

Willow had missed years with her brother. She'd experienced so many firsts without him. First days of middle and later high school. First time she sang for an audience. First crush and later her first heartbreak. So many took family for granted, assuming the ones they loved would always be there simply because that was how it had always been. But Willow knew better, and because of that, she knew how special this moment was, even if all she was doing was lying on the ground staring up at the sky.

"I've never seen one before," she told Jenna and Colt.

Jenna responded by tilting her head to lean it on Willow's shoulder.

Colt cleared his throat and replied, "It's a first for me too, Wills."

Willow's throat tightened, and everything inside her seemed to bloom. Maybe this was it. Maybe every little moment like this *was* the good part amid the beautiful, the sometimes not so beautiful, and the ordinary. She just had to open her eyes and look.

The meteor shower culminated in a predawn bonfire and sing-along, the song list consisting of a little John Denver, a little Neil Diamond, and even a few Willow Morgan originals. When Willow returned home to find the guesthouse still empty, she strode straight into the bathroom, tore another sticky note from the pad *someone* had left on the counter, and next to the one that simply said, *I'm all in*, she added a second.

I am too.

Willow could wait for the other shoe to drop, for some sign that this—whatever she and Ash were doing—was *right*, or she could open her eyes and look at what was right in front of her. Or what would be right in front of her in the next day or two when Ash returned.

She crawled into bed just as the sun began to peek above the horizon, exhaustion covering her like a weighted blanket so that despite the light creeping in through the shades, she sank into the mattress and, soon after, the oblivion of sleep.

She woke to the windows still framed in dim light and to solid arms clasped around her torso, her back pressed against a strong, solid chest.

Willow sucked in a sharp breath.

"I hid all the vases," Ash said groggily. "Just in case."

She spun to face him, taking in the sight she never imagined she'd be so happy to see.

"Your hair is wet," she whispered, reaching to trace a line from his forehead to his cheek. And he was doing that no-shirt thing again that made it hard for her to think.

"Showered," he replied, his closed eyes fluttering open. "Figured if that didn't wake you that I was fairly safe from ceramic harm."

Willow winced. "Thank you for your note," she told him. "I'm sorry I let you leave without saying goodbye." He was so close that she saw his blue eyes crinkle at the corners before lowering her gaze to confirm that he was smiling.

"You were spooked," he replied, and she nodded.

"Still am. It's going to take some time."

He pulled her to him so that she had no choice but to hook her leg over his hip so she didn't knee him in the groin.

"Thanks for your note too," he continued, tracing lazy circles on the small of her back. "But are you sure?" he asked. "Because if it's too fast, the couch isn't *that* bad," he teased. "I just might have to take you with me."

It was fast. And being this close to him, feeling him already hard against her, made her want to ignore every rational thought from now until eternity if it meant even an eighth of the pleasure she'd felt the other night. But Willow couldn't let her libido make the decisions when her heart and both their careers were on the line.

She slowly lowered her leg and placed her knee carefully between his.

"I'm all in, Ash...for the song, first. We have to finish what we started professionally before we officially make it personal again."

His finger stopped mid-circle on her back, and Willow swore she heard the sound of a record scratch.

"Oh," he replied, all playfulness vanishing in one simple syllable.

"I almost lost everything before my career even started," she continued. "And right now, I feel like I'm on a ship that could just as easily hit an iceberg as it could make it safely to port. If I want the freedom—and income—to make music on my terms, I have to give the label what they want for this album."

Ash swallowed, and she watched a muscle in his jaw tick. "So…" he began with a soft laugh. "I guess while I was out of my mind missing you for two days, you were here drumming up a metaphor that makes you the Titanic…and me the iceberg." There was no menace in his words, only simple resignation. "Guess that sounds about right."

Willow shook her head and then cupped his face in her hands. "*We're* the ship," she explained. "And we just need to steer it in the right direction. But that means one destination at a time." She stroked her thumbs over his cheeks.

He nodded. "I get it," he admitted. "Your career is important to me too."

She furrowed her brows. "And *your* career. They're both important."

"Sure," Ash replied absently. Then he slid his hands up her back, to her shoulders, and down her arms until he was gently clasping her wrists. "I should let you get your sleep. Heard it was a late night."

"Wait!" she cried. "This is just a pause, Ash. You know that, right?"

He nodded and gave her a weary smile. "I know," he replied softly.

Without another thought, she kissed him, a soft brush of her lips against his, and Ash let out a shaky breath.

"Let's steer the ship, okay?" he whispered, then

lowered her hands as he climbed out of the bed. "It's a little past noon," he added. "I'm going to head over to the clinic to check in with Eli and see how the dapples are doing. When you're officially up and ready, why don't you pop out to the barn and meet the new residents? Then we can get to work."

Willow sat up in bed and pulled her knees to her chest. "You're really okay with all of this?"

He leaned against the doorframe and crossed his arms over his chest. His bare chest that—pause or no pause—made Willow's mouth water. "I'm okay with whatever you need to be sure I'm not going to mess up this time." He nodded toward her with a soft smile. "Go back to bed, Wills. There's no rush, okay?"

He pivoted away from her and out into the main area of the house, pulling the door closed behind him.

Willow closed her eyes and counted to ten, letting out a long, steady breath as she reminded herself that despite the ticking clock, he was right. They could take their time and do everything right this go-around.

Chapter 19

"Jack and Rose?" Willow asked as she stood cross-armed outside the new mare's stall. "Seriously?"

Ash gave her a patented Ash Murphy wink. "Since Eli and Boone were dicks the whole trip, making me sit in the back of the cab and torturing me by giving zero control over the music selection, I called dibs on naming the dapples."

"Dibs?" she let out an incredulous laugh. "Are you eleven?"

He shrugged. "Boone got dibs on shotgun. I got dibs on the names. That's how it works."

She shook her head. "Men are forever boys, aren't they?" She sighed. "But Jack and Rose?"

"It's on brand, isn't it?" he asked.

"They *hit* the iceberg!" Willow replied, throwing her hands in the air. "Jack *dies* right before the rescue boats arrive," she added with a hitch in her breath.

"Wait…" Ash said. "He does?"

"Have you even seen the movie?"

He answered her with a wince.

Willow gasped and then backhanded him on the shoulder. "You named these beautiful horses after fated lovers who *lose* each other after just falling in love! I don't know if I've ever cried so hard watching a movie before."

Ash bit back a laugh but not soon enough because Willow was staring daggers at him, and if he didn't know better, he'd have said Rose was side-eyeing him through her gate. "Wait…" he began, opting for defense. "You saw a movie about a real-life ship that sank, and you're getting choked up just talking about someone in the movie dying when over a thousand people died in the actual incident?"

Rose snorted and stomped a hoof on the bedding of her stall.

"See?" Willow continued. "Even Rose objects. Don't you, girl?" But Willow's cooing tone caused Rose to poke her nose over the gate and whinny for a pat. "Or maybe she just likes me so much that she's setting aside her feelings about her tragic name." Willow sighed. "She *is* pretty, isn't she? I've never seen a… What did you call her?"

"A dapple," Ash told her. "She's a quarter horse by breed, but the coloring—the gray with the sort of white snowflake pattern—it's called dappling." He gave the mare an affectionate scratch between the eyes. "It's the reason the owners were trying so hard to breed them. Probably thought they'd make some easy money, but malnourished and neglected horses don't always behave the way you want them to. And if they knew anything about horses at all, they'd know there's no way to guarantee a dapple anyway." He felt his teeth clench as he spoke. He had to remind himself that Jack and Rose were going to be okay because of Eli's skills and reputation as a vet and because he'd rehabbed the family ranch and turned it into a rescue.

"Where's Jack?" she asked, and he could hear the hesitation in her voice. "I wouldn't have teased you about the names if—"

"No!" Ash interrupted with a firm shake of his head. "Jack's fine. Eli...uh...*fixed* him before we left Tahoe. Geldings bounce right back after surgery, but just to be safe, Eli's keeping him in the grazing field over by his place for the rest of the day and night."

Willow nuzzled Rose's nose. "She's too thin," she said softly. "I can't believe they were withholding food from her."

"Wanna feed her?" Ash asked with a hopeful smile. He patted the pocket of his jeans to indicate where the treats were hidden. "I've got a few carrot slices in here," he whispered, just in case Rose understood the word.

"Like...right now?" Willow asked.

He shook his head. "I was going to walk her a couple of laps around the arena. If she cooperates, she gets a treat." He leaned in conspiratorially and whispered in Willow's ear. "And even if she doesn't, I'll probably still give her the treat just because she's pretty."

"I see how it is," Willow told him. "I say we should hit pause and you're already on to the next pretty girl to cross your path."

Ash cleared his throat. "No one could ever…" he began. "I mean, I wasn't wasn't—"

"Joking!" Willow blurted. "Yes. Let's take her for a walk. I'd love to get to know her."

Ash nodded once. He disappeared into the tack room and returned with a halter and lead. He slipped inside the stall and gently affixed both, all the while cooing to the gentle yet still-apprehensive mare.

"My girl's a good girl, isn't she?" he whispered. And then, because anytime he said something that reminded him of a lyric led to singing, his gentle whispers morphed into him singing "My Girl," by The Temptations as he led the mare out of the stall and danced her toward the doors to the arena.

Once out in the open, the afternoon sun shining down on them, he paused and held the lead out toward Willow, but when she reached for it, Rose snorted and began pawing and stomping at the dirt.

"Whoa," Willow said, holding her hands up. "I do *not* think she wants me to lead her around the arena."

Ash lowered the lead, and the mare ceased her stomping and pawing. "Huh," he remarked, brows furrowed.

"She doesn't like me," Willow told him as Ash began walking, and Rose was in full cooperation.

"She can tell you're nervous," Ash replied as Willow hung to his left while Rose was on his right.

Willow crossed her arms and set her jaw. "Hard to compete when she's being serenaded by *you*," she mumbled.

Ash laughed and gently patted the mare on her snowflake-spotted flank. "Well, Ms. Rose, I'm pretty sure someone's jealous I've got a fan. What do you think?" He launched back into "My Girl," this time giving the chorus his all as the mare's ears perked up while she eagerly listened.

Willow threw her hands in the air. "See?" she cried. "How am I supposed to compete with that?"

Ash glanced at her and raised an eyebrow. "Why compete when you can join the show? We're writing a duet, yeah? Maybe we should try singing one together."

Even in the sun he could see her cheeks turn pink.

"Here?" Willow asked. "With an audience?"

He laughed. "It's not like she can boo us. 'Course, I've only known Miss Rosie for a few days, so there's no telling how she'll react if we botch the song. But it looks to me like she's a big fan of The Temptations, so we at least have that going for us." Then he stage-whispered, "Unless you don't know the words."

She scoffed. "Of course I know the words." Then she cleared her throat and took it back to the first verse without waiting for him to begin. But that was fine by him. He let her take those first five lines by herself just to listen to her sing and then came in on the chorus.

It was…messy for a couple of lines, but then they found their footing, with Ash taking the melody and Willow coming in higher with the harmony.

It was *them*. Messy to start, and maybe they were still in the thick of it, hacking at painful memories and wounds still unhealed like overgrown weeds hiding a garden and just itching to grow.

After two laps and one full successful run of the song, Ash slowed and offered the lead to Willow once more. "Even if you're scared, pretend you're not," he told her.

Willow gave him a curious look and then reached for the lead confidently—or at least with an amazing performance of confidence—and Rose pawed the dirt. But once the lead was in Willow's hand, the mare stopped. She looked Willow in the eye and seemed to be waiting for direction.

"Good girl," Willow told her, then petted her gently between the eyes.

"Give her this," Ash told her, and Willow glanced his way to find him holding out a chunk of carrot. "Flat in your palm with your fingers pressed together. So she doesn't mistake your fingers for more carrot."

Willow rolled her eyes. "This ain't my first rodeo, cowboy," she told him. Then she grabbed the carrot and held it out carefully for Rose to sniff and immediately gobble up from her hand. "Good girl, Miss Rosie!" she cheered, stroking the mare's mane. "Good girl!"

Rose snorted in response and then stomped in place.

"Okay," Willow replied with a laugh. "One more lap, and then Ash hopefully has one more treat." She urged Rose to start walking again, and the mare obliged. Willow darted a glance in his direction. "You do have more carrots, right? I didn't just lie to her?"

Ash laughed. "Yes I do, and no you didn't. And I like how you called her Miss Rosie too."

Willow's cheeks flushed again, or maybe it was the afternoon heat. "It suits her," she told him.

"It does," he agreed. "It can be *our* name for her."

Willow smiled. Then she fished her phone from her pocket and tossed it to him. "Take a picture of us? Me and Miss Rosie. Need some more fodder for social media, right? Keep Sloane happy and keep the fans guessing who might be on the other side of the lens. Make it a candid one, okay?"

She turned away from him and kept walking, leaving him to decide on the shot. He snapped several, not caring which one made the cut because he took the liberty of texting them all to himself. Well, his actual number since he had no idea what the number was to his loaner. He really needed to get to a phone store. It was either that or ask Sloane to do it, but that meant Sloane making another trip to the ranch, and that was the last thing on his list of things he wanted to make happen.

"Hey, Wills!" he called, and she glanced over her shoulder with a knowing grin.

"Candids!" she called back, then raised her brows.

He laughed, and she turned back to her mare.

They continued like that for another couple of laps before pausing to give Rose another snack and then taking her back to her stall for some water and rest. Then they walked back to the guesthouse, Willow heading straight for the fridge where she removed the pitcher of water and filled two tall glasses.

"Here," she told him, offering one in his direction.

"Thanks," Ash replied, suddenly not sure how to talk to her when there wasn't a horse's well-being to discuss. "Oh," he continued, pulling her phone from his pocket. "You probably want this back."

She set her glass down on the counter and retrieved the device. Ash leaned against the fridge and continued to nurse his drink while she scrolled and tapped, her expression morphing from pensive to curious. Then she seemed to bite back a smile as her top lip grazed her bottom lip before she let out a breath and met his gaze again.

"There," she announced. "That should hopefully keep Sloane satisfied."

He raised a brow. "You posted one of the photos already?"

She nodded. "I…um…I like the one you took when I turned around," she admitted, her lips curling into a soft smile.

Ash nodded. "I like that one too. You're not worried about people speculating in the comments about who took the photo?" He winced as soon as the question left his mouth because he knew he'd just given himself away.

"Why…Ash Murphy, have you been stalking my Instagram?" Willow asked, a teasing lilt in her tone.

He groaned but then opted for the truth, the whole truth, and nothing but the truth because what did he have to lose? "Yes," he told her matter-of-factly. "I follow your account. Not officially… I mean, Sloane pretty much runs my socials, and my professional accounts only follow my label's account and a couple of brands we've partnered with for advertising. But I've looked at your account since we set up our whole arrangement."

She eyed him warily. "So you don't follow me with a finsta or anything like that?"

He let out a nervous laugh. "No finsta." He scratched the back of his neck. "Not that I hadn't thought about it over the years. But… I don't know. I felt like that would be an invasion of your privacy or something."

Willow picked up her glass and took a long, slow sip before responding. "It's a public account," she mused.

"Still felt wrong to follow you without you knowing it was me." Ash shrugged. "But I saw the comments after the bonfire post. This is only going to add fuel to the fire."

She nodded. "Which is what we want, right? To build anticipation about what I'm doing and who I'm doing it with? Speaking of which… I have an idea for the chorus, but if you don't like it—"

"I figured it out," Ash blurted. "The melody, I mean. Sorry. I shouldn't have interrupted. I've just been wanting to tell you, but I got sidetracked by…" His voice trailed off, and Willow nodded. They both seemed happier to reference their new arrangement—putting the brakes on what they'd started—without actually mentioning it. "And same goes for you. If you don't like the melody…" He ran a hand through his hair. "Can I hear the chorus?"

She grinned and nodded, grabbing her phone where he guessed she'd written the lyrics down. "Can I hear the melody?"

He found himself smiling too. "I'll go get my guitar. Couch or patio?" he added.

"Patio," she replied. "I want to soak up as much of this Meadow Valley air as I can before I have to hit the road again."

"See you out there," Ash replied, swallowing the tightness in his throat. Regardless of what they'd started or paused, what happened when the song was written and the festival ended? The hotel incident had followed a local radio interview and performance. He'd had a couple more scheduled, not that he was even sure why. He was between albums and tours, had nothing new to promote.

"You need to promote yourself in the offseason," Sloane insisted. "Stay in the public eye…in a *positive* way," she always added, so much so that Ash was able to mouth the words along with her every time she said them. Not that she was *wrong* to remind him of the necessity. He just seemed to care less and less these days about what anyone else thought of him.

Except Willow. And…okay…maybe Eli and Boone too.

When he met her outside, she was curled up on a cushioned lounger. Ash opted for one of the wooden bench chairs surrounding the small outdoor table.

"No guitar?" he asked her, noting that the only thing in her hands was her phone.

Willow shook her head. "I want to hear your melody, and then I'll sing you the lyrics. We'll see if it all works together or what we might need to fix."

"Okay," he told her, then slung his guitar strap over his shoulder and gave the strings a quick tune.

"Should we record it on one of our phones?" he asked. "So we can listen to playback and see how it sounds?" And then he started to play.

She smiled. "Great idea. How about yours since I'm using mine? That way we can put it midway between us so no one's voice overshadows the other's."

Ash dragged the chair close enough to the foot of her lounger that his shins were touching it. He pulled his phone out of his pocket, set it at her feet, and hit Record on the voice memo app. "Ready?" he asked, and Willow nodded. Then he sang the two verses they'd already written...

> *Didn't feel like the right time to unpack*
> *With the whole damned world*
>   *cracking a whip at my back.*
> *So I hopped on a horse and rode until dark,*
> *Knowing with each step I'd never*
>   *recapture the spark.*
>
> *Everyone wants me to fix what I broke,*
> *But it took me this long to get in on the joke.*
> *Maybe I'll sit in my life, give it time to soak in*
> *'Stead of letting 'em clean every mess I get in.*

He almost stopped playing until Willow's voice cut in, so he did his best to follow her lead as she built from the melody he began with and took it to the chorus.

Starin' up through the clouds, nothing
  seems to have changed.
Beautiful and ordinary, my life rearranged.
Notes on the mirror still making me cry,
Collecting 'I'm sorrys' like stars in the sky.
Should have known from the start
  we'd still end in goodbye.

She sang the last line again, eyes closed and nodding her head to the soft rhythm as he played a few more bars. Finally, when they'd both gone quiet, she looked up at him with a tentative smile.

It was beautiful and haunting, his melody with her voice. He knew right then and there the song would be exactly what her label wanted. He knew for it to be considered a duet, he'd have to come in on a verse or two. But the chorus was all hers. It had to be. The words were hers. The words were the truth, or at least the version of the truth Willow Morgan believed.

"The melody is perfect," she told him. "I love it, Ash."

He pressed his lips into a smile because she was right. Their collaboration worked seamlessly. And yet he couldn't ignore the sort of prophecy they'd fashioned, wondering if—or rather, *how*—it would come to fruition.

"That's how you think it's going to go, isn't it?" he asked, keeping his voice even. He motioned between them with his guitar pick still pinched between his thumb and forefinger.

Willow rolled her eyes. "It's just a song."

He laughed. "Wills, we both know that is the biggest lie any musician can tell."

She froze for a second and stared at him.

"What?" he asked. Did she remember what he'd said the night she was drunk? Would it even matter if she did? Just because a guy wrote some songs about the one who got away—the one he *let* get away—didn't make it all better. She didn't trust him, and he didn't blame her. It still stung to see her put it in their song.

Willow shook her head. "Nothing. Just déjà vu, I guess?" She dropped her phone in her lap and crossed her arms. "But if you want the whole truth, fine. Your note on the mirror got the creative juices flowing, but that doesn't mean I'm predicting the future with it. If you disagree, then just vow right now never to leave me a sticky note on the mirror that says *I'm sorry*, and voilà! Crisis averted!"

He groaned, and Willow sat up straighter in the lounger, leveling him with her gaze.

"Ashton Elias Murphy, I did not write that chorus as a premonition, prediction, or prophecy. The only nugget of truth was the note on the mirror. The rest is fiction."

Ash's cheeks warmed. "You remember my middle name?"

She dropped her feet to the ground on either side of the chair and inched toward him as close as she could without tipping the chair forward.

"All three Murphy men carry both their mother and father's surnames. Eli's full name is Elias, your mom's maiden name, though he's never gone by it. And you and Boone were both given the same as your middle names. I know we were only together for a few months, but I listen when people talk."

He lifted the guitar over his head and laid it on the table behind him.

"Well, Willow Mae Morgan (legal name Hammond), I listen too."

"It's actually Willow Morgan Hammond now. Legally," she admitted. "But still Morgan professionally." She swallowed, and her eyes took on a sheen that wasn't there before. "I love my adoptive parents," she continued, her voice rougher than it had been before. "And I'm grateful for all they've done for me. But just like your parents made sure your mom's name lives on with the next generation, I wanted to do the same for both of mine." She cleared her throat and stood, brushing out the creases in her shirt. "That's enough work for tonight, right? I'm hungry. We should eat. Order in? Or I could run out and pick something up? Maybe there's a frozen pizza. I'll go check."

She spun toward the door as fast as the string of words erupted from her lips. But before she made it to the door, Ash was on his feet, his arms wrapped around her shoulders as he pulled her back to his chest.

"What are you doing?" she asked, a tremor in her voice.

He rested his chin on the top of her head and exhaled a long breath. "Hugging someone I care about when she might be sad remembering her mom."

Willow froze for a moment before finally letting her shoulders fall as she relaxed against him, clasping her hands over his.

"Thank you," she whispered. "I needed that." After another moment of silence, she continued. "You know, I never thought about the kind of friend you might be, but you're really good at it."

He laughed softly. "Friend, huh?"

She squeezed his hands. "For now," she assured him.

The funny thing was, no one had ever told him that before. Outside of Meadow Valley, everyone who surrounded him was either making money because of him or wanted to make money because of him.

Was he a good friend? Did that mean Willow was finally starting to trust him? This somehow felt bigger than he'd expected, something that—if he messed it up—would be irrevocable this time.

That night Ash lay awake on the couch, thinking

about the lyrics she'd written for the chorus of their song.

Notes on the mirror still making me cry,
Collecting 'I'm sorrys' like stars in the sky.
Should have known from the start
     we'd still end in goodbye.

He'd make sure *I'm sorry* never found room on that mirror by filling it with everything but.

He swung his legs off the couch and padded to the kitchen to grab the notepad, only to remember he'd left it in the bathroom, and based on its absence from the kitchen drawer, Willow hadn't put it away either.

He headed toward her bedroom door ready to knock, only to find it slightly ajar.

"Wills?" he whispered, but he was answered with a soft, adorable snore followed by a dreamy hum.

She was out like a light and he was nearly naked, in nothing but his boxers, about to enter the bedroom of a woman who—the last time he'd done so unbeknownst to her—knocked him out cold.

He squared his shoulders and pushed the door open enough to slip through, then padded to the bathroom where the only thing illuminating the space was a slip of moonlight mostly obscured by the small glass-block window on the shower wall.

It was enough for him to find the notes and the

pen still resting on top of the pad. He quickly scribbled the song title that popped into his head, one he remembered from a movie he made his brothers watch with him over and over again when he was a kid. It was one of the first songs he ever learned to play on the guitar even though it was meant for the piano.

Ash hesitated for a moment, wondering whether or not Willow would take it the wrong way, but the second he heard a soft sigh as she stirred in bed again, he knew he had to either make a move and get out of there or end up possibly concussed again. So he quickly scribbled, "You've Got a Friend in Me," stuck it on the mirror and hightailed it out of the room and back to the couch.

He found himself smiling as he finally drifted off to sleep.

Things were different this time.

He was different. Better. Willow could already see it, and he would prove to both of them that she was right.

Chapter 20

THERE WAS A WOMAN OUTSIDE HER BEDROOM door. A *Scottish* woman. Willow was sure of it.

"Ash...*Babe*...you *knew* what was meant to happen on that day, and it *happened*. Can you blame me for being over the moon about finally getting what *I* wanted?" After a beat of silence, the woman's voice continued. "Are you really going to just bugger off and out of my life because I held up my end of the agreement?" The woman spoke in a hushed tone, albeit an exasperated hushed tone, which made it sound all that much less *hushed*.

So...yeah. There was a Scottish woman outside Willow's door calling Ash *Babe*. Which shouldn't matter because they agreed days ago to dial it back to friends while they finished the song. She had a mirror full of song titles about friendship to prove it, from Ash's initial nod to *Toy Story* to Willow countering with *The Golden Girls* theme song, "Thank You for Being a Friend," all the way to songs that evoked the idea of friendship even if they didn't have the word *friend* in the title, like "Count on Me" by Bruno Mars or "I'll Be There for You" by the Rembrandts. She had days' worth of evidence that she and Ash were, in fact, friends and nothing more, yet the sound of a woman's voice outside her door calling Ash *Babe* while sounding like a Spice Girl was throwing her into a tailspin.

Willow might have still been groggy with sleep, but she was certain of two very important things. One, a stranger in her house calling her *friend* Ash *Babe* was not on her bingo card for this week, and two, she had to pee. Like…*now*.

Willow hopped out of bed and ran for the bathroom. In her haste, she stubbed her pinkie toe on the doorframe, *hard*, and let out a string of whispered expletives through gritted teeth as she simultaneously shimmied out of her underwear and took care of business.

Only after she'd risen to wash her hands and face and to brush her teeth did she realize how badly she'd jammed her poor little toe. Hot tears pricked her eyes as she put weight on her foot, and when she looked down, she could see that the tiny toe was already visibly bruised and not as tiny as it used to be.

"No, no, no, no, no," Willow told herself as she splashed cold water on her face and attempted to continue her morning routine. She needed a game plan for how she was going to react when she walked out into the living room to find Ash with the only Scottish woman she could imagine in connection to Ash. His *wife*… Or, she guessed, *ex*-wife.

With clean teeth, a fresh face, and morning hair piled into a messy bun on top of her head, Willow hobbled back into her room, absently threw on a hoodie over her tank and leggings, and then sniffed back the tears that were surely from her throbbing toe and nothing else. Then she squared her shoulders and threw open her bedroom door.

"Morning!" she cried, way cheerier than anyone should greet *anyone* first thing, but Willow Morgan was a singer. An actor, she was *not*.

Ash was mid-pace on the floor in front of the couch while the woman—yep, that was Annabeth Calder-Payne—stood in a fitted white tennis dress with her sleek blond bob parted down the middle, arms crossed as she glanced from Ash to Willow.

Ash's eyes widened. "Wills, I'm sorr—" but he cut himself off before finishing the word, clamping his mouth shut as Willow watched the wheels turn in his head.

"*I'm* sorry," Annabeth interjected, striding toward Willow with a hand outstretched. "Annabeth Calder—" But the other woman stopped short as well when Willow limped in her direction. "Are you injured?" she asked instead.

"I'm fine. Totally fine." Willow waved her off. "Just stubbed my toe on the way to the bathroom," she added with a nervous laugh. "Or I guess you call it the loo, right? Or toilet?" Willow offered the other woman her hand. "You must be Annabeth."

The young woman—she was barely twenty when she and Ash got married, right?—smiled tentatively with perfect red lips as she glanced down at Willow's outstretched hand. She looked like the perfect combination of Taylor Swift and Posh Spice.

"Don't worry! I washed my hands after," Willow joked then cringed at what was *not* at all funny. Nothing about this situation merited laughter.

Annabeth gave her hand a firm shake, firmer than Willow had been expecting, so much so that she lost her balance, put extra weight on the outside of her foot, and then yelped at the sudden onslaught of pain.

"Jesus, Willow." Ash finally spoke again as he strode not around but *over* the couch to meet Willow where she stood precariously, balancing mostly on her left foot. His eyes widened. "What the hell happened? I think you freaking broke your toe."

Oh god. This was not happening. Willow was not interrupting a reunion between her…her…*housemate* and the woman who was very recently her housemate's *wife* without finding out *why* she was here and what it meant. But Ash was suddenly guiding her toward the couch, almost carrying her as Annabeth clapped her hands together and announced, "Right. We'll need some ice, cotton, and surgical tape so we can use the next toe over as a splint. Have you got all of that, Ash?" Annabeth was already at the freezer, pulling out the ice tray as Ash helped Willow lower herself to the couch.

"It's my brother Eli's place," Ash called back to her as he situated Willow in the corner of the couch so she could extend her legs. He propped the right one on top of a throw pillow.

"Ah!" Annabeth replied. "Then that means Dr. Murphy has the place stocked. Will I find a first aid box in one of the cabinets, then?"

"Yep!" Ash answered. "Pretty sure it's the one by the sink."

"I'm *fine*," Willow insisted, but when Ash's thumb brushed so much as the outside of her foot *near* the toe, she hissed in a breath that gave away her big, fat lie.

"Sorry!" he said. "About hurting you…your *toe*, I mean. I didn't… This isn't…" He pinched the bridge of his nose, then soft enough so only Willow could hear, added, "I can explain. This isn't what it looks like."

"What does it look like?" Willow asked in the same hushed tone, but then Annabeth was there. In one hand she held a tea towel tied around a mound of ice and, in the other, the same first aid kit Willow had used to patch Ash up the night she mistook him for an intruder all those weeks ago.

"Right," Annabeth began, shooing Ash out of the way so she could sit beside Willow's propped foot. "Now look, this will do bugger all for the pain at first until you're good and numb, but it will help with the swelling so you can hopefully still fit into a shoe." She raised her brows, which Willow realized was the other woman asking for permission to do whatever she was about to do, so Willow nodded.

Annabeth then unceremoniously lowered the sack of ice over Willow's foot, and Willow swore through gritted teeth, this time not caring who heard her.

"Ah, yes," Annabeth replied matter-of-factly. "Maybe I should have warned you better, but the quicker you ice it, the quicker we can tape you up and have you on your feet again." She pressed her mouth into a red-lipped smile. "Broke the same toe in the middle of a three-hour match during the U.S. Open last year. Played through it so I didn't have to forfeit or even take a time-out. It was so swollen and hurt so bad that my trainer had to cut my shoe off. Can you believe that? I could barely walk for two weeks after that."

"Did you win the match?" Willow asked.

Annabeth nodded. "Aye, but I had to forfeit the rest of the tournament on account of the whole not-being-able-to-walk thing."

Willow's throat tightened, but she forced a smile. "Thank you," she told the other woman. "For the ice and for the story to distract me from the ice." Then she groaned.

"What's wrong, love?" Annabeth asked. "Did

my distraction not do the trick? Do you want to see my toe? It's crooked for life now unless I let them break it again just to set it right."

Willow laughed. "No... I don't want to see it." Although maybe visible confirmation that the beautiful woman almost five years her junior had at least *one* physical imperfection might not be the worst thing in the world. "It's just..." She nodded toward where the ignored Ash sat sulking with his arms crossed on the other end of the couch. "You're...fantastic. I get why Ash wanted to marry you." She cleared her throat. "Did you come here to work things out?"

Annabeth burst into a fit of laughter. Ash shook his head and sighed. And Willow, who could no longer feel her frozen toe and almost half of her foot, furrowed her brows.

"That's...funny?" Willow asked. Because neither she nor Ash were laughing, but somehow Willow didn't think it was for the same reason.

Annabeth slowly let go of the bag of ice, and once certain it was balancing just fine on its own, slid back on the couch so she was sitting next to Ash. She took her ex-husband's hand and clasped it between hers.

"Ash, love," she began sweetly. "Did you not tell her the whole story?"

Willow's stomach dropped, and she felt the familiar sting behind her eyes again, though she wasn't sure why. Whatever the other woman had to say wouldn't change what happened four years ago. But…would it change what was happening now?

Ash glanced up at Willow with the kind of look she swore she never wanted to see on his face again…apologetic.

"I tried," he replied to Annabeth, but his gaze held firm on Willow.

"Right," Willow mumbled. "Texts and emails that never quite made it my way."

"I swear I did, Wills. You did block me and get a new number, but I understand if you don't believe me."

Willow straightened, and the towel full of ice fell to the floor. Both Annabeth and Ash made a move to reach for it, but Willow gave them one sharp shake of her head, and the two retreated like reprimanded toddlers.

Ugh. She hated that she couldn't simply stand and give herself the higher ground. The two of them sitting across from her felt like a united front through which she had to break.

"I was humiliated and heartbroken," Willow finally replied. It was one thing to admit those words to Ash, but it stung even more to say them in front of Annabeth. "I was escorted out of your tour bus so you could greet your new *wife* and take announcement photos. Did you honestly think there was anything you could have texted or emailed that could have erased that sort of mortification?"

She heard Annabeth breathe in sharply before whispering, "Oh god."

The muscle in Ash's jaw pulsed as he shook his head. "No," he admitted. "You're right. There's nothing I can say that will fix that, and I hate myself for it." He scrubbed a hand across his stubbled jaw and sighed.

Willow shrugged. It was time to rip off the Band-Aid. After all the curated social media posts she'd seen over the years of the happy couple splitting their time between Nashville and Edinburgh when their schedules allowed…the magazine interviews that talked of the mutual love, respect, and support that kept their relationship going despite it sometimes being long distance…Willow needed to hear it all, and she needed it to be done quickly.

"Tell me, Ash. Tell me what you should have told me before you ever threw around that four-letter word."

Annabeth whistled, brushed her hands together, and crossed one leg over the other. "Here we go," she said, and Willow thought she detected a hint of nervousness in the overly confident woman's voice.

"Here we go," Willow repeated and hoped she wouldn't regret it.

Chapter 21

FOUR AND A HALF YEARS AGO, ASH HAD STORMED out of the nearly empty pub, guitar still slung over his back, and paced the dark, puddle-ridden parking lot. Before the door could snick shut, Sloane had followed him outside.

"That's another canceled contract," he called over to her, as if she didn't already know. "That's the sixth venue so far that has booked me for two nights and canceled after the first…in case anyone's keeping count." He let out a bitter laugh. "And I use the term 'venue' lightly." He nodded toward the blinking red sign that read THISTLE AND DRAGON. "If I'd actually sat on that stool, my knees would have been bumping the table in front of me. Not that it would have mattered since it was an *empty* table." He ran a hand through his damp hair. Was it raining? Or was there just a constant mist in the air? "Why are we even doing this, Sloane? It's not like I'm Dolly Parton or something. We're doing fine in the United States. We must be losing money right and left trying to make me a thing over here."

Over here, of course, was the United Kingdom. Sloane had assured him that country music was on the rise in the UK and that listeners were champing at the bit for someone new. But a two-week stint gigging off-the-beaten-path pubs had proven otherwise.

"We just need to find our angle," Sloane assured him. "Your U.S. tour kicks off in a few months, and if we can generate some buzz over here before we head home…just get your name and your sound in people's ears…" Her voice trailed off, and the silence made Ash stop pacing. Silence and Sloane either meant she was drumming up a brilliant idea or she already *had* the idea and was simply using a dramatic pause to get his attention. Either way, it worked.

"What?" he asked as she tapped her index finger against her lips as if pondering her next move. When she grinned, Ash's pulse quickened.

Five years ago, when he was only eighteen years old, he'd sent demos to music labels in California, New York, and Nashville. No one responded. So that summer, in between his shifts on the family ranch—and sometimes sneaking out on his brothers *without* finishing a shift—he'd hop a bus to Lake Tahoe to busk. When he'd socked away enough cash, he started doing the same in LA, crashing on couches when he could. It took six months, but once Sloane dropped her business card in his guitar case, the rest was history. He had a freaking career.

"We go back to your busking days," she told him, and Ash barked out a laugh.

"I played the main stage on the concert rodeo circuit last year. I played the damned national anthem at Dodger Stadium and the Oakland Coliseum this past summer. And I *almost* headlined at Stagecoach."

Sloane snorted. "Your name was in the *third* row of artists listed."

He winked at her. "Out of *six*. Third row out of six ain't half bad."

"*Or* half good!" she countered. Then she strode toward him and gripped him by the shoulders. In her heels, they almost stood eye to eye, but Sloane's presence was always larger than life. "Believe me," she told him. "After this U.S. tour, you won't be able to blow your nose without someone trying to snap a photo of it. But right now, and especially *here*, you're not a headliner. And the busking? It'll only be for a day." She booped him on the nose, which Ash hated because it reminded him how young and green he still was, even at twenty-three. But Sloane had gotten him this far, so he had to trust whatever came next.

"One day?" he asked. "How is that going to get me any exposure?"

Sloane raised her brows. "Because that, my friend, will be the meet-cute heard 'round the world." Then she shrugged. "Okay, not around the world but across the UK, and that is all we need."

And that was how he met Annabeth Calder-Payne, a nineteen-year-old tennis prodigy who'd recently been splashed all over the tabloids for sneaking around with the brother of her biggest opponent. She'd been accused of everything from using the French teen to spy on his sister to sabotaging her matches. At least, that was what the beautiful blond Scot had told him after she'd slammed his guitar case shut with her foot and boldly proclaimed to the small crowd that had surprisingly been appreciating his impromptu concert, "Show's over, folks. This cowboy's mine for the rest of day, ay?" She shooed folks away as a very strategically positioned photographer snapped photos of the dramatic display.

"Thanks for this," Annabeth said as she nodded down at her to-go cup of tea once they were nestled safely in the back of a café.

"I didn't buy it," Ash reminded her. "*You* did."

She laughed, brightly painted lips parting to reveal a slightly crooked right tooth that did nothing to lessen her radiant smile. She was gorgeous, but despite Sloane telling him *nothing* else about today's events other than suggesting he just "go with it so it looks natural," Ash was sure that their orchestrated meet-cute had nothing do with anything real happening between him and the UK's tennis darling.

"You're not interested in me," Ash stated matter-of-factly.

She barked out a full-on belly laugh. "God, no!"

she exclaimed, and confident as Ash Murphy was, he couldn't hide the wince at such a blatant bruise to his ego.

"Please," he continued drily. "Don't hold back."

She reached across the table and gave his hand a conspiratorial squeeze, reminding him that, *Hey... we're in this together...* even if Ash had no idea what *this* meant.

"Look outside the café window," she told him, and Ash leaned to his left to get a better look at the front of the café. "How about some subtlety, Babe?" she added. "Ay, you stick out like the tourist you are, don't ya?"

He straightened and cleared his throat. "I like your accent," he told her. "Even if you are *takin' the piss.*"

She raised her brows, clearly impressed, and Ash gave himself a mental pat on the back.

"Okay. Okay. You brushed up on your colloquialisms, I can see." She climbed onto her knees on the wooden chair and leaned across the table so her mouth was so close to his ear that he could feel the warmth of her breath, which surprisingly did nothing to him in the region below the belt. "Right now, there's a photographer outside who thinks I'm leaning in for a kiss. You'll be all over *The Mirror, The Sun,* and the *Daily Mail* as the guy Annabeth Calder-Payne *literally* picked up off the street and made a household name. You're welcome, by the way."

She leaned back and lowered herself into her seat again, crossing her arms as she grinned triumphantly.

"I don't get it," he told her. "Why would you do that for me? You don't even know me."

She took a sip of her tea and then shrugged. "If I'm your girl, Britain loves you. And if you're *my* guy... in public, at least...then Freddie's family might let me within three feet of him again someday."

Ash saw the tiniest crack in her confidence with this admission. "Is Freddie on board with this?" And did people really do this? Staged relationships to hide their private lives?

Annabeth pressed her lips together and nodded. Then she sniffled, sat up ramrod straight, and squared her shoulders. "Will you do it, then? Trade me a few fake public snogs for launching another leg of your career?"

He learned early enough that when it came to his career, every relationship was some sort of transaction, which meant this was no different.

"I head out on tour soon in the United States," he told her. "So we'll have to make the most of the time I have while I'm here."

She beamed. "Is that a yes, then?"

This time he leaned forward, resting his cheek against hers as he whispered, "As long as you promise me you'll never step on my guitar case again. Took me three months of *actual* busking to buy that thing, and it's lasted me five years, thanks to *no one stepping on it.*"

Annabeth laughed as he straightened in his chair. "I like you, Ash Murphy."

He raised his brows. "If I didn't know any better, I'd say we were becoming friends as well as business partners."

She kicked his boot under the table. "I would like that," she admitted. "I don't have many at the moment."

Ash cleared his throat. "The boots…they're off-limits too."

Annabeth laughed, and then she told him all about growing up on the tennis court, trading traditional schooling for private tutors and friends for coaches. He told her about the ranch, his brothers, how he never felt like he quite fit into his small-town life, and how he'd gotten fired from six British pubs in less than two weeks.

Maybe this wasn't just a transaction orchestrated by their respective handlers. Maybe, for the first time since his career had begun to take off, Ash Murphy had found a very unlikely friend.

———

Willow blinked and then cleared her throat. "Okay…" she began, drawing out the word. "So your managers orchestrated a public swoon fest. That still doesn't explain a four-year marriage that turned me into a homewrecker." She pulled the pillow out from under her ankle and swung her feet onto the floor. "You know what?" she continued. "This is actually too much. Your lives are too much. I got into this business to make music. I don't have any sort of cultivated persona. Hell, I don't even have a manager. I just…" She glanced at Ash who looked at her with those sad, stormy-blue eyes and at Annabeth who—under different circumstances—Willow might have really liked. But…

She sprung up from the couch, forgetting why she'd been trapped there in the first place, and yelped as she put weight on her poor injured toe and promptly fell back onto the cushion, a prisoner of her own clumsiness once again.

Annabeth rose and clapped her hands together. "Well then," she began. "It looks like we've got your attention for a bit longer, so why don't I just grab my phone and show you what Ash cannot since he got his knickers in a bit of a twist when Freddie and I got engaged and his mobile had a proper run-in with a hotel telly, ay?"

Willow pinched the bridge of her nose.

Ash sighed. "We can get out of here for a while if you want. Me and Annabeth, I mean. I can call Colt to see if he or Jenna can come look after you for a bit."

She rolled her eyes and threw her head back

against the arm of the couch. "It's fine," she told him. "But only Annabeth gets to talk this time. Things just sound…I don't know…better when she says them."

She noticed him bite back a grin as Annabeth returned with her phone in hand, sat at Willow's feet, and then carefully pulled Willow's legs onto her lap.

"Okay," Willow said with a nervous laugh. "I guess we're slumber-party close now?"

Annabeth waved her off. "I dunno what that means," the other woman admitted. "Never had a slumber party, but I don't waste much time with the pleasantries of getting to know someone when I already know I like them."

The corner of Willow's mouth twitched, but she wasn't ready to admit aloud that she already knew she liked Annabeth too. Except how was that even possible? Annabeth *and* Ash were the reason her career had almost ended right when she'd gotten her first break. They were the reason for Willow's saddest and angriest songs, which—sure—were some of her best. But the humiliation doesn't end with forgiveness.

What would happen if and when she and Ash went public not only with the song but with their reconciliation? Even if the present was good, their painful past would be dredged up and shared again with everyone who had an opinion and was happy to share it while @ing her in the comments. Was Willow really strong enough to weather that storm again?

"Here, love." Annabeth offered Willow her phone.

Willow hesitated for a second but then took the device from the other woman, glanced at the screen, and began to scroll through what looked like a boilerplate publicity contract.

She shrugged. "I get it. Your relationship was a publicity stunt. That doesn't change anything that happened that morning on your tour bus." She glanced at Ash who could only respond with a slow nod.

"Here's the part where you're going to probably toss me out on my bum. The only parts of the contract Ash ever looked at were the signature lines because he trusted his manager and he trusted *me*."

She nodded, encouraging Willow to keep scrolling. And there it was in the last few pages…a marriage license followed by an NDA, where Ash would have been sued if he mentioned Annabeth's…

Willow gasped. "You were pregnant? Ash is a—"

"NO!" Ash finally cried, flying up from the couch and running a hand through his hair. "Jesus, A.B., just say it because you know your lawyer will still come after me if *I* do."

Annabeth nodded and blinked back tears. "I was nineteen and still at the beginning of a very successful career. I made the decision that was best for me at the time and terminated the

pregnancy. My parents and Freddie's determined
we were a detriment to both my career and his sister's, so they cut us off from each other, and my
publicity team married me off to a daft American
who could spin my image in another direction."
She placed a gentle hand on Willow's knee. "I'm
sorry," she added, her voice cracking on that
second word. "I didn't know Ash had met you or
that he wasn't made aware of the full extent of the
contract until...well...that day."

Willow let the other woman's words sink in,
trying to make sense of the fact that for all of
them, doing this thing that they loved—whether
it was tennis or music or simply *loving another
person*—was at the whim of a public who knew
nothing about any one of them. How was any of
it worth it?

Willow reached for the first aid kit that Annabeth
had left sitting on the floor. Inside it she found the
surgical tape and did as Annabeth suggested, taping
her broken toe to the healthy one beside it. Then
she tore open a packet of ibuprofen and popped
both of the small pills in her mouth, swallowing
them without any water yet wishing she hadn't.

This time when she rose from the couch, she did
so with care, making sure to focus her weight on
the heel of her right foot rather than the ball.

"I'm sorry for what you lost," she told Annabeth.
"For what we all did. But I need to process this in

my own way." She hobbled out of the room and straight toward the front door.

"Wills…where are you going?" Ash called after her.

She stepped into her square-toed riding boot, zipping the soft leather up over her left calf. Then she sucked in a breath through gritted teeth as she did the same with the right.

Wow. How did one tiny appendage cause so much pain? Stupid, stupid bathroom doorframe. But the ibuprofen would kick in soon, right?

"To the barn!" she replied, trying to keep her voice even. "I'm fine, okay? I'll be back soon!"

And before she let anyone—least of all herself—talk her out of it, she threw open the door and limped out, letting it slam shut behind her.

Chapter 22

ASH FOUND HER BOOT FIRST, KICKED OFF against the wall where leads hung from a row of hooks above. Great. So she was walking around half barefoot in here? Or worse. If she took off on a horse with only one...

He breathed a sigh of relief when he rounded the corner and found her leaning on Jack's gate, bare foot held aloft like she was a flamingo while she patted the gelding's nose.

"Jesus, Willow. I thought you took off on one of the horses. *Injured.* Do you know how dangerous that is?"

He watched her shoulders deflate, and something inside of him did the same. When she turned to look at him, balancing now on her bare heel along with her boot, he saw what looked like defeat in her brown eyes.

"That was the plan," she admitted. "It's the best way to clear my head, but..." She shook her bare foot and shrugged. "Ibuprofen is kicking in, but the boot was definitely a mistake." She nodded toward Jack's gray nose still poking over the top of the gate. "So I'm getting to know Jack a bit better. He's a good listener."

Ash strode toward her but stopped a few feet away. He knew she'd left the house because she needed her distance from him and the four-year-long mess he'd gotten himself tangled up in. But he also knew he could help if she'd let him.

"I can take you out on him, *just* around the arena. He's been healing up really well." He leaned closer for a conspiratorial stage whisper. "Might even be on his way to riding faster than Cirrus."

Cirrus snorted in his stall at the mention of his name, and the corner of Willow's mouth twitched. An *almost* smile. Ash considered that a small victory.

"On a lead?" she asked, then pressed her lips together and shook her head. "It's not the same. Something about going slow makes me think too much. Does that make sense?"

Of course it made sense. Ash hadn't been on the back of a horse for who knows how long before he hopped into Midnight's saddle and took her to the clearing. That short ride off the property was the most peace he'd felt in years. He and Willow might be miles away from where they were for one glorious night in a tent, but at least here, in the barn, they were on the same page.

"Then let's take Midnight for a spin," he told her. "According to Eli, she's the best at riding double."

Willow's eyes brightened for a second before her expression fell. She opened her mouth to protest, but Ash held up his hands.

"Hear me out. For however long we're out there"—he pointed to the arena and the field and forest that lay beyond—"I don't exist other than pulling the reins. It's just you, the mare, and the wind. We don't have to talk. I'm just the vehicle to get you where you need to go."

She bit her bottom lip, and he could see the wheels starting to turn. She was considering the offer, which meant she *wanted* this even if she didn't exactly want it with him.

"Let me do this for you, Wills. Please?"

After a few more beats of silence, she finally nodded her head.

Ash blew out a breath. "Great. Okay. I'll tack her up, and we'll go." He glanced down at her feet. "But you can't go like that. Can I grab you a pair of sneakers or something? You still have those red Chuck Taylors?"

Her cheeks flush slightly as she nodded again. "You remember my shoes," she told him, a statement rather than a question.

He remembered everything. Well, save for the few days following her departure when he somehow survived performing while subsisting on nothing other than an overabundance of liquid courage.

"Yeah," was all he said. "I'll be right back."

Once he had Midnight ready to go, Ash sat Willow down on a storage bench outside the stalls and let her pull off her remaining boot.

"Do you want help?" he asked, holding up the well-worn pair of Converse sneakers.

Willow rolled her eyes. "I can put on my own shoes."

That she could, and she did. Ash said nothing as she winced—but only slightly—sliding her right foot into the very loosely laced shoe and tying it just enough so it wouldn't fall off. When he held out a hand to help her back up, she reluctantly took it, though she seemed steadier on her feet now as she limped toward the arena door where Midnight waited for them outside.

"Feeling better?" he asked.

And although she nodded, she reminded him, "No talking, remember?"

Ash let out a nervous laugh. "Right. Guess that starts now."

Willow greeted Midnight with a pet between the eyes, and the mare responded with an affectionate nuzzle.

"So…mounting…" he began, scratching the back of his neck. "I didn't think about that."

It made sense for him to hop in the saddle first since he'd be sitting in front, but then how would he help Willow up?

She waved him off. "It's a stupid, silly pinkie toe," she informed him. "I can still mount a horse."

He raised his brows and shrugged. Then he removed Midnight's lead, stored it in her small pack, and hopped into the saddle. He immediately removed his boot from the left stirrup so Willow could use it to do the same, but he could already tell that the stirrup was too far forward for her to use it as the sole means for climbing into the pillion saddle. She'd have to put all her weight on her right foot to even attempt it, and Ash could tell by the frustration in her stare that she had realized the same thing.

Ash held out his left hand and mimed zipping his lips with his right, assuring her that he would by no means violate the *Pretend I'm not here* policy unless acknowledgment of his presence was an absolute necessity.

She sighed and grabbed his hand, which gave her the leverage she needed to reach the stirrup, and then he hoisted her the rest of the way until her chest was flush against his back, her arms wrapped tight around his torso as she steadied herself in on the pillion.

His pulse quickened at her touch. There was no way Willow couldn't feel his heart hammering away like an overeager drum solo. But if she noticed, she didn't let on. Instead, she simply squeezed him tight and said, "Ready whenever you are."

So Ash gripped the reins, gave Midnight a soft nudge with his heels, and pointed her in the direction of the open gate on the other end of the arena, the one that would take them wherever Willow wanted to go.

For a few minutes, that was how they rode, Ash in control of the mare with Willow hanging on from behind. Slowly, though, she loosened her grip on his waist and slid her hands behind his so they both were holding the reins. He leaned slightly to the right and felt her lean to the left.

"Can you see?" he asked.

"Yes," she replied, her cheek almost flush against his.

"Then she's all yours," Ash told her, letting his hands trade places with hers. "You're in charge."

"Yah!" Willow called, tapping her heels on Midnight's flanks, and they sailed across the field and toward the woods.

Even though he couldn't see her behind him, Ash imagined Willow smiling, letting go of everything he'd put her through both in their time together *and* apart.

He expected her to pull the mare left as the field gave way to trees, but instead she pulled up on the reins, slowing the horse until they came to an opening in trees where the oft-trodden trail would take them to the clearing where she found him that first day a month ago.

He didn't ask why or if she was sure. He simply let her take the lead as Midnight slowly led them deeper into the trees, the only sound the buzzing of cicadas and the rustling of leaves as a small animal scurried by.

Finally, sunlight began to peek through the leaves until they were exactly where they'd been four weeks prior when they'd made their truce and agreed to work together on a song.

Midnight paced back and forth in question, so Ash decided to ask what both he and the mare were wondering.

"Is this just a pause or a destination?" he pondered. "Because I think Midnight wants to know."

He felt her let out a long breath before she spoke. "I want to lie under the maple and watch the clouds."

"Okay," he replied. "I'll help you down. Midnight and I can hang by the grazing tree."

She was quiet as he dismounted first, careful to swing his leg in front of him rather than behind. Then he let her dismount mostly on her own, only grabbing her hips to help her land softly once she was close enough to the ground.

He was ready to turn in the opposite direction from the maple when Willow grabbed his wrist.

"Come with me," she told him simply.

"Okay," he answered again, daring to let a spark of hope ignite.

He tied off Midnight to a tree where the mare was happy to graze and then followed Willow, who seemed to be limping less with each step, to where the sun flickered through breeze-blown leaves, speckling the grass like flickering stars.

She lay down first, patting the grass beside

her. Ash dropped his hat to the ground and then reclined on the warm patch of earth.

"Meditating on clouds," Willow said softly as they both stared up at the sky. "I like what you called it when I asked if I was a weirdo for liking this."

A smile tugged at his lips. "I like that you like doing it." He cleared his throat. "Probably should have asked for permission to speak. You could have just been thinking out loud."

Willow reached over and backhanded him on the shoulder. "*You're* the one who said you weren't going to talk. I never said you couldn't."

"Ahh," he mused. "But you never said I could either."

She sighed. "Your life was a circus before I even met you, wasn't it?"

"That's putting it mildly," he agreed.

A wisp of white streaked slowly above the leaves, seemingly carried by the soft wind. What a contrast this place was to the chaos he'd been living since he was a teen. Ash *loved* the chaos, didn't he? Why else would he have kept at it for a decade now?

He wasn't sure how much more to say, how much she still wanted to hear.

"Is knowing everything even more exhausting than hating me?" he asked.

Silence stretched between them for several seconds before she finally responded.

"You've been playing a fictional version of your-self for *four* years, Ash. How is that not exhausting for *you*?"

He shrugged. "Despite her being a little less than honest about our initial agreement, Annabeth really has become a good friend over the years, and those are hard to find in this line of work. I play the part I need to play so I can make the music I want to make. It's all part of the game, isn't it?"

Willow hummed a soft sigh. "I don't play it," she told him.

Ash huffed out a laugh. "Then what are you doing holed up with me in a guesthouse writing a song you never intended to write before trying to bludgeon me to death?"

Willow rolled her eyes. "Touché, I suppose, but I wasn't actually *trying* to kill you. I was just hoping not to get unalived myself."

They both laughed. Several beats of silence fol-lowed before Willow spoke again. "You know I never actually hated you, right?"

Even though he hadn't heard her move, he could feel that her eyes were on him now rather than the sky. So he tilted his head to meet her gaze, expect-ing to see the same hurt and frustration he'd seen back in the barn. But her brown eyes were clear and intent, a stamp of approval on an admission of truth.

"How?" he asked.

She reached for his fingertips, brushing her skin against his and nothing more, yet sending a surge of electricity through him like only Willow Morgan could.

"I hated what happened. I hated that for months after everything happened, I was caught up in that circus. I hated that I actually cared what strangers were saying about me. And I hated that the only person who might understand what I was going through was the one who put me in that position in the first place."

He gritted his teeth and swore. "I'm so sorry, Wills. I know it's just words and that I can't take any of it back, but you have to believe how much I hate that *I* did that to you."

Willow nodded. "I believe you." Then she pushed herself up, pulling her heels together so she was sitting like a butterfly. "I think we're getting really close with the song, which is great. But I need a reminder of why we got into this business in the first place."

Ash crossed one boot over the other and propped himself up on his elbows. "What do you mean?"

She already had her phone out, her thumb scrolling through something on her screen.

"Casey's parents own that bar, right? What is it called?"

This got him to sit up. "Yeah. Midtown Tavern.

She still tends bar there a couple times a week if her parents are short-staffed."

"Right!" Willow exclaimed. She tapped on her screen and then held it up for him to see. "They have a small space for live musicians, but it doesn't look like they have anyone booked for tonight." She beamed at him, suddenly lit from within at the mere thought of getting to do this thing that she loved. Ash missed that feeling.

"What are you getting at, Willow Morgan?" he asked, her smile and excitement too contagious to resist.

"Think Meadow Valley's one and only night-time establishment would be up for a little pop-up acoustic set?"

Ash pulled his loaner phone out of his pocket. "I'll call Boone right now and see what we can do." He stood, then held a hand out for Willow.

She grabbed it, her grip firm and assured. Once standing, her hand still in his, she added, "The space looks big enough for two. What do you say to a pop-up duet?"

His eyes widened. "Are you serious?"

She nodded. "I only have one condition."

He didn't care if she had two hundred conditions. He'd jump through a ring of fire doused in gasoline if it meant sharing the stage with Willow tonight. "Anything you want. Name it."

"None of these." She waggled her phone in her

hand. "Closed set. Phones at the door. No public evidence of the show…and *no* communication to Sloane about it. Our show. Our terms."

"Done," Ash replied without hesitation. "*Our* show. *Our* terms."

Chapter 23

AT TEN THAT NIGHT, WILLOW AND ASH STOOD just behind Midtown Tavern's swinging kitchen door. They decided that a late-night set would work best since families often came in during the earlier evening hours when the kitchen was still open.

"I know your music is kid-friendly enough," she'd told him. "But they might not be the most willing audience if they have to hand over their electronic devices to yours truly."

So they waited now as Casey walked out with an empty milk crate that would soon be packed with cell phones and tablets.

Willow wanted to be at peace with the fact that any sort of connection to Ash Murphy meant a connection to a very vocal public. Logically, she knew that what strangers said didn't matter. But she was made of more than that. Sometimes the mind outweighed the heart, but sometimes the heart made you forget that logic even existed. Tonight she'd settle for home-field advantage...or, in Ash's case, home*town*.

"If there's one thing I can promise you," Casey

assured her. "It's that Meadow Valley takes care of its own. The surrendering of devices is only a formality."

Ash grabbed her hand and gave it a gentle squeeze, pulling her back to the moment. "You okay?" he asked. "Say the word, and we can run out the back door just as easily as we came in."

She smiled. "I'm good," she assured him. She even picked up her loosely sneakered foot and wiggled it in the air. "Even standing on my own two feet!" *After* staying off of it for the rest of the day after their ride to the clearing. Rest and pain medication at regular intervals had done the trick enough that she could stand while she played or perch on one of the two stools Casey and Boone set up for their performance.

She squeezed his hand back, this man she fell for years ago. This morning everything about him had seemed so complicated. But tonight, when he smiled at her from the kitchen of a small-town bar, he just looked like a guy with a guitar about to do the thing he loved.

"Thank you for your cooperation with the devices!" they heard Casey call out to the crowd. "We have something very special in store for you all tonight. While he's been keeping a low profile on his family's ranch, I know some of y'all might have seen a certain Murphy brother around town these past few weeks."

"We see Eli Murphy every day!" a man's voice called in reply. "That's nothing new!"

Ash shook his head and chuckled as laughter bubbled up from the tavern patrons. "Once an asshole, always an asshole, huh, Boone?"

Even when they were separated by a door, Ash's brothers brought a smile to his face that Willow hadn't seen before their time in Meadow Valley.

"*Not* Eli, darlin', but let's give it up for my husband, the dad-joke comedian!"

Rueful *ooohs* followed Casey's remark, which only made Ash's smile grow.

But the anticipation was building. Willow's pulse quickened. This was always the part where she was the most nervous, right before the audience knew she was heading out onstage. Everything after was cake, and she *really* wanted to get to the cake.

"Should we put her out of her misery?" Ash asked, and while he was referring to Casey, Willow understood.

Either he could feel her hand go clammy in his, or he just knew that she needed to burst through the door—to rip off the bandage—*now*.

She nodded, and without another second of hesitation, Ash pushed the door open and nodded for her to take the lead. But this was *his* town, and she wanted him to get the welcome he deserved... One that maybe didn't involve blunt objects being aimed at his head.

"You go first," she told him. "I'm right behind you." He hesitated for a moment, but she shooed him forward. "This is *your* homecoming, Murphy. Go get it."

He answered her with a swift nod and pressed his palm to the door, but when she loosened her grip on his other hand, he only squeezed her tighter.

"Oh, no you don't, Morgan," he told her. "This is *our* entrance."

Ash might have been the one to stride through the door first, but he made no move toward their makeshift stage until she was standing beside him.

Whistles and hollers erupted from the crowd, and Casey spun to see that her time as emcee had just ended prematurely.

Sorry! Willow mouthed, but Casey answered her with a beaming smile.

"Well, folks!" she called over the din. "I should have known he'd upstage me. Let's welcome—well, I guess you already are—Ash Murphy and Willow Morgan!"

Colt and Jenna flew up and out of their seats. Eli, Beth, and Boone followed as Casey joined the group at a table right in front of two wooden stools and two mic stands, otherwise known as the stage.

Ash started playing before they'd even made it to the mics, and Willow waited for recognition and then reaction. The credit went to Jenna who yelped with laughter and backhanded an unsuspecting

Colt on the shoulder right as he was about to take a sip of his beer.

Willow bit back a laugh as Ash finished the opening guitar riff and then launched into the first verse of Taylor Swift's "We Are Never Ever Getting Back Together." Was it too on the nose? Maybe, but sometimes words were just words, and a song was just a song. Singing with Ash beside her strumming on his guitar, she realized how much she hoped she was right.

They'd roughed out a set list that afternoon. They'd intersperse their original songs with duet covers. Right now Willow sat on her stool, leaning into the mic for the harmony on the chorus as he sang the song she'd always wondered about.

"I Loved You Once."

Something niggled at the back of her mind while Ash launched into the bridge and then the final verse. It was the same sense of déjà vu she'd had when they were arguing about the words she'd chosen for the chorus of the duet.

It's just a song. They're all just songs. And they're all about you.

The wine at the bonfire. Ash holding her hands so the room would stop spinning and then staying with her in case it happened again.

She'd flat out asked him if the song was about *her*, and he told her what she'd never in her wildest dreams thought she needed to hear.

She stared at him as he sang the final refrain, his eyes closed as he went somewhere other than the sticky floor of a local bar.

I loved you once and broke your heart.
Spun out of reach and called it art.
Made my bed and played my part.
I'd trade it all to go back to the start.
I loved you once.
I loved you once.
I loved you once.
I loved you once. I love you still.
And every damned day between then and now,
All the days to come, this is my vow.
I'll love you. I'll love you. I'll love you. I will.

Everyone in the bar sang the last three lines with him, but Willow sat transfixed, forgetting her part as she let it all sink in. Every word he'd written... Every song he'd sung...

When the last string had been strummed and the whole audience broke into applause, Ash finally opened his eyes and glanced her way.

Willow flung her guitar over her shoulder so it hung across her back, slid off her stool, and threw her arms around Ash's neck.

"They were all for *me*," she said. And then she kissed him, not caring who saw, what they thought, and what they might decide to post on social media once they got their phones back in their possession.

"Every last song," he admitted, his lips parting into a smile against hers. "A song is never *just* a song, Wills. At least…not mine."

The tavern patrons had plenty to say about Ash moving his own guitar out of the way so he could plunge his fingers into her hair and kiss her like only he could. There was continued applause, some whistles, and even a *Get a room!* that sounded an awful lot like Boone.

Willow kissed a trail along his jaw and then whispered in his ear. "We're supposed to do one more song," she reminded him.

"They don't know that," he whispered back, sending a wave of goose bumps over her flesh and setting her on fire from within. He kissed her again and then spun toward the crowd.

"Willow Morgan, everyone! Get your tickets to see her at Acoustic Acres next month!"

Before she had a chance to give him the same recognition, Ash's hand was around hers, and he was pulling her through the crowd and back toward the kitchen. Like a couple of teenagers fleeing a party that just got busted, they ran toward the back door, stopping only to toss their guitars into their respective cases before bursting out into the night.

"Wait!" Willow cried before they got twenty feet from the tavern. "Eli drove us here!"

Ash stopped and spun back to face her. "We can walk. It's only a mile back to the…" His expression fell, and Willow's shoulders sagged.

Willow sighed. "Should we go tell Mom and Dad we need a lift home?"

"Or…" Ash replied.

Five minutes later, their guitars rested in the bed of Eli's truck, and Ash was giving her a piggyback ride down the dimly lit street.

"This is insane," she told him. "You can't carry me for a mile."

"Do you plan on kissing me again when we get back?" he asked.

She laughed and then planted one right on his cheek. "I plan on doing *lots* of things to you when we get back," she teased. "If that's okay with you."

He picked up the pace, almost breaking into a jog.

"Whoa there, wild stallion," she cried. "If you fall and put us *both* out of commission, the only thing I'm going to be doing to you is calling 911."

Ash slowed to a more respectable pace.

"Fine," he relented. "But maybe you should tell me some of those things you plan on doing to me… just to make sure I can handle it."

"Hmm," she began. "Before or after I throw you down on the bed and take your pants off?"

Ash swore. "You know what?" he added. "I think I'm better off being surprised. Otherwise I'm not going to be able to walk very well for the rest of the way."

"Fair enough," Willow replied. "If the whole point is to *get* home before I properly thank you for carrying me there, I should probably let you concentrate."

He paused, resituated her on his hips, and then said. "Can we maybe not talk at *all*? Even words like 'properly thank' get my imagination going, and then things start happening below the belt, and *then* the whole walking thing becomes much more difficult than it has any right to be."

"Sorry," she replied, then kissed him gently on the side of his neck.

"*Willow*," he pleaded, and she laughed.

"Sorry again! Lips sealed and promising to refrain from all kissing activities...until we get home."

He thanked her, and she enjoyed the quiet sounds of summer as Meadow Valley's town center gave way to the quiet country road that led to the ranch.

Crickets chirped, frogs croaked in a nearby pond, and Ash was *carrying* her home.

"Are you okay?" she asked after a few more minutes. "I can probably walk the rest of the way."

"No way," he told her. "Besides, I can see the light outside the guesthouse already."

Willow squinted, sure he was lying just to make

her feel better. But there it was. A beacon calling them home.

Ash must have heard the call too because his pace quickened as the Murphy property grew near.

Willow grinned. She couldn't wait to get there either.

Chapter 24

ASH SANK BACK AGAINST WILLOW'S WARM embrace, steam rising from the bubbles as water sloshed over the side of the tub.

"Careful there, cowboy. You can't hop into a bathtub like you're hopping on the back of a horse."

He leaned his head on her shoulder and looked up at her, a grin spreading across his face. "I'm sorry," he told her. "But if patience and grace is what you're looking for, then you should think twice before you get naked, cover yourself in bubbles, and ask me to lay between your legs."

She laughed and grabbed the soft bath sponge from the side of the tub, soaked it in the water, and then gently scrubbed it up and down his chest.

Ash sighed and sank even further against her, his shoulders relaxing. "When you said you were going to do all sorts of things to me when we got home, I don't think I realized what you meant."

"You worked hard carrying me all the way home. Maybe I wanted to pamper you a bit before getting you all worked up again." Willow kissed his neck. "Are you disappointed?"

"God, no…" he replied. "This is…" His eyes fell closed. "Why have we never done this before?"

She continued dragging the sponge up his torso, down his arms. She filled it with water and held it above him, letting a steady stream of water trickle over his skin, and Ash thought he might just want to call the whole career thing quits and live here, in Willow's arms, letting her pamper the hell out of him.

"Because you had a closet for a shower on the tour bus, we didn't see each other for four years, and then I backpedaled when things were getting too serious too quickly after the camping trip. Which was amazing, by the way."

"But you got spooked," he replied.

"I got spooked," Willow admitted.

He wrapped his arms around her thighs, and his hands on her skin must have made her lose concentration because she dropped the sponge right on his face.

Ash laughed and then shook his head like a golden retriever. "Did I spook you again?" He grabbed the sponge and tossed it gently over his head in mock retaliation, but Willow caught it.

"You did," she confessed. "I mean, not by touching me because I *really* do like that, but with Annabeth this morning."

Ash sat up straight and clumsily spun himself in the tub. A pile of bubbles joined the small puddle on the tile, but he was facing her now in all of her naked, bubble-spotted glory.

"So why are we here now, Wills?" He scrubbed a palm over his face, trying to hide the worry in his expression. They didn't *have* to talk this out. He knew she was ready and willing to just let whatever was happening between them happen. But he needed to know if tonight was any different from the night in the tent. He needed to know how to keep her from getting spooked again.

Willow bit back a laugh. "Sorry... Let me just..." She wiped the bubbles from his chin and jaw. Then she draped her legs over his, slid closer, and cupped his face in her palms. "Bubble stubble," she told him.

He rested his hands firmly on her hips. "Are you sidestepping my question?" he asked, brows raised.

She made a move to scooch forward, but he held her in place, waiting for an answer.

"Oh...you want me to answer you now?" she asked, feigning innocence. "Because I thought it was time for me to do all of those fun things to you."

Ash growled softly. "You are *not* playing fair. But yes...answer now. Please. Complete and total honesty, no matter what. You can do anything you want to me after."

Willow grabbed his hands and slid them considerably lower so that he was now gripping one very naked cheek in each palm. She laughed as he gritted his teeth, jaw pulsing as he held on to every last shred of his resolve.

"Okay," she relented. "You win, but if you ever try to tell me I'm irresistible, I'm going to remind you of this very moment when you *resisted*."

He exhaled a shaky breath through his nose but said nothing, so she had no choice but to fill the silence.

"We're here now, cowboy, because performing with you tonight was the most fun I've had onstage in years, even if that stage means the soles of my sneakers will be sticky for weeks to come."

This made him smile. "Me too," he told her.

"We're here now," Willow continued, "because it turns out that you were just as young and naïve as I was four years ago. You made a mistake, one that hurt me more than I knew I could hurt..." He flinched, and she cupped the side of his face in her palm. "Complete and total honesty, right?" Ash nodded slowly, and she sucked in a steadying breath. "We're here now because after what you did for me tonight—what you've *been* doing for me since the moment you came to after I knocked you out cold—I trust that you would never hurt me like that again."

He let her move closer, so close that he was right there, between her legs. But he needed to *not* be holding her ass when he said what he was going to say next. So he wrapped his arms around her back, holding her as tight and as close as he could while still being able to look her in the eye.

"I will never hurt you like that again, Willow." He kissed her, slowly and sweetly, letting his lips linger on hers before he spoke again. "Do you really trust me?" he asked, his voice rough.

"Yes," she whispered.

"And if people post about us on social media after tonight?"

She shrugged. "Let them post." Then she hooked her legs over his hips and whispered, "I loved you once too."

Ash's breath caught in his throat. He's spent four years dwelling on how he'd loved her and lost her, and he hadn't realized until that moment that Willow had never uttered those words. Even if they were past tense, they were an admission...a redemption...and maybe, if he was lucky, a promise.

"Willow," he whispered, but that was the only word he could manage. So he lifted her slightly and placed her exactly where he needed her to be.

"Wait..." She lowered her knees to the base of the tub and braced herself. "I was supposed to do all the things," she reminded him.

He gazed up at her, knowing that even if she couldn't say the words now, there was love in her dark eyes, a love for him that he would do his damnedest to earn every day from here on out.

"There's only one thing I need," he whispered.

In answer, she sank down, burying him inside her, her lips parting as they brushed against his.

———————

Later, after they'd cleaned up and dried off, Willow padded into the kitchen combing her fingers through her damp hair, wearing nothing but a pair of white cotton underwear that looked like a tiny pair of shorts.

"Okay, that's my favorite outfit you've ever worn," he teased.

She looked him up and down, raising a brow at his similar attire, a pair of black boxer briefs.

"Likewise, my friend," she replied.

He handed her one of the two glasses of water he'd poured and held his up for a toast.

"Should we drink to never wearing clothes in the house again?" she asked.

"Hmmm..." Ash mused. "Might get awkward if one of our brothers pops by unannounced, especially if they bring their children."

Willow nodded sagely. "True. True. Okay. I'd like to amend my proposal to no clothes after dark, once we assure any surprise family visits are off the table."

"Like...after a toddler or baby's bedtime?"

"Exactly!" she agreed. "Like, right now, all babies

and toddlers are totally asleep, right? So we can continue this mostly naked thing we have going until we wake up tomorrow!"

They clinked their glasses together just as someone pounded on the front door.

Willow yelped, keeping hold of her glass but managing to toss its contents in Ash's face. Then she dropped her glass on the counter and covered her breasts with her hands.

"Ash?" Eli called from outside the door. "It's supposed to rain early in the morning, and your guitars are in the bed of my truck."

Ash shook his head and huffed out a laugh.

"And Colt wants to make sure Willow got home okay since you two kind of disappeared without saying goodbye."

"Shit!" Willow hissed glancing down at her *handmade* bikini top. She made a beeline back for the bedroom but stopped short when she heard her name.

"Wills?" It was Colt's voice this time. "I left you two voicemails. Is everything okay in there?"

"Oh my god!" she whisper-shouted. "He's *here*?"

Ash was full on laughing now as he strode toward the door.

"You're answering like *that*?" she cried. "You know my brother doesn't exactly like you yet, right?"

Oh, Ash knew. "Do you want to hide this from him?" he asked, his resolve faltering.

Willow bit her lip and shook her head.

He blew out a breath and clapped his hands together. "Then I guess there's no time like the present." So he strode toward the door while Willow scurried into the bedroom to grab something other than her own palms to wear as a top.

Ash threw the door open and crossed his arms over his bare chest. "Evening, gentleman. What can I do for you?"

"Jesus, Ash!" Eli exclaimed. "You could have just told me through the door that you'd grab the guitars later."

"Where is my sister, Murphy?" Colt asked. "And why the hell is your face wet?"

"Right here!" Willow called.

Ash heard the pitter-patter of her bare feet behind him until she was standing at his side wearing the white T-shirt he'd been wearing at the tavern for their performance.

Colt's eyes darkened as he glanced from Ash to his sister and then back at Ash.

"Come on, Colt," Willow said playfully. "You saw me kiss him. What did you think we were sneaking out to do?"

Colt covered his ears and shook his head. "Baby sister. Baby sister. Baby sister," he chanted.

Willow snorted, then grabbed her brother's hands and yanked them away. "Your baby sister is almost thirty years old. She's a grown-up who does grown-up things like have *sex*."

Colt winced. "With the asshole who broke your heart?"

"Hey," Eli interrupted. "He might be an asshole, but he's still my brother."

"Sorry," Colt mumbled.

"Um…thanks?" Ash replied to both of them.

Willow threw up her hands. "It's not like this is the first time we've slept together since I've been here. What did you think we were doing when we disappeared overnight to the campgrounds? What do you think we were doing on the tour bus four summers ago?"

"All right! All right!" Colt relented. "I know you're an adult, but that doesn't mean I'm going to stop wanting to protect you, okay?"

Willow grabbed Ash's hand and threaded her fingers through his. "Your protection sounds an awful lot like judgment right now," she said coolly.

Colt's mouth fell open, but no words came out.

"You don't have to defend me," Ash told her. "He has a point."

She looked at him and shook her head. "I'm not. I'm defending *me*." Then she turned her attention back to her brother. "Whether you agree or disagree with my choices, you need to respect them because they are *my* choices. And that means no more of your big-brother chats with Ash when you think I'm not looking."

Colt raised his brows. "You told her about that?" he asked Ash accusingly.

Willow laughed. "No! *You* did. Just now."

Colt's mouth fell open, and Ash bit back a grin.

"And no more looking at me like I kicked your puppy if the subject of me having sex ever comes up again."

"You know what?" Eli said. "I think I'm just going to go and grab those guitars." He spun back toward his truck without another word.

"He looks like he might need help," Ash suggested, attempting a getaway even if it meant heading outside barefoot in his underwear. But Willow only squeezed his hand tighter.

"Oh, no you don't," she told him. "We're settling this right here, right now." She let go of Ash's hand only to grab his wrist. She did the same with Colt, grabbing his right wrist. "Now shake hands and be friends."

Ash had a sudden sense of déjà vu. Hadn't she done the exact same thing with him and Boone? Willow had been instrumental in getting him to reestablish a relationship with his brothers, and now she was trying to smooth things over with him and Colt.

Ash grabbed Colt's hand first, and Colt responded with his own firm grip, which he guessed was more competition than it was acquiescence.

"I care about her, Colt," Ash told him. "I'm not going to hurt her."

"I care about her more," Colt replied.

Willow sighed, then placed her hand over theirs.

"Then I'm one hell of a lucky girl to have you both in my corner. Time to shake on it, boys."

And because underneath it all, Ash knew Colt Morgan would do anything for his sister, the other man nodded, and they both shook.

The two men dropped their hands as Eli approached, a guitar case in each hand.

"Thank you, Eli," Willow said, grabbing her case as Ash grabbed his.

Eli laughed. "Always happy to escape an awkward situation." He turned to Colt. "Can I take you home to your wife now?"

Colt nodded.

"I'll call Jenna, and we'll have you all over for dinner sometime in the next week. You and Beth and Boone and Casey, too," Willow added, turning her attention to Eli.

"Sounds great," Eli replied.

Colt forced a smile. "Yeah, Wills. Sounds great." He kissed her on the forehead and then said goodbye, following Eli back to his truck.

Willow grabbed Ash's hand and led him back to the bedroom where they both plopped down on the side of the bed.

"Well, your brother definitely still hates me, *and* I think it's safe to say that our after-dark naked pact is a thing of the past."

Willow stood and lifted his T-shirt over her head so she was very much naked again.

"Are you kidding? Those two are *never* knocking on that door again without calling first, and I'm sure they'll spread the word to Boone. We can be naked *all* the time now if we want." She pushed him down on his back and climbed over him. "And while you might be right about my brother, I think I know how to take your mind off of your troubles."

She shimmied out of her sexy little shorts and yanked his boxer briefs down to his knees.

"What troubles?" he asked.

And…naked time was officially reinstated.

Chapter 25

WILLOW DREAMED THERE WAS A CHICKEN VIO-lently squawking outside her window, so loudly that it woke her with a start. She sat bolt upright in bed. Except, she could still hear it.

She glanced to her left where Ash lay on his stomach holding a pillow over his head.

"Are you dreaming about chickens too?" she asked him.

A muffled groan sounded from beneath the pillow. "It's *not* a dream." He sat up, finally, his dark hair sticking up every which way. It would make her want to climb on top of him—after brushing her teeth, of course—if it wasn't for the incessant squawking that sounded like it was coming from inside her head.

"Is this my new internal monologue?" Willow asked. "Because I can't live like this."

Ash sighed. "It's coming from over there." He pointed toward the window, which they left cracked open but covered by the shade, and crawled out of bed, striding toward it.

"Hey!" Willow called in the space between squawks. "You want to change out of your birthday suit?" She pulled the sheet up to cover her breasts.

"Nope," he replied, his morning wood on full display. "If our brothers are going to play this way, then I'm going to make sure they regret it."

He spun back toward the window, at least leaving Willow with an excellent view of his ass to help make up for the rude awakening at... What time was it? She glanced at her phone on the bedside table and swore. "It's 6:30 a.m. On a *Saturday*."

Ash flipped up the shade without a moment of hesitation, and the squawking was replaced with a mixture of yelps and screams. *Female*-sounding yelps and screams.

"Oh my god!" Willow cried, staring out at Jenna, Casey, Beth, and Beth's sister, Delaney.

Ash had the decency to cover his erection with his hands as best he could, but he didn't budge from the window. "Did your husbands warn you of nothing?" he mused.

Willow threw a pillow at him, but it fell short, landing a couple of feet behind him on the floor. "All right, Greatest Showman," she teased. "Time to close up the tent and let the viewers collect themselves." She turned her attention to the audience that had unsurprisingly not yet dispersed.

"Show's over, ladies!" she called. "Wait for me at the front door, and I'll be right out."

"You should get dressed too, sugar," Jenna drawled at Ash, and the chicken in her arms, Lucy, squawked in agreement. "The boys are waiting for you in the barn."

Willow wrapped herself in the sheet like a mermaid and penguin walked over to the window. "Sorry, ladies. But he's all mine." She pulled the shade closed and spun to face her naked bedfellow. "I think you enjoyed that a little too much."

Ash grabbed the edge of the sheet and unraveled her so they were both in their birthday suits. "Not as much as I enjoy this," he told her. He wrapped his arms around her and pulled her to him. He dipped his head, giving each of her breasts a good-morning kiss that made her ache between her legs. Then he trailed kisses up her chest to her neck, the side of her jaw, and eventually her lips.

So much for brushing their teeth.

Willow whimpered as he pressed up against her. "We can't," she whispered. "We're being kidnapped."

As if being summoned, one of their kidnappers knocked on the front door.

Ash growled. "What are the odds of them thinking we somehow left if we don't answer?"

"What are the odds of Beth using their key to just walk in?"

"Shit," he whispered. "Is there a conspiracy to keep us apart now that we're finally together?" He cleared his throat. "Wait...we are together, right?"

"I love how you can be bold enough to open the window naked and yet adorable enough to ask me that." Willow leaned up and kissed him. "We're together, cowboy. No matter how hard they try." She slapped him playfully on his beautiful behind. "Though I think the conspiracy is more on keeping us clothed than keeping us apart."

He winced. "Somehow, that sounds worse."

She kissed him one more time before letting him go and scrambled toward the bathroom and into her robe.

"Get dressed while I let them in. If I put them to work getting the coffee going, maybe we can steal a few more minutes after that."

Ash's shoulders sagged as he let out a sigh. "Fine," he relented, and Willow's heart grew about ten times its size. Here was this big, beautiful, confident man pouting like a child to be taken away from her.

"I'll see you soon," she told him, blowing him a kiss before running out and toward the continued knocking at the door, grinning the entire way.

When she threw it open, she found Jenna still holding Lucy. What she'd neglected to notice before was that Casey was carrying a drink holder filled with four iced coffees while Beth held the solo fifth one in her hands.

"Girls' day!" Jenna cried as all five of them filed inside. "We have so much planned for my baby sister-in-law, don't we Lu-lu?" And then she put the hen down on the floor. *In* the guesthouse.

"Okaaay," Willow replied, following the train of

women back into house. "But why at the crack of dawn? With a chicken?"

Casey set the coffees down on the breakfast bar and pulled one free. She spun and handed it to Willow. "I don't know if salted caramel is your thing, but this is the best salted caramel cold brew you'll ever taste, courtesy of one Ms. Trudy Davis at Storyland bookshop."

Willow accepted the decadent-sounding concoction, swirled the contents around in the perspiring cup, and took a sip.

"Oh my *god*," she said. "This almost makes up for you all waking us at the crack of dawn."

Jenna waved her off. "Dawn was over an hour ago. I had to get some fresh eggs over to the farmers market. Colt's manning the booth today so I can partake in the festivities."

Willow let out a breath. "So Colt's *not* one of the guys waiting for Ash in the barn?"

Delaney, who was visibly pregnant, lowered herself onto the couch and sunk into the cushions. "Bethie...can you bring me my pathetic decaf?" She gasped and pressed a palm to the side of her belly, then added, "The little hellion does not like when I complain about my coffee."

Beth laughed and grabbed the one coffee clearly marked with a big D on the side and a high-octane one for herself, dropping down on the spot next to her sister.

"No," Jenna finally replied to Beth's question as Lucy pecked about along the perimeter of the sliding doors that led outside. "Only Ash's brothers are out there waiting for him." She nudged Willow's shoulder with her own. "He told me about what happened last night. I'm sorry for all that, honey. When he left to come back here with Eli last night, he told me it was just to make sure you got home safe since you weren't responding to his texts. I should have known better."

Ash emerged from the bedroom fully clothed… in what he was wearing the night before since the rest of his clothes were in the front hall closet.

"Mornin', everyone," he called with a grin. Then he held up his loaner phone. "Apparently, I need to get my 'better-be-covered' ass out to the barn ASAP before they drop me at the farmers market and make me sell eggs with your brother?" He glanced at Willow and shrugged.

Willow sighed. "Guess that means it's my turn to get dressed." She set her coffee on the breakfast counter and briefly turned back toward her guests. "Excuse me for a few, everyone. And feel free to avert your eyes while I plant one on my guy before he leaves for the day."

She strode toward a resigned Ash, likely with the same resignation on her face, and wrapped her arms around his waist.

"You're not limping," he noted, a smile tugging at the corner of his mouth.

"You're right," she replied, realization in her tone. "Huh. You know what? I don't think anything could hurt me today."

He beamed at her. "And you called me your guy. In front of everyone," he whispered, as if the room weren't small enough for everyone to still hear.

"I did, didn't I?" she mused. "Guess I felt like claiming what was mine in case anyone got the wrong idea after your little window display."

"Hoo boy!" Jenna called. "There ain't nothin' little about that earlier display!"

His cheeks darkened, and Willow gasped.

"You're *blushing*!" She craned her neck to glance back at the five women who were definitely *not* averting their eyes. "Look at that, ladies! Country music's Mad Man Murphy is blushing!"

"You did *not* just call me that."

She clasped her hands behind his neck and pulled him down to her. "I did. And your sudden attack of modesty is adorable." She kissed him and ignored the *oohs*, *ahs,* and low whistles from their small audience.

"Tell me we get to sleep in tomorrow," he pleaded. "I don't even want to see a.m. on a clock."

She kissed his cheek and whispered in his ear. "We're not leaving the bed tomorrow." She unclasped her hands and straightened to her full height. "Have fun with your brothers," she told him.

He sighed and kissed the top of her head. "Only because you asked me to." He offered a salute to the rest of the room, grabbed his well-worn straw hat from the small table by the door, and headed out into the sun.

Her cheeks warm and every part of her feeling all tingly and light, Willow turned toward her guests to find them all still staring. "There is no such thing as personal space around here, is there?"

She was greeted with a chorus of, "Ha! *No*," and "Absolutely not," and "Welcome to small-town living." But despite the unwelcomed morning interruption, Willow suddenly felt surrounded by a sisterly kind of love she hadn't experienced before.

"I guess I should go get dressed then," she added and made to pivot back toward the bedroom door.

"Wait!" Jenna called. "Can I…uh…borrow your phone? I forgot to tell Colt something really important about running the tent today."

Willow's brows furrowed. "Sure but…don't *you* have a phone?"

Jenna laughed. "Of course. But I left it in Delaney's minivan."

Delaney rested her decaf iced coffee on her pregnant belly and pouted. "I can't believe I'm a minivan person now."

"Hey!" Casey chided. "Don't knock that sweet ride. It's got automatic doors and super-comfortable seats. Plus, we all fit!"

Delaney perked up. "It is comfortable as hell. I can't believe it's going to have two car seats soon!"

Willow padded into her room, unplugged her phone from the charger, and then brought it out to Jenna, making sure to unlock it before handing it over.

"He's saved in my contacts under ICE Morgan… You know…in case of emergency?" Willow only had three ICEs in her life, her adoptive parents and Colt. Somehow, though, she felt like after this visit to Meadow Valley, that might change.

"What?" Jenna asked, taking the phone. "Oh… right. Your brother…the guy I'm callin' with your phone."

Willow's brows furrowed, and then she laughed. "How much did you drink last night, Jenna?"

Her sister-in-law laughed. "I guess more than I thought."

Lucy abandoned her exploration of the back door and strutted her way over to Willow's bare feet. The hen gently pecked at her bruised pinkie toe that Ash had carefully retaped the night before.

"Ahhh," Jenna mused.

"Ah *what*?" Willow asked.

"She can tell you're still healing and that you might not be ready. Otherwise she would have pecked the hell out of you."

"For real!" Beth chimed in. "I wasn't in this house for two seconds before my sister brought the hen in to greet me, and that monster drew first blood."

"You're *welcome*!" Delaney singsonged.

Jenna scowled at Beth. "And look where you are now, all because my girl *knew* you belonged in Meadow Valley with Eli, and that was the only way she knew to tell you."

Willow scoffed. "So we're back on the chicken being psychic again?"

"Oh, she is," Beth and Delaney replied in unison.

"She's just not always gentle about it," Beth added.

Willow narrowed her eyes. "Uh-huh. Right. So her knowing my poor little toe is still broken is supposed to be some revelation?"

Jenna shook her head. "It's a metaphor, darlin'. She can tell something else still needs to heal before you can truly let love in."

Willow huffed out a laugh, shook her head, and pivoted back toward her bedroom to change. She could have sworn she heard a few whispers as she turned her back, but they were drowned out by a hen's deafening, "SQUAWK!"

Chapter 26

ASH FOUND HIS BROTHERS WALKING JACK around the arena, Eli on foot and Boone atop Cirrus a few paces ahead of the new gelding.

He climbed and hopped the fence partly to show off and partly to prove that he still could, just like he had when he was a teen and this ranch was his life.

"You boys mind telling me why I'm dressed and out of bed this early on a Saturday?" he called to his brothers.

The two elder Murphys rounded the final corner of the arena and stopped where Ash stood at the gate leading to the barn.

Eli shrugged. "Maddie woke us at five, so I got up and fed her. An hour later, Beth comes into the living room where we are enjoying a riveting episode of *Bluey* and tells me all the women are surprising Willow within the hour and that we should think of something to do to keep you busy for the day."

Ash barked out an incredulous laugh. "Glad to hear it's not because my asshole brothers were itching to spend time with me."

"Don't get your panties in a twist," Boone called

down from Cirrus's saddle. And so the good-natured ribbing began.

When Ash was younger, he often wished he could come up with some of the zingers his brothers tossed his way. But Boone and Eli were always quicker on the draw. But now Ash was the one who slung words for a living, and he found himself holding his own and sometimes even winning.

They started the morning by walking all five horses to the grazing field outside Eli's place and then putting on gloves to muck out the stalls.

"You didn't have any better ideas for how to keep me busy today?" Ash called from Holiday's stall as sweat trickled down his neck and his shoulders began to ache.

"Honestly?" Boone replied from Cirrus's gate. "No. We've never really done anything else together other than this."

Eli poked his head out from Midnight's stall as he shoveled droppings into his bucket. "We used to ride," he added.

"Is anyone getting hot?" Boone asked. But before either of the other brothers could answer, he popped out of Cirrus's stall with a hose in his hand, the sprayer aimed at Ash.

"Don't you—" But Boone cut him off with a shot of icy water straight to the chest. Then he whirled on the already retreating Eli and got him right in the ass.

And now Ash knew why Boone had insisted they store the wheelbarrow of clean bedding *outside* the barn.

———————

They were drenched, filthy, and sporting several bumps and bruises by the time the stalls were clean, because of course no water fight between brothers was complete without three grown men rolling on a barn floor trying to kick each other's asses.

They sat in Eli's Adirondack chairs facing the horses grazing in the field, nursing cold bottles of beer.

Eli snorted, "No, I don't think the thirties are supposed to hurt this much."

"Speak for yourselves, old coots," Ash replied with a laugh. "My age still starts with the word 'twenty.'"

Eli kicked Ash's boot with his own. "Oh yea, twentysomething? Then why do you have a bag of ice on your knee?"

Ash winced and then nodded his head back toward Boone. "Because this asshole tackled me to bare, wet concrete in Holiday's stall."

Boone snorted. "You did go down pretty hard."

"Oh yeah?" Ash retorted. "How's that tailbone feeling?" Boone might have gotten him on the first tackle, but Ash took him down in round two. If there were actually rounds, which there weren't.

Boone grumbled something under his breath and then readjusted his own ice pack where it rested just above his ass.

Eli laughed. "If this was twenty years ago, Dad would have ripped us a new one for almost flooding the stalls. It'll be after dark before they're dry enough to lay the bedding again."

They were all silent for several moments as they watched the horses graze before Ash spoke again.

"I was always too young when you two would get into this kind of trouble. When I was old enough, Dad couldn't work anymore. You were already in charge." He toed Eli's boot. "And this kind of *trouble* didn't really happen." He hadn't meant it to sound so somber, but Ash didn't realize until right that moment that he'd missed out on some of the prime *brothering* of his brothers.

"Because I would have been the one cleaning up the mess," Eli replied. "And by the time you were old enough, you weren't interested in anything other than that guitar."

"Ouch," Ash said, then took a long swig of his beer. "I mean...noted, but still...*ouch.*" Just because Eli was right didn't ease the sting of the truth. "Because what used to be fun suddenly felt like barely keeping our heads above water. I needed something that made me feel like *me.*"

"Cut the kid some slack, Eli." Boone stretched his arms up toward the sky and let out a long sigh. "The ranch was always work, but I think we all got a little lost when Dad's legacy became our responsibility."

All three of them nodded in unison and then quietly tended to their beers. Despite his bruised knee and overall sore *everything*—not that he'd admit that to his brothers—Ash was awash in contentment.

"So… Willow, huh?" Boone asked after several minutes of contented silence. "Is it for real this time?"

"This time?" Ash tilted his head back against his chair and let out a long exhale. "Shit. You waited a whole ten minutes before going there, huh?"

Boone laughed. "It's noon. I waited five *hours*."

"How about four *years*?" Eli added. "You think it's time to let us in on what really happened?"

Ash set his beer down on the ground and leaned forward, elbows on his knees as he hung his head. He'd sent Boone and Eli tickets to the show that night not only to see him play but so he could introduce them to the girl who had turned his whole world upside down, in the best possible way. They were the only ones who knew, when the marriage announcement hit the internet the next day, that it was total bullshit. And to protect Annabeth…and to hide his own shame…he'd pushed them away.

"Yeah," Ash finally replied. "I think it is."

Because more than the past twenty-nine years of his life, the past month had taught Ash the importance of trust when it came to the people he loved. He should have trusted his brothers to have his back even when he made the biggest mistake of his professional and personal life. He should have, and he didn't. But that was all going to change now.

"So…" he continued. "Here's the story…all of it. And if you realize I'm the world's biggest asshole when it's done, don't worry. I'm right there with you."

_____

Willow sat in one of Casey's salon chairs, a black cape snapped around her neck and her wet hair hanging at her shoulders.

"Are you sure?" Casey asked, wiggling the shears at Willow in the mirror.

Jenna spun back and forth in the chair beside her. "We should have kept Lucy with us to help you decide," she mused.

She could see Beth and Delaney sitting behind her in the mirror's reflection. They nodded sagely in agreement with Jenna.

"It's just *bangs*," Willow insisted. "I don't need a psychic hen to tell me whether or not it's a good idea."

"Ha!" Jenna cried. "So you *do* believe in Lucy's talents!"

"That's not what I…" Willow groaned and then

tilted her head up at Casey. "I got that new dress at your friend Ivy's shop, and we were looking at all of those fashion magazines at the bookshop. It just feels like it's time to change something up, you know?"

Casey nodded. "The girl has a point. Remember when I singed my hair on my curling wand and *had* to cut bangs to fix it? That was the morning I ran into Boone in my brokedown car in the middle of the highway, and now look where we are. All thanks to my bangs."

Willow gasped. "You hit Boone with your car?"

Casey burst out laughing. "*No!* I hit a speed limit sign, and then Boone showed up on his motorcycle out of the blue and got me to my cosmetology school interview on time after we hadn't spoken to each other since *high school*!"

Willow's eyes widened. "Do *all* of you somehow have a chicken involved in your romantic relationships?"

Every single one of them nodded her head, even Jenna.

"She's a wise old hen, Miss Willow. And the sooner you accept that, the better."

Willow gripped the armrests of the chair beneath her cape and steadied her resolve. She didn't need a supposed metaphor-squawking hen to tell her whether or not *bangs* were a good idea. She squeezed her eyes closed and forced away thoughts of every meme she'd ever seen declaring that cutting bangs was a cry for help because Willow didn't *need* help! She was happy...really and truly happy for the first time in years. A new look was simply a stamp of approval on what she deemed a new start.

"Do it!" she declared, blinking her eyes open and meeting Casey's gaze.

Casey set down the blow dryer, gave Willow's waves one final shake with her fingers, and then unsnapped and removed the cape.

"What do you think?"

The rest of the group was silent, waiting for Willow's reaction.

She stared at the woman in the mirror who didn't look completely different but also not completely the same. The long fringe hung just below her eyebrows, and her brunette waves seemed to have a bounce and fullness they'd lacked an hour ago. She looked younger, somehow. Less world-weary. And seeing it made Willow believe it.

A smile slowly spread across her lips until she was utterly beaming.

"I love it," she replied, and everyone else let out a collective sigh.

"You're gorgeous, girl!" Casey declared. "You're going to drive 'em wild when you get up on that stage in a few weeks." She spun Willow so she was facing them.

"Thank you," she told Casey. Then she surveyed everyone else in the room, a group of women she'd only known for a little over a month—save for Jenna—yet who all felt like family. "All of you, truly. This has been the best morning."

Jenna climbed out of her chair. "So...now?" she asked the other women.

Willow's brows furrowed, and her stomach instinctively tied itself in a knot. Something about Jenna's tone wasn't right.

Casey took a step back, allowing Jenna to pivot in front of Willow's chair. Jenna pulled a phone out of her pocket and held it out toward Willow, and that was when Willow realized it was *her* phone she'd handed Jenna that morning before she got dressed.

Willow stood and let out a relieved laugh as she took her phone back. "Oh! Is that all this is about? You had me freaked out for a second there like you were about to dish out some really bad news." She unlocked the phone and scanned the home screen. Nothing looked amiss. Then she glanced back up at her silent audience and laughed again, but this time it came out sounding a bit more nervous than she'd expected. "If I didn't know any better, I'd have guessed you all were keeping me busy today so I would forget I even had a phone."

Jenna barked out a laugh. "No! Of course not!"

Willow crossed her arms and raised her brows. "You are the *worst* liar, Jen."

Her sister-in-law winced. "Okay, fine. I would have told you earlier, but after Lucy pecked your little toe, I realized you might not be ready." She worried her bottom lip between her teeth. "We were going to pamper you either way... It was just a matter of *when* we told you."

The knot in Willow's stomach tightened and then twisted itself in a double knot. "Okay, now you're freaking me out." She looked at her phone again and noticed what she hadn't a moment before. Willow was used to not being able to keep up with the notifications on her social media, but she prided herself on reading every comment and responding when she could. At most she'd have fifty to one hundred to read at the end of any given day unless she posted something like the bonfire post with Ash's form obscured through the flame. But Willow hadn't posted anything in over a week, yet the little red square on top of the Instagram thumbnail was now a rectangle indicating she had over five *thousand* notifications.

"What the...?" She looked up at Jenna. "You all saw whatever it was this morning, didn't you? And you waited hours to tell me about it? Because of a hen pecking my toe?"

Beth pushed the hooded dryer up as she answered Willow with a nervous nod.

"Maddie woke up *before* the crack of dawn, and Eli was the best and took one for the team, letting me sleep off our late night. Except once I was even semiconscious, I had to pee. And once I got out of bed to pee, I felt like I should brush my teeth, and once I brushed my teeth, well… I was wide awake, you know?"

Delaney rolled her eyes. "I just aged five years, Bethie."

"Sorry!" Beth exclaimed. "I just wanted to put it all in perspective. Okay. So, what do we all do when we should be sleeping but *can't* sleep? We scroll social media. And because I just started following Ash, his profile keeps popping up at the top of my feed."

"What did he post?" Willow asked, trying to keep her tone even. She trusted him, right? So whatever it was would be fine. *They* were fine.

"We waited because of Lucy pecking your toe and until we got confirmation on *how* what happened…*happened*." Jenna grabbed her hand and gave it a reassuring squeeze. "I guess you should take a look."

Willow tried to hide her trembling thumb, but what was the point? She tapped the icon and opened the app.

"Haircut's on the house, by the way," Casey blurted out. "And not just because I feel partially responsible."

Willow still didn't follow Ash on social media,

but it didn't matter now because she'd been tagged in whatever the post was, which was why she was getting notified of all the reactions and comments.

Then there it was. Not only was it a photo of them from their impromptu performance the night before, but it was a photo of a moment Willow thought they'd shared only with the small crowd in the tavern...the kiss. And the caption of the photo simply said, "Together again. Just wait to see what we have in store for you next."

The comments went from excitement and encouragement to posts that gave her déjà vu from years before.

wmstanfan: i knew it was an Easter egg!!! SOOOO stoked for this!

morgansminions: happy for wm if she's happy but still don't trust AM.

cntrylvr: YASSSSS

annabash4life: And...now we know the real reason behind the divorce. Why am I not surprised? Hope they call the duet "The Other Woman."

Willow sniffed back the threat of tears and then gazed up at the other women who were all giving her pitying looks. She shook her head and squared her shoulders. "Ash had nothing to do with this. How could he have? I was clearly devouring the man for all to see when the photo was taken." She turned her attention to Casey. "And you collected phones from all the patrons, right? So I don't understand how this is even possible." She knew they had no control over what patrons did *after* the show. But those would be personal posts from accounts that likely didn't have a lot of reach. Plus, *Meadow Valley takes care of its own.* Casey had said those exact words. This wasn't adding up.

Casey cleared her throat. "I did collect phones from the *patrons and my line cooks…*" she began. "Drew, Hank, and Isaac are great kids. They're all seniors at Meadow Valley High School, and I've known them all their lives. But it gets so damn hot in that kitchen, so we usually prop open the back door on cooler nights to get some fresh air circulating for the line crew." She blew out a breath. "The boys are huge fans, and they admitted to leaving the kitchen unattended for a few minutes while they popped up front to watch.

"I think someone snuck in through the back and then blended into the crowd. I'm so sorry, Willow. Whoever it was somehow knew about the pop-up and…" Casey's eyes turned glassy and she ran a finger under her suddenly damp lashes. "Did you see the second image?"

Willow felt sick. She hadn't even noticed the second dot beneath the post, an indication to swipe in order to see what came next.

She swiped.

Instead of an image, she saw only a black screen with a green, wavy shape moving across the screen. An audio track. It took another few seconds for her to register what she was hearing…the raw recording of their yet-unfinished duet.

Chapter 27

ASH FOUND HER IN THE BEDROOM PACKING HER suitcase, but Willow didn't look up even when she noticed him lingering in the doorway.

"Going somewhere?" he asked, daring to sound playful at a time like this.

She let out a bitter laugh, doing her damnedest to hold on to the anger to keep from falling apart in front of him. "Yeah. I'm going to hole up in my bus near the fairgrounds for the next couple weeks before the festival."

"What? *Why?*" Ash strode into the room—was he limping?—and stood so close she could smell the sweat on his skin. His brothers had obviously put him to work today, and it pained her not to ask him about it. To hear how he likely bonded with Eli and Boone and hopefully got closer to the family he hadn't seen in years. But everything was different now. Or maybe it had never even changed in the first place.

She took her time as she finished folding her last pair of jeans before laying them neatly on top of the rest of her clothes and zipping up the case. Then she finally dared to tilt her head up and meet his eyes.

"Oh my god! What happened to you?" She instinctively reached toward the small cut on his cheek but then snatched her hand away.

"What?" he asked again, still seeming confused. Then he lightly touched his cheek. "Oh," he continued. "Nothing. Just a little roughhousing with the boys." He laughed, but then his brows furrowed. "Your *hair*." He lightly brushed his fingers over her new bangs and smiled. "You're beautiful, you know that?"

She shook her head and took a step back.

Ash let out a nervous laugh. "No, you're not beautiful, or no you don't know that you're beautiful."

Willow groaned. "Ash! Stop, *please*. I know, okay?"

He ran a hand through his hair, making it look wild and unkempt like it had earlier that morning. Was it really the same day she'd woken up next to him after the best night she'd ever had onstage... or off?

"Know *what*, Wills? Jesus, you're freaking me out." He took a step toward her and placed his hands on her shoulders. "Tell me what's going on, and I'll fix it, okay? Whatever it is, I'll take care of it."

She crossed her arms and took another step back, stopping short as she bumped into the wall.

Ash stepped with her, not letting her go, so that now she was both physically and emotionally pinned.

"Can you take care of my label threatening to drop me because of an unauthorized leak?" she asked, her voice beginning to shake. "Can you take care of me having to possibly pay back my advance for a second album that might not ever release?"

He flinched but continued to hold her, and she hated how his hands on her felt reassuring rather than revolting, how her heart hadn't yet caught up with her mind.

"Willow…" he began, his tone careful and measured. "Please tell me what happened."

All she had left in her was a tired, half-hearted scoff. "I saw the Instagram post, Ash. It's over, okay? Transaction complete."

This made him stumble back like he'd been socked in the gut. He pulled his phone from his pocket and unlocked the screen. A few seconds later, Willow heard it again, Ash's hopeful, earnest voice as he said "Ready?" and then launched into their song.

Willow squeezed her eyes shut as she listened to the recording. God, they sounded good. She knew it then, and she knew it last night when they performed together.

"I learned quickly that everything I do is some sort of transaction," she finally said, opening her eyes after the audio clip finished. "Isn't that what you told me *four* years ago?" She laughed, and her throat tightened. "I can blame what happened then on my naïvete. But what about now? What excuse do I have for putting myself in the exact same *humiliating* position when I should be smart enough to know better?"

Ash stared at the phone and then tossed it on the dresser like it had suddenly caught fire. "Willow, I didn't... You can't think I had anything to do with this."

She pressed one hand to her stomach, the other to her chest as if she might come apart at the seams if she didn't hold herself together. "If it was just the photo, Ash..." She shook her head. "The only place that recording existed was on your phone. *Your* phone."

"I know," he replied, holding his hands up. "Which was *your* suggestion, remember?"

Willow nodded slowly. "Did you send it to Sloane?"

All the color drained from his face. "I can't believe you'd even ask me that."

She shrugged. "Well... I'm asking."

"What happened to trusting me? That lasted, what, barely more than twelve hours?"

She couldn't believe he had the audacity to sound angry. At *her*! "You're not answering the question, Murphy," she told him.

Ash pinched the bridge of his nose and blew out an exasperated breath. "I shouldn't *have* to. Not if you meant what you said."

She finally threw her arms in the air. "Just say it, okay? Say you gave Sloane the recording, and we can be done with this. I'm too tired, Ash. I don't want to do this anymore."

He grabbed his phone and shoved it back in his pocket. "Right. I forgot. *Hating* me is exhausting."

He moved in front of her again and pressed his hand to the wall beside her head, leaning in so he was close enough to kiss her…so she almost wanted to *let* him because her stupid, aching heart didn't know any better. But instead she pressed herself against the wall, clenching her teeth and daring him to say what they both knew was the truth.

"I sent Sloane *nothing*," he told her, a rough tremble in his voice. "I sent her nothing, and I *knew* nothing about the post. But you were never going to actually trust me, were you?" he asked.

"Isn't this where you tell me you're retiring from the industry because you broke my heart again?" She blinked and felt the first tear fall, and Ash's steely gaze melted.

He cupped her cheeks in his hands and stared at her with pleading, stormy-blue eyes.

"Wills…" His thumbs brushed at the tears that fell freely now. "I'm so—"

"Don't!" She interrupted. "Please don't say it." She sucked in a shaky breath. "Remember when I told you I never actually hated you?" He nodded slowly, and she hated the glimmer of hope she saw in his eyes. "Trying to love you is what's exhausting," she admitted. "I have lost too much in my life to *keep* losing." She shook her head. "Did you see what they're saying about me? Calling me a homewrecker just like they did last time? I thought I could handle being a part of your life and your career, but I just keep getting knocked down again and again."

He tilted his forehead against hers. "Don't do this, Wills. I'm begging you not to do this." His lips brushed against hers, and she couldn't help but kiss him back. Not because she believed they could fix this but because when she kissed him this morning, she didn't know it was their last kiss. *Now* she knew.

She tasted salt on his lips, and when she pulled away she saw that she wasn't the only one failing at holding back tears. The sight of a broken Ash wrecked her, but she couldn't do this anymore, always waiting for the other shoe to drop because it just…kept…dropping.

"I have to go," she whispered, gently pushing him away so she could free herself from the wall.

"No you don't," he replied. "You don't have to. You're *choosing* to."

"No," she told him, sure of at least one small thing. "I'm choosing *me*." She cleared her throat. "Colt's going to be here soon to pick me up," she added. "I should probably go wait out front so a bad situation doesn't get worse…"

Willow slipped past a speechless Ash and grabbed her suitcase from the bed along with her own phone from the bedside table. Then she rolled the suitcase out of the room and toward the front door. She glanced back, taking in the empty room that had just begun to start feeling like home. Then she counted to ten, exhaled, and turned back to the door, opening it and stepping through.

Once outside, her phone vibrated in her hand. She didn't recognize the number but answered it anyway.

"Hello?"

"Hi…" the voice on the other line replied. "I'm looking for Willow Hammond."

"This is Willow Hammond."

"Oh good. Ms. Hammond, I'm calling from Mobile One, your cell phone provider. You came in several weeks ago asking about retrieving texts from an old number?"

"Yes…" she replied hesitantly, a faint glimmer of hope rising in her chest.

"Sorry for the delay," he continued. "Your number is in use by another customer and has been for some time, so it took a bit of untangling, especially since it involved retrieving texts from a blocked number. Lucky for you, your old phone's backup was still on our server."

"And the texts?" she asked.

The man on the other end of the line read Ash's

old number back to her, double-checking that the company had, in fact, researched the correct number.

"Yes," she confirmed. "That's correct."

The Mobile One man sighed. "I'm sorry, Ms. Hammond. But there were no undelivered texts from that number. Would you like us to send a record of the texts from the dates preceding the number getting blocked?"

Willow's heart sank. "No," she told him. "That won't be necessary. Thank you for your time." She ended the call.

A few minutes later, Colt's truck pulled up in front of the guesthouse. He climbed out and grabbed her suitcase, tossing it in the bed. Then he opened her door and helped her in before returning to the driver's seat.

"Where did you tell him you were going?" Colt asked.

"My bus." She stared at him with watery eyes. "You and Jenna are the only ones who know I'll be at your place?"

He nodded.

"Okay," Willow told him. "I just need to lay low until the festival and do some damage control with my label. You guys sure you'll be okay not having anyone over to the house until then?"

Colt squeezed her hand. "Whatever you need, Wills. But...if I see him, do I get to go all big brother on him now that he did what we all knew he would do?"

She pressed her lips together and shook her head. No matter what role Ash played in this mess, he was hurting too. "Just let it go, Colt, okay? There's nothing else to do."

"Okay," he agreed. Then he turned the car around and slowly rolled off the Murphy property.

Willow watched over her shoulder as the guesthouse receded in the distance, ignoring the figure of a man standing on the front porch, watching her drive away.

Chapter 28

ON THE FOURTH DAY OF NO CONTACT, ELI BROKE the unwritten rule of knocking before entering. Ash heard the metal grind of the key entering the hole, heard the *thunk* of the tumbler releasing, and simply sat where he'd been sitting for the past ninety-six hours, give or take a time or two to get up and pee.

"*Shit,*" Eli hissed. "It smells like a goddamn locker room in here."

"Ha!" Boone replied.

Great. There were two of them.

"I'd say a locker room smells like a meadow compared to what our boy Ash has going on in here," the middle Murphy brother continued.

Ash heard their boots on the hard floor as they approached but didn't bother to turn around.

Boone went straight for the back door and threw it open, the cool afternoon breeze mingling with the stagnant living room air.

"What the hell is this?" Eli asked, standing next to the television in the corner of the room at which Ash had been staring for hours on end.

"*Titanic,*" Ash replied. "Have you seen it?" He stared up at his brother with eyes that stung.

"Of course I've seen it," his brother told him. "Who hasn't seen *Titanic*?"

"Uh...me. At least when I named the dapples." Ash let out a mirthless laugh. "You could have told me it was bad luck or something. But don't worry. I know Jack and Rose's fate now, and it's sad as fucking hell."

Boone turned around after attempting to usher in more fresh air and then crossed his arms. "Um... Ashton Elias? How many times have you watched the movie *now*?"

Ash shrugged. "Today or since she left?" God, he couldn't even bring himself to say her name. "Because I bought it so I could stream it on repeat."

"Holy shit," Boone uttered, incredulous.

Ash pointed at his brother. "Watch that language. You don't want my niece picking up any bad habits." But his attempt at teasing fell flat. Probably due to the monotone timbre of his voice. Or maybe it was because he wasn't sure his face even remembered how to smile.

Eli ran the tips of his fingers over the bottom corner of the screen, and it went completely dark.

Ash flew up from his lived-in corner of the couch. "What the hell do you think you're doing?"

"What the hell do you think *you're* doing, Ash? We've been calling and texting for four days!"

Ash shrugged. "My phone died. Didn't see any point in charging it after that." Especially when all of his calls to Willow went right to voicemail and all of his texts went undelivered. Blocked again.

"And what are you *wearing*?" Boone added.

Ash glanced down at the white terry cloth that had been his sole garment for the last four days. "A *robe*. You've heard of them, right?"

Eli sighed. "Is it Willow's robe, Ash? We know what happened, okay? Hell, the whole *town* knows what happened. We just wanted to know—"

"How I could be such an asshole?" Ash interrupted. "Does it even matter that I didn't do what everyone thinks I did?" It wasn't like he could prove it, and his voicemail to Sloane asking for an explanation earned him nothing other than a text in response assuring him that his back catalog was getting more streams than ever and to enjoy some *good* publicity for a change. Regardless of whatever the truth was, everyone was going to believe what they believed. And the town that took care of its own wouldn't see him as one of theirs anymore.

Eli took a step forward and shook his head. "We just wanted to know if you were okay."

"Because *clearly* you are not," Boone added. "Have you tried to contact her?"

Ash threw up his arms. "Of course I tried to contact her. She blocked my number. I even tried her brother, but he only answered the phone long enough to tell me what I should do to myself and then hung up. Hell, I even stole Eli's truck after he went to bed the other night and drove out to the fairgrounds to try and find her bus, but the only thing I found were people on the festival crew building stages. *No* tour buses. It's like she disappeared, so...you know...what the hell else is there for me to do?"

Boone actually took a step back. "How about you hop in the shower, buddy? Then we can figure this all out."

Ash sighed, his shoulders sagging. "You're not going to leave until I do, are you?"

Both older Murphys shook their heads.

"So if I clean up, you'll leave me, Jack, and Rose alone?"

Boone huffed out a laugh. "No, I'm unplugging your router and taking it home with me."

Ash gave his brother a half-hearted shrug. "Fine. But I'm really not in the mood for visitors." He trudged toward the bedroom and into the master bath, turning on the water and letting the room fill with steam. He stared at himself in the quickly fogging mirror, shocked to see the wild-eyed, wild-haired, practically *bearded* man staring back at him.

How had he gotten here? How did his life feel more out of control now than it had when he was a couch-surfing busker in his teens? Ash was more successful than he'd ever imagined he could be. This was supposed to be the easy part, wasn't it?

When he emerged again, cleaned but not shaven,

he found Eli standing in the doorway, talking to someone on the porch.

"Willow?" he called, practically jogging for the door in nothing but his boxers. But when he pushed Eli out of the way, he found a man in a purple Mobile One polo shirt holding a package and tablet Eli was about to sign.

"Oh," Ash said, deflated.

"Ash Murphy?" the guy asked, then laughed. "I mean, of course you're Ash Murphy. Recognize you even with the beard. Sorry. I'm new. First week on the job. Never made a delivery to a celebrity before." Mr. Mobile One's cheeks darkened. "Um, especially a half-naked one? Anyway, I was delivering your replacement phone and would be happy to come in and set it up but was telling your brother that I was confused about the directions on the account."

Ash's brows furrowed. "What do you mean confused?"

"About the call and email forwarding? The note on the account is from four years ago, so I wasn't sure if that was still in effect or..."

"Forwarding?" Ash asked. "What the hell do you mean *forwarding*?"

Mr. Mobile One or *Tad* as Ash now noted from the guy's name tag, let out a nervous laugh this time. "Well, there is a note on your account..." He tapped the screen on his tablet and then seemed to scan some text. "Here!" he exclaimed, turning the tablet toward Ash so he could read. "See right there? It lists one number and one email address to be forwarded to a secondary number."

"What the actual...?" Ash recognized all three. The first two were Willow's old number and her email address. The forwarding account? Sloane's.

"Can you retrieve those emails and texts if they were somehow deleted from my sent folders?"

Tad shook his head. "Anything permanently deleted is...well...permanently deleted. But they're saved on the forwarding account. You can just check them there."

Ash was confused again. "Even if the account they were forwarded to belongs to someone else?"

Tad's brows drew together and he laughed. "Mr. Morgan, you *own* the 'forward *to*' account."

Ash felt the hint of a smile tugging at his lips and a tiny spark of hope ignite in his chest. He stepped back and opened the door wide. "Come on in, Tad. We have some work to do."

Then he glanced at Eli. "And when he's done, I need your truck."

———

Ash pounded on Colt's door. "I know you're in there, Morgan! I stopped by the ranch, and they told me you're off today." He pounded again until he was sure he'd bruise his hand, and then he pounded some more. He was going to pound until someone opened the door, and then—

The door flew open, and Ash stopped short right before he knocked on Colt Morgan's face.

"Come on," Ash told him.

"What?" Colt asked. "Where? And also, *no*." His dark-brown eyes, looking so much like Willow's, only spurred Ash on.

He grinned. "Even if I tell you it's time to enact Article A?"

"Article A?" Colt asked, looking at Ash like he was crazy. Then his eyes widened with recognition. "Our contract. We never notarized it, Murphy. Why don't you count your blessings you got off on a technicality and get the hell out of here?"

Ash shrugged. "I don't need a notary to hold me to our agreement. I did what I promised not to do, and now I'm here to pay up." Ash heard a commotion somewhere beyond the entryway, and suddenly the reluctant Colt took a step forward.

"I'll be back in a few, Jen!" Colt called as he stepped the rest of the way onto the porch, quickly slamming the door behind him.

"Wow," Ash said with a nervous laugh. "You are really excited to kick my ass, aren't you?"

Colt crossed his arms and looked Ash square in the eyes, a muscle ticking in his jaw. "You have *no* idea, Murphy."

They rode in silence the few minutes it took to

get to the Meadow Valley Fire Station. Once out back in the workout facility, they found Captain Carter Bowen and some of his company using the free weights, but the ring was empty.

"Don't mind us, boys!" Colt called with a salute as he led the way to the other side of the ropes. "Just here to give this asshole what he deserves."

Ash and Colt stood at opposite corners, bouncing on their toes and shaking out their arms.

"Not gonna lie," Ash began. "Your enthusiasm is a little intimidating. I'm going to do my best not to block or retaliate, okay? But I can't help what I might do on instinct." He strode toward the center of the ring and nodded at Colt. "Gimme all you got, Morgan."

Colt had begun moving in Ash's direction but stopped short. "What the hell are you talking about? Not going to block or retaliate? Do you have a death wish?"

Ash let out a nervous laugh. "I mean, I'm hoping it won't go *that* far. But Eli said he can treat a broken nose without me going to the ER. Hate to mess up this pretty face, but I feel like there's less chance of internal injuries if we keep it up here." They had now amassed a small audience, so Ash added, "And these guys are all EMTs, so if I have any injuries requiring emergent care..."

"What the hell is the matter with you, Murphy?" Colt ran a hand through his hair, his eyes volleying from Ash, to the small crowd of firefighter/EMTs, and back to Ash again. "I'm not hitting a defense-less man."

"If you don't at least put on the gloves," Lieutenant Hayes called from down on the ground, "either one of you could be charged with assault. I'm just sayin'…"

Ash held up a hand and gave Colt the *bring it* gesture.

Colt closed the distance between them, and Ash braced himself for where the blow might land. When Colt grabbed the collar of his T-shirt, Ash gave himself a mental pat on the back for not yet having flinched.

"What the hell *is* this?" Colt asked through grit-ted teeth.

Ash exhaled a shaky breath through his nose. "I broke her heart, man," he replied, unable to mask the pain in his voice when he recalled the look of betrayal in Willow's eyes. "I didn't mean to," he con-tinued. "And I'm doing everything in my power to fix this whole situation even though I know I can't win her back." He shrugged. "Figured I'd start by getting the ass kicking I deserve, then move on taking back control of my professional life and my goddamn cell phone. Then… I don't know. Maybe I can convince you to tell me where Willow is so I can at least tell her the truth I didn't know four days ago, and then I promise never to bother her again. I

just want her to be happy and to know despite my
many, many, *many* mistakes…I've always loved her."

Colt yanked at Ash's collar, and Ash closed his
eyes, readying himself for the blow. But a second
later, Colt growled and shoved him backward,
swearing under his breath. He ran a hand through
his hair and threw his arms up. "How the hell am I
supposed to deck you after that?"

Ash raised his brows. "Because I'm an asshole
who signed away his life at nineteen and took ten
more years to grow up and take it back?"

"Shit," Colt replied. "You really do love her, don't
you?"

"More than anything," Ash told him.

"Enough to just stand there and take a beating?"

Ash nodded. "I mean, I probably wouldn't stay
standing for long."

Colt rolled his eyes, then scrubbed a hand across
his face. "I'm only telling you this because Willow
has been a wreck all week, and I don't want her to
have to perform like this next weekend." He sighed.
"She's staying at my place."

———

Ash barreled through the door as soon as Colt
opened it. "Willow?" he called. "Wills?" He ran
straight into the kitchen and living area, but it was
empty. He ran up the stairs, throwing open doors

and calling her name, but every room and every closet was empty. When he made it downstairs, he found Colt standing in the kitchen with a sticky note in his hand.

"I found this on the fridge." He handed the note to Ash.

You better not have touched him. Can't stay in MV anymore.

Jenna taking me somewhere to crash until the festival.

She'll fill you in. Thanks for being there for me.

See you at the show. Love you,—W.

"Okay. Call Jenna, man." Ash's heart was racing. "She'll tell you where they're going and we can go after them."

"Don't you get it?" Colt asked. "She knew I wouldn't hit you...even though I *really* wanted to. And she obviously knew I'd crack and tell you she was here." He clapped Ash on the shoulder and sighed. "She doesn't want to be found, Murphy. I'm sorry."

Chapter 29

WILLOW STOOD IN THE WINGS, GUITAR SLUNG over her shoulder, and waited as the rest of the band finished their tuning and sound check. She closed her eyes and centered herself in the moment, reminding herself that while it wasn't the promised duet, her label liked the rough version of the new song she'd sent them and promised she'd get to a studio to record it in the next couple of weeks after the festival. Her career hadn't ended, and despite the mixed press she'd received after the leak, her agent told her that morning that her set at the festival was completely sold out.

She should be happy, right? She *was* happy, wasn't she?

Oz, her drummer, started in on the beat to "This Time," a crowd favorite, and the fans began to cheer. She waited a few measures, sucked in a deep breath, and then headed out onstage.

For the entirety of the song, Willow never sang alone. Every word, every chorus, and even the bridge…the fans were with her each step of the way. And right there in the front row was everyone she loved.

Colt and Jenna, Boone and Casey, Eli and Beth. Even the Hammonds, her parents, drove up to catch the set.

Everyone she loved. Except one.

This time I'll pick myself up when I fall;
This time I'll block your number before you call.
This time I'll hold the needle and thread;
Jagged stitches 'cross my heart…cold
   sheets on your side of the bed.

Her throat felt raw as she sang the final refrain.

Jagged stitches 'cross my heart…
Jagged stitches 'cross my heart…
Jagged stitches 'cross my heart…cold
   sheets on your side of the bed.

She strummed the last chord with a little too much vigor and snapped a string.

"Whoops!" she cried into the mic once the applause died down. Then she laughed, lifted the strap over her shoulder, and handed the guitar to a crew member who ran onstage. "While my girl Mel restrings this for me, or finds me another guitar, I'm going to just…" Willow strolled over to the stool where three bottles of water waited for her and opened one up. She downed half of it in one breath before carrying it back to the mic. "I'm not sure if y'all heard…but I got myself tangled in a tiny little scandal a couple weeks ago. *Again.*" She wasn't sure what the hell she was doing or why she'd just said what she said, but she needed to fill the dead air, and something propelled the words out of her mouth.

"We love you, Willow!" someone in the crowd called out.

"I love you too!" she replied with a laugh. Then she felt an odd pang in her gut. "You know what?" She grabbed the water stool and dragged it over to the mic stand, set the unopened bottles on the stage floor, and then parked herself on the stool. "It's so easy to say 'I love you' to y'all when we've never officially met, so how come it's so damned scary to say it to the *one* person I've loved for years? Who knows what I'm talking about?"

There were cheers and a few murmurs from the crowd, but for the most part, they'd gone silent as they stared up at her, waiting for what came next.

"Here's the thing," she continued, because why not go for broke now that she'd made it this far. "I loved someone once, a few years ago, but I never told him. I get a second chance…and I chicken out. Anybody else here a chicken like me?" *Chicken.*

Lucy might be able to spot the real deal, but she can't do your part of the job…

Clucking and hooting and hollering from the crowd. She was baring her heart more than they knew, and they were still entertained. God, she loved her fans. Willow let out an incredulous laugh and then glanced down at her brother and Jenna. "A wise woman and her hen once told me that I have to believe I deserve the fairy tale just as much as the rest of you do."

"Woo-hoo!" Jenna cried. "That's my girl!"

Willow blew her a kiss and then stared back out into the crowd.

"Hey, Wills…" A voice sounded through the speakers.

"Y'all heard that, right?" she asked.

Again, Jenna shouted, "That's my girl!"

"It's just you and me, Wills," the voice said again, and Willow realized it was coming from her ear monitor, not the speakers.

"I know you blocked me, and I don't blame you. But I need to explain, so I'm hoping you'll read this. 'The Annabeth thing isn't what you think. I fucked up, but I never lied about loving you. Please call me. Let me make this right.—Ash'"

Willow's gaze darted from side to side, but there was no one else onstage other than her and her band. She held up a finger as fans started giving her quizzical looks.

"Um… Just a second," she said into the mic. "My…uh…stage manager is giving me an update on my guitar."

"'I'm gonna email every day until you respond,'"

Ash's voice continued. "'You can hatr me, buy at leash you'll know the trth.'" He paused. "Sorry... I was drunk when I wrote this one, but I wanted you to get the full effect."

She let loose something between a laugh and sob while he kept going.

"'It's been a week, Wills. I'm a mess, which is a shitty thing to say because I'm sure it pales in comparison to what you're going through. Just one phone call. That's it. Please. I love you.—Ash'"

The audience started to cheer, and for a moment Willow wondered if they were actually applauding her having what looked like a very emotional reaction to news about her guitar. But then there he was.

Willow stood as she held her breath...and hoped.

She saw her guitar first, newly strung and slung across his chest. Then the setting sun shone on her favorite straw hat as Ash Murphy strode across the stage amid the crowd's thunderous roar.

He lifted her guitar over his shoulders and set it on the stand next to the mic. His own guitar hung across his back.

"How? What?" she asked, voice shaking. And even though she was facing him, the sound carried out from the speakers.

"It's a long story," he replied. "The short version is I'm here, and I fired my manager and record label." Murmurs and gasps arose from the audience. "That costs a pretty penny, let me tell you. Don't try this at home." That earned him some laughs. "The long story…" he continued. "Let's just say your inbox is full of four years' worth of a broken-hearted man begging for forgiveness. But for now we should probably just sing these folks a song."

He skimmed his fingers across her forehead and tucked her hair behind her ear before resting his palm against her cheek. Willow felt her heart rise into her throat. "I just want to tell you one thing, Willow Morgan, in front of all these witnesses. I have always loved you, even when you didn't love me back."

Willow strummed her guitar, cleared her throat, and said into the mic, "Didn't love you back?" She glanced out at the sea of people who, despite everything that had happened, were there for her. "What do you think, folks? Is it possible to have stopped loving this man?"

The crowd began to roar.

Her throat tightened as she spoke softly, as if only he could hear. "I always have, Ash, every day."

Ash dipped his head toward hers, then turned directly toward the mic, pulling it free from the stand, and sang in his deepest baritone, "Always… have…*what*, Willow Morgan? Just in case there's any confusion."

He handed her the mic, and Willow didn't hesitate for a single second, singing softly in a breathy voice as the crowd began to go wild.

"I loved you once, Ash Murphy. I love you still.

And every damned day between then and now…
All the days to come, this is my vow. I'll love you.
I'll love you. I'll love you. I will."

She leaned up on her toes and kissed him. Ash's
face lit up with the broad, beautiful Ash Murphy
smile she knew was meant only for her but decided
she could share it with her fans for tonight.

"That sounds an awful lot like a song I know,"
he said.

She covered the mic and leaned up to whisper in
his ear. "When I say it for the first time for real, it'll
be for you and you alone." Then she leaned back,
biting her lip as she grinned. "I don't suppose you'd
want to sing it with me. I feel like these folks were
maybe hoping for a duet tonight."

Willow's long-lost guitar-stringing crew member,
Mel, strode out onstage carrying a second mic on a
stand. Willow narrowed her eyes at the conspirator
as she set the mic in front of him, and Mel simply
smiled and shrugged.

Willow snapped her mic in the stand and
strummed her guitar again. "What do you think,
folks? Should we let him sing?"

The crowd went wild, clapping and cheering.
Even her brother, which made her think that Ash
had more than one coconspirator that night.

"I'm glad you agree," Willow continued.
"Because after that sob fest, I'm gonna need a little
help until my voice returns to normal." She grabbed

her half-full bottle of water from the floor, finished it up, and then nodded toward Ash who mouthed, *One, two, three.* And then they both launched into the song. Together.

It was well past two in the morning when they finally collapsed onto Willow's tour bus bed, her exhausted, elated, naked body curled up against his.

"What are you going to do now that you're a free agent?" she asked as he combed his fingers softly through her hair.

He kissed her cheek, her nose, and then her lips, and Willow hummed a soft sigh.

"I don't know," he finally replied. "I think I want to set up a new base camp in Meadow Valley...help my brothers with the ranch. There's room on the property to add on to the guesthouse. Was thinking of building a small studio, make the music I want to make *when* I want to make it." She hooked her knee over his, and he pulled her closer. "But mostly," he continued. "I'm just waiting for this great new album to drop and hoping I can be a roadie for the band when they go on tour to promote it."

She wrapped her arms around his neck. "And after this promotional tour, if the band's singer wants to regroup but doesn't really have a home base of her own, are you open to sharing yours?"

Ash leaned his forehead against hers. "Will I have to sleep on the couch?"

Willow laughed, but then her expression softened. "I love you," she told him, and it suddenly felt like the most natural thing to say. No more hiding behind fear or lyrics or anything that might keep him from knowing how very real those words were.

"I love you too," he told her. "But you and everyone else in the world pretty much knows that by now."

She brushed her lips against his. "I'm sorry it took me so long to say it."

His lips parted in a smile against hers. "Then I guess you're going to have to make up for lost time."

"Oh?" Willow asked. "I should probably get started, then, shouldn't I?" She kissed his forehead. "I love you, Ashton Elias." She kissed his cheek. "I love you, Ash." She kissed his *other* cheek. "I love you, Murphy." She kissed his nose. "I love you, cowboy." She kissed his mouth.

"That one's my favorite," Ash told her.

"Which one?" she asked.

"All of them." He grinned. "And you, Willow Morgan Hammond. *You're* my favorite."

She crawled over him, throwing the blanket over their heads as they lost themselves in each other, finally drifting off to sleep as the sun peeked above the clouds and somewhere, not too far away, a wise old chicken squawked to greet the day.

As it turned out, Willow was wrong. Loving Ash Murphy wasn't exhausting at all. In fact, it was the easiest thing she'd ever do.

Need more cowboys?

Read on for a taste of how
Boone Murphy and Casey Walsh fell in love in
Holding Out for a Cowboy

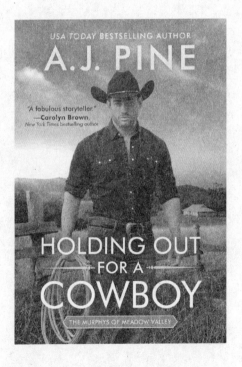

Chapter 1

CASEY WALSH SWORE SHE HEARD THE SWEET melodic sound of harp strings, as if heaven were opening its gates to welcome her—or more like the serene reception area of one of those fancy Chico spas she'd been to once, but that was a lifetime ago.

She hummed out a soft sigh and pulled her quilt tight over her shoulder, snuggling deeper into her pillow as whatever dream she was having played out in her subconscious. Heaven or spa, it didn't matter. She'd wake to the same reality either way.

Again, the soft refrain chimed, a sound so familiar she could almost hum it, yet it still felt out of reach.

Over and over, the same few notes twinkled, pulsing like a wave.

"Casey," it cooed softly. "Casey. Casey. Casey."

"*Casey!*"

Her eyes flew open, and Casey bolted upright only to knock her forehead against what felt like a boulder, but she had zero recollection of a boulder dangling over her bed.

"Ow! Jesus, Case. If that was my nose, you would have broken it!"

Ivy Serrano, Casey's best friend since childhood, rubbed her temple, her lips pursed in a pout.

The harp from Casey's dream was still there, playing on repeat just off to the right.

Her *phone* alarm.

"Oh my god!" Casey cried. "What time is it? How much did I oversleep? Why the hell did I say yes to shooting whiskey with Pearl right before closing?"

Pearl Sweeney—Meadow Valley matriarch and owner of the Meadow Valley Inn—had popped into Midtown Tavern just as Casey was closing up the night before.

"You didn't think I was letting you off the hook without a shot for luck, did you?" Pearl had asked. "It's not every day a girl gets a second chance at her dream."

Only one shot had turned into two, maybe three, which was fine because Casey's interview wasn't until 1:00 p.m. Only now it was…it was…

"Ivy," Casey croaked, her voice not yet caught up to the fact that it and *she* were awake. "What time is?"

"Eleven fifteen," Ivy said. "You told me you were leaving at 11:30, so of course I came to see you off, but when you didn't answer, I used my key, and—long story short—I think we might both be concussed."

"Shit," Casey swore, scrambling out of bed. "Ives, what am I gonna do?"

Ivy tossed her bright yellow scarf over her shoulder and brushed off her navy wool coat. "Give me your keys. I'll warm up your car while you get ready. Your good-luck pumpkin spice latte is on the counter in the kitchen."

Casey grabbed her keys off the dresser and tossed them to Ivy with a snarl. "There had better not be pumpkin spice *anything* in my kitchen, and you know it," she said with half a sneer.

Ivy snorted. "It's black coffee with a dusting of cinnamon, the same way you've had it since high school. But I do adore how much you hate autumn's most beloved fruit."

"Are you gonna start my car or what? I haven't driven Adeline all week, so she's gonna need some extra love." She patted her head, feeling a knotted tuft of what needed to be her perfectly beach-waved silver balayage.

Ugh. What had possessed her to grow her hair out when she'd been doing the wash-and-go pixie for years?

This morning had. Today. This interview. After twelve years, she was going to reclaim part of what she'd lost all those years ago. But that meant wowing the board of directors at the prestigious Salon and Cosmetology Institute in Reno, Nevada. The same Salon and Cosmetology Institute she dropped out of over a decade ago. The *same* Salon and Cosmetology Institute that needed to readmit her with the credit hours she'd already completed so she could finally put her tavern apron to rest and open her own salon.

But if she was late for her interview, there would be no wowing of any board, no matter how fabulous a specimen her hair was.

She stumbled out of her room and into the bathroom where she plugged in her hot iron, threw her hair in a shower cap, and hopped in the shower to rinse the late night at the tavern from her body.

Two minutes later, she stood wrapped in a towel as she sprayed her homemade detangler—a mix of water, her favorite conditioner, and a few drops of rosemary and peppermint essential oils—in her hair, brushed away her bedhead, and then reached for her waving iron.

She wound the first lock of hair around the barrel of the wand and squinted at herself in the mirror.

"Is that a...?"

She leaned closer to the reflective glass, rolling her eyes at herself as she confirmed that—*yes*—that certainly was a bruise forming above her left eyebrow from coldcocking Ivy as she flew out of bed. Nothing a little concealer couldn't take care of.

But wait... Did she smell smoke?

Casey sniffed, looking to her left and then to her right. Something definitely smelled like it was burning. Like burning—*hair*.

"Shit!" she yelled, practically ripping the wand from her hair.

Her *smoking* hair.

"Do I smell burning?" Ivy called as Casey heard the front door slam. "Because this is some *really* bad déjà vu, Case. Are you okay?"

Casey didn't have time to ruminate on how Ivy had almost burned her clothing boutique down just days before her grand opening. Because—her *hair*!

"Um…Ives?" she asked quietly at first, too nervous for her friend to see what she'd done.

"Case?" Ivy called, louder and a bit frantic.

"In the bathroom!" Casey called back, but the words came out as more of a whimper.

Ivy stopped short in the doorframe, a hint of smoke still wafting in the air.

"Oh, Casey," she said, the corners of her mouth turning down. "What happened, sweetie?"

Casey's eyes burned, but she swallowed the threat of tears. She'd been putting on a brave face for twelve years now. She'd played the long game, trained for the marathon when it came to caging her emotions. Because the alternative was what? To let everyone know that she might be broken— might have been broken ever since the day…

Nope. She wasn't going there, not now when she had burnt hair, a bruised eyebrow, and mere minutes to get on the road.

"I can fix it!" she exclaimed, pulling a pair of salon shears from one of the bathroom drawers.

And she did. Because if there was one place where Casey Walsh didn't falter—even if it meant recovering from a monstrous blunder like singeing a lock of hair—it was hair.

"You always did want bangs," Ivy said with a forced smile.

Because Casey had *never* wanted bangs. Every time she thought she did, she'd cut them, hate them, and then grow them out. It became a running joke. Every time Casey needed to change something in her life, especially when it was one of the pesky external factors over which she had no control, Ivy would say, "You always did want bangs," and Casey would grab her shears.

Ninety seconds later, Casey Walsh had blunt silver bangs that fell just below her eyebrows.

"It's a win-win!" she admitted as realization set in. "Covers my bruise from our unfortunate headbutting."

Ivy pouted and rubbed her temple. "I'm sure I'm bruised too," she insisted. "Just because you can't see it doesn't mean it isn't there."

Casey laughed. The morning started out as a disaster, but she'd turned it around. After a quick change from her towel to the denim jumpsuit Ivy had insisted she borrow from her boutique, she dabbed some gloss on her lips and gave her on-the-fly haircut another look of approval.

"How do I look?" she asked Ivy as she slid her arms into her red puffer coat and slung her bag over her shoulder.

"You look like my gorgeous, take-no-prisoners friend who is going to knock the socks off that board of directors and get all her credits reinstated. But you don't want to forget this." She handed Casey the travel mug of coffee that otherwise would have tragically been left behind.

Casey blew out a long breath. "And Addy?"

Ivy winked. "Only a couple of mild coughs before she purred to life. I can't believe you're still driving that thing."

Casey scoffed, then shushed her friend. "That car was bequeathed to me by my great-grandma Adeline when she passed. It's all I have left of the woman I barely knew, and it was *free*. No car payment. Just insurance. Plus, I've barely driven it since we graduated high school. And she was given a full Boo—" She stopped herself before completing the thought.

A full Boone Murphy tune-up before she'd ever been allowed to take it on the road.

Because besides Boone Murphy being—or having been—Meadow Valley's best and only mechanic, he was also Casey's ex, a man whose name went more the way of Voldemort in Casey's presence—*he who shall not be named*.

"You think," Ivy started hesitantly, "that maybe

your oversleeping and being a little scattered this morning have something to do with Boo—"

"Nope!" Casey interrupted.

It had nothing to do with today—the day Casey Walsh finally got her life back—also being the day that Boone Murphy was getting married. And leaving Meadow Valley for good.

No possible way all the setbacks that happened this morning had *anything* to do with that. Not when Casey had some rocking new bangs and Great-Granny Adeline's car purring in front of her building.

"This is *my* day," she added, ignoring the slight tremor in her voice.

"Right. The day of Casey," Ivy said. "You got this!"

Acknowledgments

I love, love, LOVE live music. One of the joys I redis-covered after the pandemic was going to concerts, and so much of 2022 and 2023 was filled with the wonderful, collective experience of being at a live show. From the Eras Tour (I could write a whole other book on how that happened) to Charlie Puth to K-Pop, I was *In. It.* And I still am, but the point is, there was a stretch of about eleven months where I was just devouring this joyful, collective experi-ence while at the same time writing this book. I am not a singer, but I love to sing. I am not a song-writer, but I love to jot down verses here and there. And thankfully, I had an editor that let me slide a country superstar and a folksy up-and-comer into a cowboy book. So thank you, Deb Werksman, for giving the thumbs-up to Willow and Ash's story. It was truly one of my favorites to write.

Thank you to my partner in publishing madness (otherwise known as my agent), Emily, for being in my corner. To Lea, Megan, Jen, Chanel, thank you for being the best besties a girl could ever want. Tracy, Mindy, Linda, and Heather, my other best besties, thank you for drinking and knowing things with me and making Thursdays my favorite night of the week…and thank you for still reading my books even when sometimes the dog dies.

A huge thank-you to the K-drama and K-pop communities that have just made life infinitely better and my stories infinitely more tropey.

A shout-out to my mom for being my Facebook and Port St. Lucie marketing manager. Keep the bookshelf growing!

S and C, you're my favorites. Always.

And of course, I'm saving the best for last. Thank you, my wonderful readers, for being the reason I get to do this thing I love to do. It means the world.

About the Author

A corporate trainer by day and *USA Today* bestselling author by night, A.J. Pine can't seem to escape the world of fiction, and she wouldn't have it any other way. When she finds that twenty-fifth hour in the day, she might indulge in a tiny bit of TV to nourish her undying love of K-dramas, superheroes, and everything romance. She hails from the far-off galaxy of the Chicago suburbs.

Website: ajpine.com
Facebook: AJPineAuthor
Instagram: @aj_pine
TikTok: @aj_pine

Also by A.J. Pine

THE MURPHYS OF MEADOW VALLEY
Holding Out for a Cowboy
Finally Found My Cowboy

HEART OF SUMMERTOWN
The Second Chance Garden